HOPE'S DELTA (SPECIAL FORCES: OPERATION ALPHA)

DELTA TEAM 3, BOOK FIVE

RILEY EDWARDS

This book is a work of fiction. Names, characters, places, and incidents are products of the author's imagination or used fictitiously. Any resemblance to actual events or locales or persons living or dead is entirely coincidental.

Dear Readers,

Welcome to the Special Forces: Operation Alpha Fan-Fiction world!

If you are new to this amazing world, in a nutshell the author wrote a story using one or more of my characters in it. Sometimes that character has a major role in the story, and other times they are only mentioned briefly. This is perfectly legal and allowable because they are going through Aces Press to publish the story.

This book is entirely the work of the author who wrote it. While I might have assisted with brainstorming and other ideas about which of my characters to use, I didn't have any part in the process or writing or editing the story.

I'm proud and excited that so many authors loved my characters enough that they wanted to write them into their own story. Thank you for supporting them, and me!

This series is special to me as the five authors writing in the Delta Team Three series took a team that I introduced in *Shielding Kinley* and made them their own.

READ ON!

Xoxo

Susan Stoker

CHAPTER 1

BEAU "JANGLES" Talbot sat on the edge of his bed, looked down at the long, wavy brown hair splashed across the pillowcase, and the area around his heart constricted.

"Babe?" he called, and watched as she stirred but did not wake.

I need to end this.

He knew it, but he wasn't going to.

"Hope, baby, wake up," he tried again, and swept the heavy fall of hair off her bare shoulder.

The pads of his fingers skimmed over her warm, smooth skin. Hope opened her pretty brown eyes and Jangles fought the urge to crawl back into bed.

"Call out?" she mumbled.

"Yeah."

"Damn."

Damn was right. Since Jangles and his team had transferred to Texas, they'd gone out frequently. Such was the life of a Special Operations Group. Terrorists didn't have a set schedule of operation. Extremist groups didn't limit their bombings to the hours between nine and five. And kidnappers and guerilla forces didn't give the first fuck he was being pulled from his bed in the middle of the night. Further, they didn't care Jangles was leaving a sexy, hot, willing woman in that bed.

"You got Buster?" Jangles asked.

"You know I do. Go save the world."

No whiny complaints he was rolling out of bed. No bitching about where he was going or when he was coming back. No questions—period.

Just easy acceptance.

That was why he needed to end this.

Whatever *this* was, Jangles had to put a stop to it. He should've done it months ago. Hell, he never should've started it with Hope in the first place.

"I'll text you when we get back."

Hope's hand came up, her fingers stroked the side of his face, and her eyes gentled.

"Be safe, Beau."

That was why he hadn't ended it. Jangles was addicted to her gentle eyes and soft pleas for his safe return.

"Always am, babe. Go back to sleep."

Jangles leaned forward, kissed her shoulder, then her forehead, and lingered just long enough to breathe her in.

Then he grabbed his bag and walked out the door, leaving Hope naked in his bed.

He did that, secure in the knowledge she'd be waiting for him when he got home. So he wasn't going to end it—proving he was a selfish prick, but not a stupid man. He knew Hope Mitchell was the best thing that had happened to him since he'd joined the Army.

CHAPTER 2

Hope Mitchell scanned the bar. For a Tuesday it was busy, not packed, but there was a crush of patrons. The mood was mellow as it would be. Baby Face, better known as BF, didn't put up with rowdy. He may have been in a wheelchair after losing both his legs in combat, but that didn't stop her boss from being well…the boss.

He also owned the shooting range next door—therefore, he had a plethora of firearms at his disposal. Not that he'd ever had to brandish one of those weapons, but everyone knew he could and would if someone cut up in his bar and made a ruckus. One of the many reasons Hope loved her boss—he took care of his people. And he considered anyone coming into his establishment to enjoy a drink, a game of darts, or time around the pool table *his* people.

"Need another, Lefty?" Hope asked when she finished her scan.

"No thanks, Hope, driving tonight," Lefty returned.

"Water then?"

"That'd be appreciated." Lefty tipped his chin and Hope's gaze slid to the woman next to him.

His woman, Kinley, was laughing at something Gillian had said and Hope knew Lefty was in for a long night.

Neither woman looked like she wanted to leave anytime soon.

The kernel of jealousy that had taken root made itself known. Hope hadn't meant to allow it to lodge in her belly, she certainly hadn't given it permission to stick, then to grow, but there it was—Hope was jealous.

Hope set Lefty's water in front of him and a fresh bowl of corn nuts to the side knowing Lefty didn't eat from a communal dish—neither did Trigger, Oz, Brain, Lucky, Doc, or Grover. Being as she was a good bartender, and not because she watched Jangles with more inspection than was necessary, she knew that he and his teammates—Merlin, Zip, Duff, and Woof—would eat anything. Although Zip and Woof did it grumbling.

Nope, I'm just being a good bartender and manager. It's my job to pay attention.

"You're too good to us." Lefty smiled.

"Yeah, yeah, you always say that. Not playing darts tonight?" Hope asked, and jerked her head toward the back room where Trigger and Oz were, in an effort to cover her reaction to his praise.

"Nope. Tired of hearing Trigger complain when he loses."

Hope's gaze went back to Kinley, then to Gillian, and a little farther down the bar to see Destiny and Gwen, and she knew he was full of shit.

That jealousy knotted tighter.

Gage "Lefty" Haskins was not sitting at the bar because Trigger complained when he lost a game of darts—though that was the truth; Trigger was a poor sport when he lost. Lefty was sitting sentry. He was watching over his woman, Trigger's woman, and even though Gwen and Destiny were two stools away because there were already patrons sitting at the bar when they arrived, he was watching over Merlin and Zip's women, too.

Hope didn't need a man to protect her—she'd been doing that herself for a long time. But that didn't mean she wasn't jealous of the women. But not for reasons one would think. Hope's envy steamed from their ability to have a normal relationship.

Hope's cell vibrated in her back pocket with a text. The sad truth was only three people had her number. Jake the other bartender at the Ugly Mug, her boss BF, and Jangles.

Jake was working the bar next to her and it was well past BF's bedtime, so that left one person.

Hope didn't fight the smile as she pulled the phone from her pocket and slid her thumb across the screen. She also didn't bother to stop the anticipation she felt. Jangles had been gone two very long weeks.

Hey, babe. Just landed. If you're not busy after you close the bar, I want to see you.

That was Jangles.

That was what they had.

No I missed yous, no expectations.

And that was a-okay with Hope. That was what she'd agreed to when she'd accepted Jangles' first invitation. He didn't mince words, he didn't sugarcoat it, he was straightforward—no commitment, no ties, no promises. Light and easy, nothing heavy, no swapping childhood stories and dreams. Fun, laughter, and loads of awesome sex.

Since Hope had no interest in ever talking about her childhood, she'd long ago given up her dreams, and she was not a woman who wanted to be tied to a man, this worked for her. Spectacularly so. Especially the sex.

Hope tapped out a quick message and stowed her phone back in her pocket.

"Only time I see you really smile," Lefty muttered.

"What was that?"

Hope lifted her gaze to meet Lefty's and she watched as something passed over his features. A look she'd seen less and less of now that he had Kinley. It was sweet, made sweeter because Hope knew Lefty was a badass Delta Force operator, even though he'd never told her that's what he was.

Hope had worked in Killeen, Texas, long enough to spot the Delta guys. They had a little more swagger, a little more confidence, a little more edge. They were also quieter about it. The Rangers came in kitted out in Ranger gear, the infantry guys came in full of bravado, but not the Deltas. They didn't need the attention nor did they want it.

The problem with that was, they were also the most observant.

Therefore they all knew what Hope and Jangles were doing and they knew what it was—friends with benefits. And cat sitting.

Though Jangles had long ago stopped texting her while he was out on a mission to ask about his cat, Buster. Oh, he still texted, but they'd changed, simply asking her how *she* was doing. The subtle shift felt awesome, but it also scared the pants off her. In an effort not to freak out when the texts came, she reminded herself they were friends and the gesture was a friendly thing to do.

At least Hope thought it was. She didn't actually have friends so she couldn't know for sure.

"That smile. You only get it when—"

Destiny cut off Lefty when she called down the bar. "Hope, when you have a minute can you please close out our tab?"

Right.

Destiny and Gwen had gotten the same text she did, or a version of it. Their men were home from assignment and they were anxious to get home.

Hope didn't have a home. She had an RV on BF's property.

"Sure thing, babe," Hope returned.

"Duty calls." Hope gave Lefty a wink and walked away.

Hours later than he thought he'd be, Jangles let himself into his house. Buster greeted him at the door. The cat meowed and rubbed her body against his ankle.

The feline had been a gift from his teammate, Woof. Being as Jangles was the only sucker of the group, Woof had dumped Buster on him when she was just a kitten after he'd found the little thing on post. Why animals of all varieties seemed to gravitate to his friend was a mystery for the ages.

Jangles hadn't wanted a cat, he didn't even want a house plant—if it needed to be fed, watered, or cared for, Jangles wanted no part of it. Yet, he'd kept the damn furball. Then he decided he liked her because she was a cat, therefore, didn't want much from him except for the occasional cuddle, full bowl of food and water, and a clean litterbox. Other than that, Buster roamed the house like she was the queen of the castle, making Hope her princess.

Hope.

The woman who was right then in his bed.

He reached down to give his cat a quick rub before he made his way through the house, not bothering to look around. He knew what he'd find, the same thing he found every time he'd come from a mission and left Hope in his house. The kitchen would be cleaned from whatever mess they'd left before he got called away. His mail would be sorted. And depending on whether or not she'd decided to spend the night and hang out while he was gone, his clothes would be washed and put away. He'd told her many times she didn't need to clean his house or do his laundry, but she simply rolled her eyes and told him to shut it.

Jangles had given her a key so she could watch Buster while he was gone. After he'd given Hope a ride home after work because her car had broken down and he saw where she lived, he'd extended the invitation for her to stay at his house while he was gone.

Truth be told, if he wasn't sleeping with her, she'd be the perfect roommate. And not because she cleaned and did his laundry—Hope Mitchell was cool people. Chill, funny, always smiling, in a good mood, and up for fun. And not just the kind they made between the sheets. She just liked to have a good time. But she also knew how to be quiet. She didn't ask questions he couldn't answer, she didn't prod and bitch.

Hindsight being what it was, he never should've started sleeping with her and instead asked her to move in as a roommate. Losing the physical part of what they had would suck, and that was putting it mildly—she was a knockout. Great with her hands, excellent with her mouth, and she knew how to work her body in ways that sent Jangles over the edge. But one day he'd cut her loose, and then he'd lose the rest of her. The funny, the sweet, the woman he could have a beer with, go to the shooting range with, run the obstacle course with even though he smoked her ass every time. She still went back for more and did it with a smile and good humor.

If Jangles was the type of man who believed he deserved a woman, Hope would be his.

But he wasn't.

He hit his bedroom and his chest started to burn.

Hope on her stomach, she'd kicked the covers off, giving him an eyeful—his tee bunched around her waist, red panties that left a lot of cheek on display, one long leg straight, the other cocked at an angle. She was turned away from him so he couldn't see her face, though he didn't need to. He'd spent a lot of hours memorizing every inch of her, including what she looked like when she slept.

Jangles quickly peeled off his clothes, careful not to pull off the bandage the major had redressed after she'd checked the stitches Zip had given him in the field. That was the reason Jangles was late getting home. The reason why Hope was now sleeping in his bed instead of awake and meeting him at the door.

Shit had hit the fan, as it often did while on a mission, and Jangles had caught the business end of a knife.

New day, new scar.

His body was covered in so many blemishes, holes, and marks that one more made no difference.

Jangles climbed into bed behind Hope, tagged her hip, and rolled her to her side so he could fit his front to her back. He did all that knowing he shouldn't, but doing it anyway because he couldn't stand the thought of not touching her.

"You're home," Hope whispered.

Jangles closed his eyes and let her words wash over him.

Christ.

"Yeah, baby, go back to sleep."

"But—"

"Baby, I'm wiped. We'll talk in the morning, yeah?"

"Okay. Welcome home, Beau."

Christ.

Beau.

It was good to be home.

CHAPTER 3

HOPE WOKE with a start and fought the last threads of the nightmare.

Jangles' arm around her middle tightened and she screwed her eyelids closed, hating that he'd felt her jolt.

He wouldn't ask, he never did.

The nightmares rarely came when he was holding her, but as rare as they were, Jangles always woke.

But never asked.

She should've been grateful, it wasn't like Hope would've told him anyway. But the lack of response was a cold hard reminder of what they had.

"You good?" Jangles' sleep-rough voice sent goose bumps racing down her arms.

"Yeah."

Her eyes slowly cracked open, happy the man whose bed she was in was behind her and couldn't see the vestiges of the dream still playing across her features. Not that he'd comment, but Hope didn't want him to see, didn't want any of her past to taint how he saw her.

If he knew the type of woman I am, he'd kick me out of his house and never let me back in.

That thought hurt worse than it should've.

That was not what they had. Never could be. Never would be.

Hope's hand roamed over Jangles' forearm but stopped when she felt a bandage.

"You're hurt."

"It's nothing," he grumbled.

Her finger continued to trace the edge of the tape. By the length of the dressing, it didn't feel like nothing. However, she knew better than to push. Not because she understood he'd never tell her what happened, but because she appreciated him not prodding into her personal life, so she'd return the favor.

"Glad it's nothing."

Seeking the warmth of Jangles' big body, Hope pressed deeper and sighed when she felt his lips press against her neck.

"You need something, smalls?"

She told herself the shiver of excitement was from the long, thick erection rubbing on her ass and not from Jangles calling her a silly nickname. But recently the lie had become harder and harder to swallow.

"If you think you're up for it." She wiggled her backside in an invitation.

"When am I not?"

"I can think of a time or two when—"

"Babe, two minutes after I've blown down your throat and you're ready to go but I need a few minutes to recover does not count. And while you're waiting for my cock, I do not make you wait without my mouth between your legs. So I'll ask you again, there ever a time I'm not ready to give you what you need?"

Cue the full-body tremor.

"If that's the case, then what's the hold-up?"

Once again, Hope's eyes closed, this time in a slow blink when she felt Jangles shaking with laughter. She knew it was coming so she braced, and when the shaking turned audible and his mirth filled the room, she soaked it in like a greedy addict. The sound of his deep, rough laughter glided over her skin and she absorbed all of it. Every last drop he was willing to give.

The tee she'd slept in was up over her head and tossed away, followed by her panties, and without further delay, one of Jangles' hands cupped her breast while the other dove between her legs and teased her opening.

"You ready for me?" Jangles asked as he trailed a line of kisses from her ear down her jaw.

"When am I not?" she parroted his earlier response.

Hope bit back her sigh when Jangles shifted just enough to slide his cock through her wetness from behind. The engorged head teased her clit and she automatically tipped her ass to give him better access. This wasn't an invitation —Jangles didn't need to be invited to the festivities, he never did. Not once, not even the first time, did the man need encouragement or direction. He knew what he wanted and he knew how to work her body to wring every ounce of pleasure from her and he did this expertly.

"Give me your mouth."

Hope turned her head, eager to give him what he wanted. The moment her lips touched his, Jangles slammed home and swallowed her cry of delight.

"Fuck." Jangles broke the kiss and growled.

God, she loved his snarled curse. In all of the months they'd been together, Hope still couldn't believe little ol' her could turn big, bad, tough Beau Talbot to a snarly beast.

"GODDAMN, it's good to be home."

As soon as the words left his mouth, Jangles knew he didn't just mean it was good to be home stateside. He didn't even mean it was good to be home in his bed.

He was fucked in more ways than one. He knew it when he'd hit his bed last night and didn't wake Hope to sink deep inside her warm, willing body. Instead, all he'd wanted to do was wrap his arms around her and sleep.

More and more, he was thinking of Hope as home.

And that was dangerous.

"Jangles," Hope moaned, and for some inexplicit reason, his heart seized.

"Beau," he corrected. In an effort to stop himself from saying more, like say, explain that while her tight pussy hugged his cock he wasn't Jangles, he captured her mouth and pounded harder.

Christ. Beautiful.

All of her, the taste of her on his tongue, the weight of her tit in his hand, the way her nipple pebbled, the way she arched her ass, wanting him deeper. All of it. And it scared the fuck out of him that the connection they shared went beyond sex. But when her pussy started to quiver around his cock and her excitement leaked down his balls and dripped on his sheets, all thoughts of the risky game he was playing were swept away.

There was nothing left but them, the pleasure they created, and the rush to climax.

"Beau. I'm—" Her moan dangled and her pussy clamped down around his cock.

Then his world narrowed further as he slammed home as deep as he could and shot off, bathing her insides with thick ropes of come.

Him. Her. Ecstasy.

When Jangles finally had some brain function back he gave Hope a slow, gentle glide of his cock and enjoyed the way her pussy trembled after her orgasm.

"You want me to clean you up or make you breakfast while you shower?" he asked, and because he couldn't keep his mouth off her, he licked the area above her shoulder and loved the resulting shudder.

Fucking beautiful. All of her.

"Neither." A pang of something that Jangles didn't want to process slithered up his throat. "I wish I could stay but BF needs my help this morning. I didn't know you'd be home or I would've pushed it to this afternoon, but now he's waiting for me. And you know him—if I'm even two minutes late I'll get a twenty-minute lecture on respect and responsibility."

The ball of unease tightened when he found he liked that she was leaving because she had plans and not because she was trying to ditch his ass.

Courting trouble.

Fucking hell.

"Need help?"

Hope stiffened and it didn't take a rocket scientist to know why.

That wasn't what they had. He didn't help her with projects she worked on with BF. She didn't hang with him and his team at get-togethers where Nori, Destiny, Gwen, Ivy, or any combination of the four were present. She didn't even hang with them when they were sitting at the bar at the Ugly Mug. She served them their drinks, joked with the guys, smiled at the women, and occasionally if no one was watching she'd flirt with him. She also did all of that with Lefty, Oz, Brain, Doc, Grover, and Trigger—

minus the flirting—and not just because some of them were taken.

"No. He just has a new ceiling fan he wants me to install. It'll take me ten minutes and besides, you just got home. Buster might protest and claw up your furniture if you don't give her some attention."

Fuck. Why were they talking about ceiling fans and cats while his semi-hard cock was still gliding? For that matter, why hadn't he pulled out and rolled away?

Because you like being connected to her, you dumbass.

"I'll clean you up before you go."

"Jangles."

"Beau," he reminded her.

Fucking hell.

"Beau. I'm fine."

He pulled out, ignoring the way his cock immediately missed her heat, and kissed her neck.

"Don't move," he demanded.

What the hell am I doing?

By the time he had a wet washcloth between Hope's legs, washing away the evidence of his orgasm, he still had no answer.

CHAPTER 4

JANGLES FELT THE IRRITATION BUILDING. It'd been three days since he'd seen Hope. Two days since she'd texted him and told him Baby Face had a long list of projects he needed her to do, which meant Hope would be doing them, therefore busy.

That was the source of his agitation—not so much that she was too busy to see him, but that she was going at those projects alone. BF's property was on the outskirts of Killeen. It wouldn't be considered a ranch because there were no animals, but he had land—lots of it. He also had a few outbuildings, an RV, two single-wide trailers, and the house he lived in. Jangles had never been in any of the buildings, but he'd seen them. He'd also seen the state of their outsides and knew they were well-kept, and it wasn't BF who was making them so—it had to be Hope.

Baby Face was not a man to take advantage, likely Hope had him snowed. There was no doubt she was tough, physically and mentally, but it still pissed Jangles off she was going at it alone. Not reaching out and asking for help with whatever tasks she'd been working on.

"Hey there, handsome. Cool surprise," Hope greeted.

He'd timed his visit to the bar perfectly, thirty minutes before closing meant that the crowd had thinned and she'd be off soon.

"You leaving?" Her head cocked to the side and her face got gentle the way it always did right after he told her he was leaving on assignment.

Fucking Christ.

That look gutted him—every time. Yet, he kept going back for more. He couldn't get enough, couldn't stop thinking about her, couldn't let her go.

"No, baby. I'm not leaving," he told her, and Hope's eyes scanned the bar. He knew she was looking for one of his teammates. He never came in alone. "Came in to see you."

"See me?"

Hope didn't hide her shock. Actually, she hid very little from him—except she did. When they were together, she gave him everything, all of her time, all of her attention. She was fully immersed in them—always, from the first time he'd taken her back to his place. But she shared nothing about her past. She didn't talk about her nightmares, the scar on her arm, how she'd met BF, how she'd learned to work on cars, what she did with the time they were apart.

Nothing.

It was time for a change.

Cut her loose or move us along.

And he hadn't known for sure which it was going to be until he'd walked in the bar, sat down, and saw the look on her face. She was exhausted. But that wasn't what had his gut tight. It was the shock in her pretty brown eyes that he'd come in to see her. *What the fuck was that*? They'd been seeing each other for months. No, they hadn't—they'd been sleeping together.

And that was going to change.

"You've been busy," he unnecessarily told her. "Wanted to come around and see if you needed any help."

Jangles watched with no small amount of frustration as Hope closed down.

"Nope. It was just some handiwork around the house and an oil change on BF's van. Easy peasy."

The broad smile she gave him was fake. At first, Jangles hadn't recognized her quick jabs and easy smiles were a lot like his buddy Zip's. Totally bogus, a defense mechanism to hide the pain. Now that Zip had reconnected with Destiny and his source of anguish had been extinguished, his smiles were real.

And right then, he vowed to find Hope's source of pain and snuff it out.

"So you're done?"

"Yep."

"Good, then you're free to hang with me tomorrow."

Jangles hadn't posed his statement as a question and there was no way Hope could miss his demand.

"Actually, I have to work at the range tomorrow before my shift at the bar. BF has some vets coming in. That's what's kept me busy. I needed to get the trailers ready because they're staying a few days. But I'm free after I close the bar until noon tomorrow."

Jangles ignored the pang of annoyance. After all, that was what they were. What they'd agreed on.

Sex. No strings.

If Hope was any other woman, he'd be doing backflips that she understood his place in her life. Yet it pissed him right the fuck off that Hope was offering him her body but nothing else.

"Grab me a beer, would ya?"

"You don't have to stay. I'll be—"

"Beer, Hope."

"Sure thing, handsome."

With a wink, she strutted her fine ass away to grab him a beer. Jangles caught the asshole at the end of the bar eyeing her and he barely contained his growl. It wasn't the first time he'd caught a man staring at Hope, she was a beautiful woman. It was, however, the first time he had the urge to rip someone's head off because of it.

~

HOPE POPPED THE TOP OFF JANGLES' LoneStar IPA and didn't bother with the pint glass she knew he wouldn't use, but she took her time making her way back to him. She needed to fortify her resolve.

She was in too deep.

At some point, she'd done what she'd told Jangles she'd never do and developed feelings. At first, those feelings were friendly, so she'd allowed herself to have them. Then slowly, they'd turned into more. Not only would Jangles be disappointed, but it was wholly unacceptable to her. She had no place in her life for a man, or for those emotions.

Feelings like that made you stupid. They made you make bad decisions, and after the second chance BF had given her, she couldn't afford stupid.

Hope had spent the last three days coming up with an exit strategy. Slowly, she'd extradite herself from his life. This wouldn't be hard because their lives hadn't truly mingled, though her heart had managed to twine with his. That was okay, too. Jangles could keep it—that way, she'd never find herself in this situation again. One she never thought she'd face again after what Went had done to her.

Wentworth Collins—the spawn of Satan.

"Hey, darlin'," the college kid at the end of the bar

drawled. "When you get a minute, you think I can get my tab?" The kid paused, and with what Hope assumed was supposed to be a sexy grin but missed its mark by a mile, he continued. "And your number while you're at it."

Totally cheesy.

"I can get you that bill, but the only number you're gonna get from me is your total."

"Can't blame a guy for trying," he muttered.

"No, I suppose you can't." Hope gave him a smile to soothe the sting of rejection. "Be right back with that bill."

Hope made her way down the bar and took in Jangles. His eyes were on her, and if she didn't know him the way she did, she'd think he was simply looking at her. But he wasn't, he was *watching*. The nuance would be subtle with another man, but with Jangles it was obvious. Watching meant assessing, evaluating, measuring a threat. Hope had seen the change many times, and not just from him but from his team, and Lefty's, too. Sometimes, the guys had gone from looking around the room to scrutinizing it. Something Hope figured was ingrained in all of them due to their jobs.

But Jangles had never watched *her*. It was unnerving so by the time she stopped in front of him to deliver his beer, she felt exposed.

"Here ya go." Hope placed the bottle on the bar and tried to interject as much happiness in her tone as she could while her heart was in her throat.

How am I going to let him go?

"That happen a lot?"

"Yep," she answered, not bothering to pretend she didn't know what he was talking about. Jangles wasn't dumb—he'd sniff the deflection and call her on it.

"They always take it that good?"

"Take what?"

"The letdown," he explained.

She didn't think she wanted to go there with Jangles. She'd never seen it directed toward her, but she'd seen it aimed at Nori, Destiny, Gwen, and Ivy—Jangles had a protective streak just like all the guys on his team. She wasn't sure what he'd do if she answered honestly. What she did know was, she didn't want to find out.

"They don't," he muttered, correctly reading her silence. "Fuck."

Hope felt something sweep over her, something she didn't want to feel, something she'd gone to great pains *not* to feel. But right then, she couldn't stop the rush of emotion as it burned down her chest and settled in her belly.

She didn't want to feel his concern but it couldn't be missed. Hope didn't want Jangles to care if a man hit on her then called her nasty names when she turned him down. But damn it to hell, the knowledge that he did felt like a warm, sunny Texas afternoon. It coated her skin and made her wish for things she couldn't have.

Something had changed. But before Hope could get a read or ask, Jangles spoke. "Go finish closing out, babe."

"Everything all right?"

"Nope."

Oh, shit.

"You don't have to—"

"Hope, do me a favor and finish closing down so we can get home."

Home?

What the hell?

"Listen, there's no reason to get wrapped around the axles because men hit on me. Some of them take the rejection and move on nice and quiet. Some are dicks and try to persuade me. Others are total assholes, don't like the hit to their ego so they say nasty shit. Which I have to tell you as a woman, I do not get. Why a man calls a woman who's turned him down ugly, fat, or a bitch seconds after he was trying to get in there makes no sense considering I wasn't too fat, too ugly, or too bitchy to want to bang—" Hope clamped her mouth closed when the low, menacing growl emanated from Jangles.

"Close the bar down, yeah?" he clipped.

That was it, just a not-so-veiled demand for Hope to get the lead out and do what he told her to do.

Hope nodded, turned, and hauled ass to the other end of the bar. She did that while thinking up a way to get out of going to Jangles' house. A place that was not home, a place she shouldn't be going to with a man she had to give up.

An hour later, she found herself in her car, Jangles in his truck behind her following her to his house. She hadn't found an excuse not to go.

Not that she'd tried all that hard.

CHAPTER 5

JANGLES FELT HOPE JOLT AWAKE. He stared into the dark, clenched his teeth, tightened his arm around her, and waited.

"Sorry," she mumbled.

Sorry.

Christ.

She said that every time. Apologized for waking him but offered no explanation.

"You good?"

"Yeah."

Hope snuggled in deeper, pressed her back against his chest as if she wanted to fuse them together.

Enough of this shit.

"Wanna tell me what keeps waking you?"

Hope went stiff as a fucking board. Then a tiny tremor stole through her and he felt it—hell, he could *taste* it. The stench of fear wafted off of her and filled his bedroom so thick and ugly he instinctively wrapped his body around hers until there was no space between them.

"Jangles."

His name was not an answer; what it was meant to be was a reminder they didn't ask personal questions.

Fuck that.

"Beau," he corrected. "When we're in this bed, no, when we're in this house, I'm Beau. You wanna call me Jangles when we're at the bar, have at it. But here, when my arms are wrapped around you, when my cock's in you, I'm Beau."

"This isn't cool," she mumbled. However, she hadn't tried to move.

"You're probably right," he easily agreed.

"Please don't do this."

"Do what?"

"Change what we have."

"Babe, you might have missed this, but I didn't. We changed a while ago."

"No, we didn't," she denied.

"You got a key to my house? You got my alarm code? You sleep in this bed, both with and without me?"

"That's because of Buster."

Fuck, is she serious?

"Right, do you think I'd give my key and alarm code to some woman I was just fucking so she could take care of my cat while I'm gone? Or maybe you think I gave them to you because you're not some woman I'm *just* fucking, but more."

"There can't be more. *I* can't be more."

Jangles' gut roiled at the terror in her tone.

"Too late, you already are."

"It's not right."

He decided to ignore that comment, wanting his original question answered.

"What wakes you up in the middle of the night?"

Silence.

"What scares you?"

Silence.

"What has you so afraid that you're shaking in my arms, Hope? Why are you so—"

"How'd you get this?" She cut him off and trailed her fingers up his forearm next to the line of stitches.

If she wanted to do this—test him, ask him questions because she wrongly thought he wouldn't tell her, thus proving her point that they were nothing more than fuck buddies—he was game.

Though Hope would find she'd made an extreme error in judgment after Jangles rolled to his nightstand and turned on the lamp, bathing the room in light. Then he rolled back, turned her so they were facing each other, and locked his gaze on her startled one.

She wanted to play, he'd play, but they were doing it with the light on so she could see he wasn't fucking around.

"Took a knife to the arm when I was clearing a house. Turned a corner and the bastard had his back against the wall and I didn't see him before he got a good long slice in."

Hope's face went pale and her eyes widened. Jangles had no idea if it was because she was shocked he'd told her, or if she was horrified he'd been injured.

"When we finished up and the house was secure, Zip stitched me up and forced me to take some concoction of vitamins he swears speeds up the healing process. As you can see, it'll leave a scar but it's healing fine."

Hope's gaze dropped to his arm and her brows pinched together.

"Your turn. How'd you get your scar?" Jangles traced the long, jagged mark from below her elbow nearly to her wrist, their scars almost a matching pair.

"Is that why you call him Zip?"

"Not tracking, babe."

"Zip. Do you call him Zip because he zips you guys up? Is he some sort of medic or something?"

"Nope. Zip is short for Zipper. He's got a gnarly scar on his thigh. He fell down an embankment when he was a kid and almost died. Would've, if his twin brother Sean hadn't gotten help. The scar looks like a zipper."

"Geeze, there's two of him?"

Jangles didn't want to think about the irrational jealousy that welled in his chest.

"There was. Sean died in combat."

"Oh my God. That's horrible."

"Yeah, it is. Sean joined the Navy, Zip joined the Army. Sean's unit was taken out by an IED. Sean's death hit Zip hard; not only were they twins but best friends. Destiny was engaged to Sean when he died."

"What?"

Time for stalling's over.

"That's a story for another time. I think you get that I've shared, now it's your turn. Where'd you get your scar?"

Silence.

This time, Jangles didn't fill it. He let the quiet stretch, his hand on her hip unmoving but heavy. Finally, she broke the stare down and glanced over his shoulder.

He'd give her that disconnect if she gave him the truth.

"My ex, Went, wasn't a good guy," she started, and Jangles felt his body tighten. "We were young, I thought he could protect me." Hope huffed a humorless laugh. "God, I was so stupid. I learned the hard way that no one could protect me, no one could save me, especially not him."

"He hurt you?" Jangles asked the question but as soon as the words left his mouth, he regretted asking.

Fear and pain flashed in her eyes, her lips pinched, and her brows drew together.

Fucking, fucking, *hell.*

"He hurt me in so many ways, so many times, there are not enough words for me to express what he did to me. The mark he left on my flesh is the least of the damage he did, yet it's the reminder to never trust my heart. Never forget that I can't be saved."

Jangles felt the fury building inside of him. It pooled in his gut, and he welcomed the rage.

"Where is he now?"

"Dead."

"Dead?"

Hope's gaze came back to his and he held his breath. Anguish danced. Dread, panic, alarm, he wasn't sure if that was what he saw in her or felt in his soul. But wherever it was emanating from, it surrounded them, blanketed them under its weight.

It was on the tip of his tongue to ask how the fucker died, but he couldn't bear the answer. He prepared to pull them from the heaviness when Hope straightened the best she could and announced:

"I killed him."

Christ.

"Good," he blurted out and watched Hope jerk in surprise.

"How is that good? I killed a man."

Jesus. He never wanted to hear her say that again. Not because it changed a damn thing he felt for her. He couldn't stomach the pain in her voice.

"I'm sorry you were in a position to take a life. I'm sorry that you have to live with it. I'm sorry it fucks with your head. But I am not sorry you killed the bastard that caused you so much pain that not only did he leave you with physical scars but emotional ones. I know you. You wouldn't—"

"You don't know me, Jangles. You have no idea who I

am and what I'm capable of. If you did, you'd kick me out of your bed, your house, and your life. You'd be disgusted with the things I've done. Don't pretty up what we have. I am not more. I'm the woman you're fucking who happens to have a key to your house so I can take care of your cat. Nothing more."

Jangles didn't bother correcting her again about using his nickname. With everything she'd spewed, that was the least of what churned in his gut.

"Tell me, Hope, what would disgust me?"

"So much."

"Try me."

Silence.

"Baby, if you think you're nothing more than a warm body in my bed, what do you care what I think? It's not me prettying anything up. You know damn well what's between us, and it's a fuck of a lot more than the exchange of bodily fluids."

"Went killed my parents." Hope's features blanked, totally devoid of any emotion and Jangles' body went taut. "They died because I was stupid. My little brother lost our parents because I got hooked up with the wrong guy. Mom and Dad warned me he was no good. Told me to stay away from him, then they forbade me from seeing him. But, stupid me, I didn't listen. I kept seeing him. I snuck out of my house, I lied, I was a bitch to Dad and horrible to my mom. I acted like my life was so bad. Poor me. The kids at school made my life miserable until Went made me his girl. Then they stopped—no one messed with Wentworth Collins because they all knew he was crazy. So suddenly, no one was making fun of me, no one was calling me names. It was a night and day difference, and for the first time in four years, I wasn't afraid to go to school. I knew he was crazy, but I fought to keep him so I wouldn't get bullied. Mom and Dad died for that. I made my brother an orphan so I wouldn't get picked on. All because I was a selfish, stupid, *stupid,* bitch."

Jangles said nothing, not because there wasn't a lot to say, but because Hope was visibly wrecked. There wasn't a damn thing she'd listen to while her emotions were raw and exposed. So Jangles did the only thing he could do. He crushed his woman against his chest and held on as tightly as he could while her pain leaked from her eyes and soaked into his skin.

He'd gladly absorb every last drop of her guilt if it meant she'd let go of it.

"Jangles—"

"No more sharing tonight, baby."

He let her go long enough to turn off the light, then rolled back and tucked his woman close.

An hour later, Hope stopped shaking. Minutes after that, she fell asleep.

Jesus.

Her parents.

Jangles didn't sleep, not a single wink, didn't even move a muscle as he lay holding Hope. He couldn't stop thinking about her eyes and the depth of pain that shone was burned onto his soul. An emotion he didn't quite understand swept over him, a tenderness he'd never felt. The desire to protect was ingrained, it was one of the reasons he'd joined the military, but this was different. It was a need. It went beyond obligation and duty.

Oh, yeah, fuck yeah, she's more. So much more.

CHAPTER 6

Hope woke up in bed alone and stretched, enjoying the delicious ache between her legs. She rolled to her side, pulling Jangles' pillow to her face, and inhaled. She did that a lot when she slept in his bed when he was on a mission. That, and she always slept in one of his tees. It made her feel close to him when he was gone. She knew it was wrong, it was too intimate for what they had, but she gave it to herself anyway.

She froze as last night came back in a rush.

Shit.

With her heart thundering and a hurricane of regret swirling inside, she remembered—everything. The nightmare that had awakened her. Always the same dream—her mind wasn't kind and wouldn't let her forget a single second of Went murdering her parents. Hope remembered every minute detail, every grizzly moment of Went stabbing them to death. The blood, her father's grunts of pain, her mother's cries of sorrow. *The blood.* All of it forever seared on her heart.

And Hope had told Jangles.

No! God, what an idiot.

Last night, Jangles had been cool about it. He'd let her cry and held her while she'd done it. But today would be different. He was Jangles, which meant he was a good guy, he would never kick her out in the middle of the night, but he would find a gentle way to ask for his key back and tell her they'd no longer be seeing each other.

Shit, that hurt more than it should.

The bedroom door pushed open and Hope lifted her gaze, finding Jangles' eyes on her. Under normal circumstances, she would've chastised herself for being caught cuddling his pillow, but now it didn't matter.

"You're awake."

Her eyes focused on the man before her and that hurt, too. Loose-fitting gym shorts that sat low on his hips exposing the sexy V, and she knew if she followed the path downward she'd find treasure. Long, thick, heavy treasure. His lean torso was cut with blocks of muscle, his chest perfect, broad shoulders, biceps that made her mouth water. Actually, the whole package made her mouth water. Top to toe, he was male perfection.

For months, he'd been all hers—now he wasn't.

And that hurt so bad she had to close her eyes.

It's time to go.

She felt the bed depress next to her but she refused to open her eyes. She couldn't face him, didn't want to see the disgust or pity. That would kill.

"Hey."

Hope jolted when his hand cupped her cheek.

No. She was wrong, his touch killed way worse.

"I…um…should get dressed."

"Baby, open your eyes."

Slowly, so slowly, she lifted her lids knowing she

needed to get it over with but dreading the moment with every fiber of her being.

Why is this so hard?

This was not what they were. *Fuck buddies.* She was nothing more than his cat sitter and part-time sex partner.

God, I'm stupid.

The breath seized in her lungs when her gaze met his blue eyes. Before Jangles, she'd never seen blue eyes that were so beautiful, so startling. She hoped one day he had kids and they got those blue eyes. The world needed more beauty, and those cobalt blue orbs would certainly do it.

"I was gonna make us breakfast, but I haven't been to the store since I've been home, so I got nothing. Thought we'd hit Twinny's before you have to get to the range."

What?

"What's happening?" she croaked, uncaring her voice sounded like a frog had taken up residence in her throat.

"What's happening is, I'm gonna feed you before you have to go to work."

"You don't have to do this, Jangles. I get you're a good guy so you'll try to let me down easy. But really, it's not necessary, I understand what we were. You've been straight with me from the start. I appreciate you being nice last night, but I'm a big girl, you don't have to do the slow, gentle escape. It was fun, we had a great time, so I'll just get dressed and leave your key. No need for breakfast."

Hope was so focused on delivering the lame speech she hadn't been paying attention to Jangles' face. She should have. She should've been watching closely. If she had, she would've shut her mouth long before she did. She would've stopped after she'd called him by his nickname.

But she was lost in her head and missed the change.

"Fun?" he clipped.

"Um..."

"Great time? Escape? Nice? Not necessary? You understand? Leave my key?"

Jangles' face was granite, each word angry, abrupt. He was pissed, not just mad but—*seriously* pissed. Before she could ask why, his hand on her cheek slid back into her hair and he fisted the strands, forcing her head back. This didn't hurt, unfortunately. It caused tingles to race up her spine. But then again, every time Jangles touched her she had the same reaction.

"Right. I see you don't understand. How's this for straight? You're not giving me back my goddamn key. We are far from over. And for the last time, you call me Beau."

"Um… But we are."

"No, Hope, we're not. We've just begun. If you think anything you told me last night changes how I feel about you, you'd be wrong. There's a lot to talk about, a lot I wanted to say last night but you weren't in the right frame of mind to hear me. Something we're gonna get straight right now before we go to breakfast is, you are not selfish and you are not stupid. You did not kill your parents. Wentworth Collins did."

Hope went statue-still as pain tore through her body. Acid churned in her belly and guilt rushed through her veins.

"Don't," she spat. "It's my fault."

"Babe, it's not."

"Let me up."

She needed to leave, needed to get far away from Jangles and the memory of her parents. The look on her little brother's face. So much pain and grief, and it was all her fault. Her parents were gone, she ruined her brother's life, and she deserved every bit of reproach. She was responsible for it all, but her brother—her sweet, smart little brother had paid for her sins.

"No, baby, we're gonna work this out of you. I'm gonna—"

"No, you're not. There's nothing to work out. I am who I am. I killed *four* people, Beau. Four. There's nothing I can do that will wash that away. That's mine. I own it. I remind myself every day so I'll never forget. I owe them that."

"Baby, that's fucked-up," Jangles whispered.

She didn't want his whispered words, she didn't want his pity, his concern, or anything else. All she wanted was to be left alone to drown in her misery.

That was all she deserved.

That was all she'd allow herself to have.

CHAPTER 7

JANGLES STARED DOWN HOPE, and he did this thinking about how strong she was. She'd never see it that way, but it was the truth. She'd been through hell and she'd survived. Knowing what he knew now, he understood. The steel-encased shell she'd wrapped around herself. The quick smiles, albeit fake—unless he had her alone in his bed, then she gave him real.

The tough-chick attitude she tossed around while serving drinks at the Ugly Mug. He'd watched her joke with Lefty, Trigger, Oz, Brain, Doc, Lucky, and Grover. The same with his team. Always pretending to be one of the guys. She'd engage the women when they were there but always gravitated to the men. Now he knew why—men didn't pry, they didn't ask personal questions, they didn't want to gossip and share stories. Especially the type of men they were—they all had secrets they'd never tell. Even if they could, they still wouldn't.

She was safe with them.

And she'd felt safe with Jangles because he was one of

those men, therefore he wouldn't pry, ask questions, or share personal information.

Until he did. Until everything changed. Now Hope wasn't safe—at least not emotionally—and she was going to retreat. But Jangles wasn't going to allow that to happen.

He just didn't know how to play this. Nor did he have anyone he could ask.

"Just let me go," she hissed.

Not a chance, baby.

Jangles yanked the pillow she was resting on away, forcing Hope to roll to her back. Then he slid in beside her, tagged her arm, and rolled her back so her head was on his shoulder. Without releasing her wrist, he held it to his chest and asked, "Four?"

Hope's body was already wound tight, stiff as a board, yet he still felt her go solid.

"Don't do this."

"Four, Hope?"

"Don't."

He figured since she blamed herself for her parents' murders, she'd lumped them into the tally, but that was only three when he added Wentworth.

"Where does your brother live?"

The solid that Hope was seconds before turned rigid, her nails dug into his chest, and her breathing became labored.

What the fuck?

Jangles clenched and unclenched his jaw. He couldn't get that fucking look out of his head, the one where Hope's eyes were cold and shattered.

"Baby? Where's your brother?"

"Texas State Cemetery. Section M, lot A, grave 3288."

Fuck.

Christ.

"Hope—"

"He was almost sixteen when Mom and Dad died. Got good grades, ran track, always happy, nothing bothered Peter. He wasn't like me, he didn't care what other people thought. He didn't care that they made fun of us because Mom and Dad worked hard but still couldn't afford to buy us nice stuff. He didn't care that people knew we wore hand-me-downs or what Mom could find at Goodwill. He didn't care that people knew we had free lunches at school, or we lived in a rundown old house. He was just him, smiling, happy, in his own world. I killed that. I killed him."

Jangles didn't believe she'd physically killed her brother. But he was dead, so something had gone horribly wrong.

"Did Wentworth get to him?"

Hope shook her head and pressed her face deeper. Just like last night, it was as if she wanted to crawl inside him, seek comfort in his arms. Jangles let that slide through him, easing some of the burn her pain caused, filling him with a different kind of warmth. Heat that felt good, that fed the need to protect her.

"He killed himself," she whispered.

Jangles fought to keep his body still, but his eyes closed.

Damn.

"After Mom and Dad. He went to live with my grandparents. They didn't want me. I mean, who could blame them? I killed their daughter." There it was again, the hollowed out, steely gaze.

Who could blame them for not being there for their emotionally damaged, distraught granddaughter who had just lost her parents? Jangles could, and he did.

But before he could point that out she continued in her cold, dead tone. "But they took in Peter. I wasn't allowed to see him. I understood that, too. But when he was eighteen, he found me. He was a wreck. Gone was my little brother. I hated what I'd done to him and he told me he hated me. He wanted money and I gave it to him. He came back months later demanding more and I gave it. I knew he was using it to buy drugs, but I still gave it to him. The last time I saw him, I begged him to get help. I offered to pay for the treatment. He was furious and rightfully so. But I wanted to get him help, not support his drug habit. He was of a different mind and took all the money I had and left. Then he left a different way. Two days later, my grandmother showed up, threw my brother's suicide letter at me, spit on me, and left."

"You didn't kill him."

"Yeah, I did. He told me I did. His final words to me in the letter were to make sure I never forgot that I killed Mom and Dad, and killed him, too. He told me. So you see, I killed four people. I'll live with that until I die. I *want* to live with it, I *want* to remember, I owe it to them never to forget."

Fucking jacked.

The tangled mess inside of Hope was so fucked he wasn't sure where to start. And if he found a starting point, he wasn't sure how to get it all untangled, especially because she was hellbent on keeping it. It was unhealthy as fuck but she wanted to hold on to the pain. Hell, she wanted to breathe it in and keep it fresh.

There were so many things wrong with what Hope said, it sliced through him like a blade, but hurt worse than any he'd physically felt cut his flesh.

God knew, if he felt shattered, she had to be shredded.

Chewed up and spit out.

He needed to find a way to break through and pull her from the hell she was purposely living in.

Jangles had seen a lot, done a lot, lived through gunfire

and bombings. He watched good men die, extinguished many lives. But never in all his years living through the horrors of war had he seen anything so cruel as what Hope was doing to herself.

He couldn't stand by and watch it.

He wouldn't have been able to do it if she was just Hope the bartender, but after finally admitting to himself all that she meant to him, there was no chance in hell he was going to watch her suffer.

Not a fucking chance.

CHAPTER 8

"Yo!" BF's loud, gravelly voice echoed in the small office. "Little Bit, you got a visitor."

Hope clenched her fists until her short nails cut into her palms.

"Stop calling me Little Bit," she clipped. "Unless you want me to start calling you Sebastiano."

"You call me Sebastiano and I'll fire your ass."

No, he wouldn't. BF threatened all kinds of crazy shit but never followed through.

"I'll save you the trouble and quit, you don't stop with the nickname."

"You gotta problem?"

Um, yeah, I have many problems.

Top of her list of problems was Jangles, one notch down was BF calling her Little Bit. A nickname said familiarity, friendship, belonging, comradery. None of which she wanted.

She preferred anonymous, lonely, nothingness.

Something that BF had never given her in the eight years she'd known him. He'd taken one look at the broken twenty-two-year-old she'd been and promptly tucked her under his wing and given her a job. She'd worked hard for him, starting as a barback-slash-janitor and had worked her way up to managing the Ugly Mug and his shooting range. He'd taught her everything she knew about cars, how to fix them, how to maintenance them, then he'd taught her about plumbing, electrical work, and how to keep his house, the trailers, and her RV in tip-top shape. And he'd taught her gunsmithing.

He did this cantankerously, which seriously worked for her because she didn't want kindness. But then the old man had slipped past her defenses and she started to like him. Now she adored him.

But she still hated the dumb nickname.

"Yeah, you coming back here bugging me when I'm trying to replace Bozo's trigger. You know I have approximately three minutes to get it done before your friend starts yelling about the reasons why a woman should never touch a firearm. And if I have to hear him say it one more time I'm gonna lose my shit, so maybe you wanna let me get back to it?"

A deep chuckle filled the space and Hope knew it hadn't come from BF. Her gaze lifted from the Beretta in front of her and there he was, Problem Number One in the flesh, leaning on the doorjamb right behind BF.

Shit.

"Goddamn! What's taking so long? It's a trigger. I didn't ask for a custom build and engrave!" Bozo shouted and Hope raised a brow in annoyance. "Shoulda done it my damn self."

"It's a two-hand job, Bozo. Shut up and let the girl work," Chief returned and Hope shook her head.

"See what you did?" Hope asked. "Now Bozo's gonna lose his mind because Chief made a crack about needing two hands. So, thanks to you, I'm gonna have to listen to all the things Bozo can do one-handed, and a lot of those things are gonna make me happy I skipped breakfast so it doesn't make a reappearance. And so we're clear, if he talks about callouses, baby oil, and self-love, I'm freaking quitting."

"Better get out of my way, Jangles," BF said as he wheeled himself around and started to roll out the door, but not before he muttered, "Maybe you can fix her pissy-assed mood."

Jerk.

Fat chance, considering Jangles was the reason she was in a pissy-assed mood.

Jangles closed the door, thankfully drowning out the men who were gathered for the bi-monthly get-together. Normally, Hope loved hanging with the old coots, listening to them rib and joke with one another. But mostly she liked being around the vets because, like her, they were all what society would call damaged. They weren't perfect. Some were missing a limb, some more than one—arms, legs, fingers. Some had burns, chunks of flesh missing. And some had injuries you couldn't see unless you looked deep. Like her injury, they were of the soul, not body. So being around the men gave her a sense of peace.

But unfortunately, Jangles closing the door meant she was locked in a room with a man she didn't want to think about.

"Trigger spring break?" Jangles asked.

"No. Bozo didn't like the stock trigger. He said it was mushy. I'm dropping in a Wilson Combat."

Hope kept her head down as she continued to work on the Beretta, hoping that if she ignored Jangles he'd go away. It was rude, but necessary if she wanted to keep her sanity intact. A trigger job didn't take three minutes but it also didn't take thirty, and she was done before she was ready to face Jangles.

"You're good at that," he noted. "BF teach you?"

"Yep."

"Hope, baby, look at me." Jangles' words might've been soft but the demand was clear.

She didn't look up. Instead, she kept her eyes trained on the now reassembled Beretta and said, "You know, it would be really awesome if for once in my life something could go right. Just once have something go my way. Like, say, when I break things off with a hot Delta operator, he walks away without showing up at my place of business a few hours later to torture me. That'd be super great."

"Hot Delta operator?" He chuckled. "I don't even know what that is. Is Delta even a real thing?"

"I'm not being funny."

"You're wrong."

Hope's gaze lifted from the gun to Jangles and her eyes narrowed. "Why are you here?"

"I'm taking you to lunch."

"No, you're—"

"Babe, I get why you bagged on breakfast. I gave you that. But you're leaving here to go directly to the bar to work another six hours. You're eating before you do that."

"How big of you to give me that," she mumbled.

Unfortunately, Jangles didn't respond to bitchy bait.

"You need to fire that before you give it to the owner?" Jangles gestured to the Beretta.

"Of course I do. I never give someone back a gun I worked on without firing it first."

"Right. Grab the nine and let's roll. I'm starving."

"Then you should mosey on out to your truck and go get food." Jangles' lips twitched and her irritation soared.

"Seriously, Jangles, you should go. I'll grab something at the bar."

Then in a supremely annoying maneuver, Jangles grabbed the gun off the workbench and turned to the door.

"I changed my mind." *Oh, thank God.* "I'm Beau. Just Beau. Anytime, anywhere, whether I got you naked in bed or having a beer at the bar. No more of this *Jangles* shit."

"That's how you introduced yourself," she returned.

"No, it's not. That's what you heard Woof call me when I was standing at the bar waiting for your fine ass to finish serving every *fucking* cowboy in the place that chose your side of the bar instead of Jake's. Which, babe, I fully understood at the time, because you're gorgeous. But now it just pisses me the fuck off when every patron with a dick would rather wait five minutes to be served by you than not wait and have Jake pour them a drink."

Hope knew she looked like a fish when her mouth opened and closed several times before she sputtered, "Are you nuts?"

"Yeah, Hope, I am. I'm totally fuckin' nuts because I fell for the one woman in Texas that's gonna fight me to the bitter end because she refuses to admit that we have something more than great sex. And so you don't twist this, what I mean by more is that I have feelings for you. I care about you. And we're gonna explore those feelings. You can bullshit all you want, say I mean nothing to you, but that'd be a lie. I know. You know. We both fuckin' know it. So let's go throw a few bullets downrange and hand this motherfucker off to whomever it belongs to so we can leave and I can feed my woman."

Hope swallowed past the lump in her throat.

The self-loathing slithered around her heart and squeezed tight.

"You can't care about me."

"Wrong, Hope. I can and I do."

"No, you can't. There's nothing to care about."

"Wrong again, baby. And straight up, I'm gonna show you just how wrong you are."

"I don't want you to."

"I know you don't. That's why I know I'm doing the right thing."

"But—"

"You got two choices, Hope. Test this gun so we can go to lunch or I lock this door and start educating you on all the reasons why I care about you. And I'll start by telling you I know this tough-chick exterior you got is bogus. I know because I've seen you with BF. He's old, he's grumpy, he's pretty much an ass to everyone unless they've served their country in one way or another. He gives you shit and you shovel it right back, but you do it in a way that shows you love him. You're loyal to him, you bust your ass for him, and don't deny it because I see it."

"You *are* nuts!" Hope shouted and threw her hands in the air.

"You already said that. What else you got?"

"You're not paying attention. Which is surprising considering who you are. You notice everything. I don't want more. And trust me, I'm not worth—"

"Now you're pissing me off," Jangles growled his warning.

"See? I'm a pain in the ass. You should—"

Hope didn't finish. In two quick steps, Jangles was across the room, his mouth slammed down on hers, his tongue shoved in—uninvited but not unwelcomed, and damn it all to hell, she kissed him back. Then her hands went to his shoulders, trailed up the back of his neck, and finally, her fingers slid through his hair as she deepened the kiss. God, she loved his hair, loved that he wore it longer than military regulations. It made him look like a step above badass but one down from a pillaging Viking.

Hope took and tasted, drank from him. It wasn't often he allowed her to control the action—not the kissing, touching, or sex—Beau was all about *him* giving to *her*. He led the way, he guided them where he wanted them to go. Sometimes that guidance was rough and demanding, sometimes it was slow and coaxing. Whatever the speed, it was magnificent. But right then, he'd passed the torch and she knew it was costing him. Hope felt it—his pent-up energy was rolling off him in waves, washing over her, upping her excitement tenfold.

More.

She needed more.

Hope didn't want to acknowledge the truth, she wanted to deny her feelings, pretend she wasn't in love with him. Beau Talbot would wreck her. If she had any chance of keeping what was left of her sanity intact, she needed to let him go.

But what if I let him in?

A sliver of hope pierced her heart and apprehension coursed through her blood. But she couldn't deny it—couldn't deny that she wanted Beau to bulldoze through all her walls and make her face her demons.

Blood-soaked dreams or a beautiful future...

She didn't deserve a future.

But Beau did.

CHAPTER 9

JANGLES SAT across the table from Hope. He'd purposely chosen the corner booth in the back of the tiny diner so they'd have privacy. He knew the only reason Hope agreed to go to lunch with him was because BF threatened to take her off the schedule and call in Brian, another bartender who worked at the Ugly Mug, if she didn't take a break and get food in her stomach.

As surly as BF could be, he genuinely cared for his employees. Hope especially.

"How'd you meet BF?" Jangles asked.

Hope glanced over the top of a one-page laminated menu she'd been studiously but unnecessarily studying, then without a word, dropped her gaze and commenced ignoring him.

"You know I don't let things go," he reminded her.

"I know. And for the record, it's annoying."

"Noted."

Deep brown eyes lifted, then narrowed. Jangles tried but failed to keep the smile from forming.

"That's annoying, too."

"I'll scratch it on the list," he mumbled and her lips pressed together. "You know the death glare only works when you don't look cute doing it."

"I don't look cute," she huffed. "Stop annoying me so I can look at the menu."

Before Jangles could call her out, the waitress greeted them with, "'Bout time I see your face."

"Hey, Suzie. How ya been?"

"Better now that I got some eye candy in my section. Boring around here, when you boys go out." Suzie's gaze slid to Hope and the older woman slowly smiled. "Hey there, sugar, what's your name?"

"Hope."

Then without warning, Suzie's head tipped to the side and she busted out laughing.

"That's perfect," Suzie shouted. "Per...fect."

"Wanna let us in on why you're laughing?" Jangles requested.

"Sure thing." Suzie looked between the two of them, her eyes dancing with mirth. Jangles had always liked the older woman. She was friendly, fast, and efficient. Quick to smile, stop for a gab, but never stayed too long. "Beau and Hope."

"Not tracking why that's worth a laugh."

"No, you wouldn't. I don't suspect a man like you would watch daytime TV." Suzie waved her hand and went on. "Anyway, I do watch daytime TV. Used to have to set my VHS to tape my shows. Pain in the backside. But now I got that satellite TV, my grandson came over and set it up. Three TVs. I don't know why I need three TVs when it's just me in the house. But Lenny insisted. That's my grandson. He's a good boy, always coming over to check on me. So now I got this DVR thingy, it records my shows for me. Never miss a' one of them while I'm working. And now—"

"Suzie, glad your grandson visits and he's set you up, but what does that have to do with Beau and Hope?"

"I was getting to that," she snapped. "He cut you off like that, sugar?"

"All the time," Hope muttered, and gave Jangles a sassy lift of her brow.

"That's rude, Beau," Suzie chastised, and with a resigned sigh, Jangles settled back into the booth. "You shouldn't cut off a lady while she's talkin'. It's important to listen, a woman will bare her soul if you just sit quietly and let her speak."

If only that were true.

Hope had settled in, she'd rested her elbows on the table and was staring up at Suzie like she was Master Yoda and if she waited long enough, the old woman would tell her the secrets of the universe.

"So anyway, Beau and Hope is my all-time favorite couple. Their love story is one for the ages. Up and down they went through the years. Eighties, nineties, and into the two-thousands. Sometimes I wanted to smack that Beauregard Brady—he, too, didn't always listen to his Hope. But they made it. And their wedding, *oh sweet Jesus,* it was beautiful. But someone shoulda told that wardrobe person that the headpiece they made her wear was too much. The dress, beautiful, that veil, ug-ly. Still, I cried my eyes out when they said the vows. So, Beau and Hope—perfect. You're meant to be."

Jangles sat back, thinking that listening to Suzie prattle on about VHS tapes, her grandson, and her scolding him, was worth it. He'd gladly listen to her drone on another five minutes if it meant Hope kept looking at him with a smile on her pretty face and humor dancing in her eyes.

Oh, yeah, he fucking loved the soft, open way she gazed

at him. He vowed right then to make her look at him like that more often.

"So, what'll be today?" Suzie asked, and the spell was broken.

Hope quickly gave her order, Jangles followed, and Suzie strolled away without writing a single thing down, but Jangles knew their order would be correct.

"She always that friendly?"

"Yep," Jangles returned. "Since the first time we all came in. She came right over, introduced herself, declared we were to only sit in her section when we came in. Then she launched straight in, telling us about her family. That grandson Lenny is her daughter's boy. She has two sons, neither live in Texas, which means the seven grandchildren they've given her don't, either. She's only got Lenny and Sunshine close. Her daughter passed away from cancer—she was young and the kids were only teenagers—and as she tells it, Lenny and Sunshine's father is as useless as tits on a bull so they spent a lot of time at her house when they were growing up."

As soon as the words left his mouth, Jangles wanted to kick his own ass as he watched the shutters slam down and dim the brightness in Hope's eyes.

Fuck.

"Babe?"

"Yeah?"

"How'd you meet BF?"

"You still making a list?"

"What?"

"A list of all the things you do that annoy me," she clarified and continued. "If you are, put that at the top."

Jangles' mouth curved up into a smile. He watched her gaze involuntarily drop to his lips and he busted out laughing.

HOPE SAT across from Beau and watched in rapt fascination as he laughed. It was not the first time she'd heard it—he laughed a lot around her—but it was the first time she'd allowed herself to soak it in. It sucked because it was truly annoying when he pushed her to talk about things she didn't want to talk about, but Beau was seriously hot when he laughed.

The sound filled her ears and wrapped around her like a cozy blanket. Open, real, honest. He didn't hold back, not from her. And when she thought about it, he never had. All the way back to the very beginning, he'd given her everything he could. They didn't talk about his job, not outright, though he never hid what he did. Hope had lived in Killeen long enough to know he was special forces. Normal calvary brigades didn't deploy as frequently, they also didn't leave in the middle of the night without warning. So, he'd never said the words, but he didn't insult her by making up lies.

With that in mind, she made a decision. Actually, she made a few, but she wasn't sure she could follow through with the others. But at least she could return the favor and be honest with him.

"When I moved here from Austin, I needed a job. One afternoon, I was having a beer at the Ugly Mug and going over the want ads and I overheard BF bitchin' his dishwasher had called in sick. I offered to work the shift. After BF was done bustin' a gut, he asked me if I was running from the law or a man. I told him I was just running from life and I'd cause him no trouble. He let me work the shift, paid me cash at the end of the night. I came back around a few days later asking if he had any other work and he let me barback. Then he asked me if I knew how to turn a wrench. I told him no, he said he'd teach me, and he did. The rest, as they say, is history."

Beau looked shocked Hope had answered. Before he could recover, Suzie was back with their drinks so she hurried and changed the subject.

"Did you always want to be in the Army?"

"Yeah. My grandad and dad both served. Never crossed my mind to do anything else. And not because they put pressure on me, I just knew I wanted to be like them. Though when I was five playing with GI Joes, I didn't have the first clue what 'being like them' meant."

"Bet they're proud."

"They were," he returned, and sadness washed over his features. "Dad died a few years ago, heart attack. Grandad's been gone longer. Old age got him."

"I'm sorry, Beau."

"Thanks. Grandad was ninety-two. He lived a long full life. He went to bed one night and never woke up. Sucked losing Dad. He was too young. Healthy, too, but he had an undetectable heart condition—that is, undetectable until it was too late. After he passed, my mom moved to Wyoming to live with my older sister. She'd divorced and has four kids, so it's a win-win for both of them. Mom can spoil her grandkids and isn't alone and my sister has her mom close and a built-in babysitter."

"Are you close with them?"

"My turn. Why do you live in BF's RV?"

Hope took a long pull of Diet Coke and fiddled with the straw, trying to find a way to explain to Beau why she lived in an RV that wouldn't make her sound like such a loser. Coming up empty, she figured there was no way to sugarcoat her reason.

"When I moved up here, I didn't have very much money. I couldn't afford to stay in a hotel *and* eat. And I certainly didn't have enough to rent an apartment. So I was sleeping in my car. One night, BF caught me. On a good day, the man can be a little grumpy and scary. The night he found me, he lost his mind. He didn't give me an option, he just told me to follow him, so I followed. We drove to his place, he pulled in front of the RV, rolled down his window, pointed at it, and told me my ass better be sleeping in it every night. So that's where I sleep." Hope shrugged, trying for nonchalance when really BF's kindness meant the world to her.

"Where'd you live in Austin?"

"Nope. My turn." He nodded in acceptance and waited for Hope to come up with her next question. "Do you enjoy your job?"

Beau leaned back, and for a second, she didn't think he'd answer. She was skirting a line they didn't cross and she knew it. But it wasn't like she asked for top-secret information or anything. So she figured she hadn't asked too much.

"Enjoy isn't a word I would use. I believe in what I do. The missions we go on are important, they make American citizens safe."

He paused and she didn't miss the turmoil swirling. His normally clear, blue eyes were stormy, and his features hardened. She'd seen a lot of Beau's expressions, but even when they argued, she'd never seen this rough edge.

"I do not enjoy taking lives. Yet, with every press of my trigger, every swing of my fist or slice of my blade, the intention is there. I aim to kill and I do so with a clear conscience. I know you know what I do. But there's a difference between knowing and *knowing*. Every time I leave you in my bed, I do so with the sole intent to complete my mission. And every time I come back to you, I do so with new stains on my hands. Those stains don't leak into my soul, they don't keep me up at night, they don't weigh heavy on me. And they don't because every time I take aim, I know that I'm saving my life, my brothers, and doing what's best for my country. But even if it was simply so I could live, I'd still take that shot."

When Beau was done, Hope felt her lungs burn. His gaze was still fixed on hers, pinning her in place, making his point. There was no missing he was talking about her, what she'd done. But she hadn't taken Went's life to save her own, not really. Because had she not been so overwhelmed with rage, wanting him to die for what he'd done to her parents, she would've let him kill her.

So many nights she'd cried herself to sleep wishing he had.

"Here you go, sugar plums, enjoy your lunch."

Suzie set down their plates, completely oblivious to the thick, ominous cloud of pain looming over Hope. The heavy weight of regret that she no longer wanted, yet held on to because it was all she knew, all she allowed herself to have. Never imagining there was anything else out there for her.

She owed it to her parents to never forget what a horrible person she was. But Beau made it hard to cling to the notion that all she deserved was misery.

CHAPTER 10

JANGLES WAS STARING down at the frying pan, watching the Teflon flake as he scrubbed the remnants of the scrambled eggs off the bottom. He was thinking he really needed to buy a decent set of pans when he heard Hope coming down the hall.

It'd been a week since their lunch at Twinny's. A lunch where Hope had shared she'd once lived in her goddamn car. One could say that that afternoon had lit a fire under Jangles' ass. He'd planned on going slow, giving Hope time to adjust to him moving their relationship from how it started to where he wanted them to be. But the more he learned, the more impatient he became.

Hope had been living in limbo for twelve years.

No, she'd been living in hell for twelve years, punishing herself for something she had no business punishing herself over.

So, Jangles was impatient to show her she deserved happiness. He also wanted her out of that goddamn RV. But that would take time and finesse. So, he'd backed off just enough to give her room to breathe, but not enough to let her retreat. That meant no more heavy conversations, but she had spent every night in his bed, coming to him after her shifts at the Ugly Mug.

Which meant something had changed. It was small, Jangles couldn't put his finger on it, but the mere fact Hope had come to him every night when he asked told him something had shifted. Hope didn't do anything she didn't want to do. If she didn't want to be in his bed, she wouldn't have shown. But she had, every night.

He also hadn't been back to the bar, even though Woof and Zip had invited him to hang since their women were out of town. Nori, Woof's woman, was on an overseas assignment with the foreign service where she worked as a negotiator. Jangles had watched the woman work, she was damn good at her job, cool under pressure, and smart. Zip's woman, Destiny, was a flight attendant and had picked up the Seattle to Dallas haul, meaning she wouldn't be back in Killeen for at least a week.

He had no idea how Zip and Woof went long stretches at home without seeing their women, but he had to admit, they made it work. He knew his teammates were in love, committed, and would wait until the end of time for their women to return. And not just Zip and Woof. Merlin and Duff had found it, too.

Jangles twisted from the sink when he heard Hope approach. She made her way to him and faceplanted on his chest. His arms wrapped around her and she mumbled something that sounded like 'good morning'.

"Morning, baby."

"Too early."

"Babe, it's almost noon. I've already been to post and PT'd."

"Well, aren't you special." Hope pressed closer and Jangles chuckled.

"I made you breakfast."

Hope lifted her head off his chest, tipped her face to meet his eyes, and scrunched her nose.

"I hope you know, I love it when you make me breakfast. But that pan is a health hazard. You need new pans."

"Noticed that?"

"Can't miss it with all the black flakes that are not pepper mixed in."

"You have today off?"

"Yes, thank God."

"We'll go to the store and get new ones."

"Beau." She started to pull away but his arms tightened. She was itching to retreat, he could hear it in her voice.

Hell to the no.

"Babe. You get I'm a man. I don't have the first clue about buying pots and pans. With safety in mind so in the future I won't poison you with flaky Teflon, help me out, would ya?"

"You're asking the wrong woman for help. I don't even own a frying pan."

That ugly ball of anger grew at the reminder she lived in an RV. She didn't own a frying pan, another slap in his face.

A loud knock at his door saved him from having to respond. His gaze moved to the front windows with a clear view of the street. He saw Merlin's black truck at the curb.

"Shit," he groaned.

"What?"

"Merlin's here."

"Um. Want me to slip out the back door?"

Jangles' eyes sliced back to her and narrowed.

"Why the fuck would I want you to slip out the back?" he asked irately.

"I'm standing in your kitchen in your T-shirt," was her asinine answer.

"So?"

"Merlin's not stupid, Beau, he'll know why I'm here."

"And?"

"Beau," she hissed. "I don't want them thinking I'm some easy—"

"Stop."

"Stop what? Surely you can understand I don't want them talking about me. I don't want rumors—"

"First, there's not a single man on my team that would talk about you behind your back. Second, there's no way in fuck my woman's slinkin' out the back door. And third, I don't know why the hell you think I'd let you."

Jangles stepped away from Hope and took her in. She was wearing his tee but she'd put on a pair of those tight leggings that women wore, so she was semi-presentable if you ignored her wild mane of long brown hair. She looked beautiful, thoroughly fucked from the night before, and Merlin wouldn't miss it—no man would.

Merlin would take one look at Hope in Jangles' tee, in his kitchen, looking sleepy, and he'd know.

Jangles didn't care about that.

He skirted Hope and made his way to the door, thinking that it was good Merlin had shown up. Jangles had been trying to find the right time to tell his team he'd been seeing Hope. The only reason he hadn't done it already was that he didn't want to explain why he'd kept her a secret for months. Something he wished he hadn't done.

"Hey," Jangles greeted when he opened the door.

Merlin smiled, something he did a lot since meeting Gwen. "Hey. We were driving by, saw your truck in the drive, and thought we'd stop and see if you wanted to hit the range with us."

Good news.

When Jangles had seen Merlin's truck, he'd thought he was swinging by to tell him they were leaving on a mission. This was better, way better, the perfect way to get Hope to go out with him in a social situation.

Jangles stepped to the side in invitation.

"Hi, Gwen."

"Hey, Jangles," she happily returned and preceded Merlin.

Jangles didn't have time to warn them he had company before Gwen abruptly stopped.

"Oh. Hey, Hope," Gwen chirped, her eyes darting from Hope to Jangles, then to Merlin, and back to Hope. "We... um...should've called first."

"Hi, Gwen."

Hope stood frozen in his dining room. Everything about this situation hit him as wrong. His woman should never be uncomfortable in his home. Hope's eyes got big as he approached, then they turned pleading when she caught on to his play.

"No worries," Jangles said, and when he was within reaching distance, he tagged Hope around the waist and pulled her to his side. "We were just discussing the state of my shitty pots and pans and the fundamental need to junk them before we die of polymer fume fever."

Hope jerked and Jangles smiled. She wanted to pull away but she wouldn't, not while they had an audience.

"Well, we wouldn't want that." Merlin chuckled. "You guys wanna hit the range first?"

"It's my weekly lesson." Gwen rolled her eyes and feigned annoyance but she wasn't fooling anyone. She loved Merlin, loved spending time with him, whether it was at the shooting range, at her bookstore, or at home.

"Um..." Hope started, but Jangles talked over her.

"Let us get showered and we'll meet you there."

Hope went solid and he knew he'd pay for that comment after Gwen and Merlin left, but his point was made.

"Right. We'll let you get to it then. See ya in a bit," Merlin said.

"Hey, I know! After I dazzle everyone with my perfect shot placement, we should go to lunch," Gwen announced and looked at Hope. "Do you work tonight?"

"No, it's my day off."

Oh, yeah, Hope was pissed and doing her best to cover it. Jangles would definitely catch shit when his friends left.

"Great. Shooting and lunch." Gwen smiled.

Jangles liked Gwen, always had, but right then, he liked her even more. She was doing her part to make Hope feel welcomed and he appreciated it.

"Come on, princess, let's let them get ready."

Jangles remained where he was as the couple let themselves out. The second the door closed, Hope turned on him.

"That was—"

Jangles didn't let her finish. His head tipped down, his mouth brushed hers, and before she could protest, his tongue darted out and tasted her lips. That was all the coaxing Hope needed to let him in. Hope's hands clutched his shoulders, and his moved to capture her face.

Her fingers curled in and pulled him closer and Jangles tilted his head, making a soft, wet kiss deep and demanding. He kept at her until she moaned into his mouth and his hard cock twitched at the sound. Then he reminded himself they needed to get a move on. He needed her showered, dressed, and in his truck in quick order before she had a chance to pull away and run.

He slowly broke the kiss and loved her mew in protest.

But today wasn't about what he could do for her in bed —he was well-acquainted with every part of her body, knew how to make it sing in pleasure. Hands down, Hope was the best he'd ever had. What she lacked in experience, she made up with enthusiasm. The woman drove him wild. It didn't matter if she was using her hand, her mouth, or he was balls-deep in her tight pussy, she had him on edge from the first stroke. She pushed him to the brink of his control—every time.

"Babe."

"Huh?"

"We gotta get goin'."

She was soft and pliant in his arms, but the moment he spoke, she turned to stone.

"Beau—"

"Get dressed. We'll hit the range, have lunch, then go shopping. Tonight I'm taking you to dinner. So if you need to stop at your place to get clothes, we'll do that."

"I don't think—"

"No more thinking."

"Stop interrupting me," Hope grunted. "It's rude and annoying."

"I'll stop if you promise me you won't say something that's gonna piss me off, like, this isn't who we are. Or, you don't think it's a good idea to hang out with my friends. Or something equally as jacked, like you don't want them knowing we're together."

Hope stared at him scowling, irritation sparking in her eyes, and Jangles smiled.

"I'm glad to see something is amusing you," she snapped.

"Baby, you're standing in my dining room, wearing my tee. Your hair's still tangled from last night, you smell good, you taste good, last night you passed out in my arms, I woke up with your head on my chest, your knee hitched up resting on my thigh. I'm gonna take my woman shooting, we're gonna go buy new pans so we're not courting death every time I cook you breakfast. Then I'm gonna take you to dinner, and after that, we'll come back here and the night will end the same way it did yesterday. I'm not amused, Hope, I'm *happy*."

He heard her suck in a breath. Then he lost her eyes because she lowered her lids before she did another faceplant.

"I'm scared."

Jangles' muscles seized.

"Scared? Of me?"

"Yes."

What the fuck?

"I would never hurt you."

"I know you'd never physically hurt me, but that doesn't mean you don't have the power to crush me. When I'm with you and you say stuff like that, you make me forget. But more than that, you make me want more."

He didn't have time to recover from the blow her words caused before she continued to rock his world. "You make me believe I could love you and we could be happy. You make me believe there's a possibility I could be forgiven for what I've done. All of that scares me so badly, I want to run far and fast so you'll never catch me."

"I'd catch you."

"I know you would. And that's why I'm so scared."

Fucking finally.

Finally, she'd admitted her feelings.

"I'd never hurt you," he repeated. "I'm not an asshole.

Nor am I stupid, I know what we have, I know what I feel. And I know I'm not letting you go."

"Please don't hurt me." Her plea sizzled down Jangles' spine and heated his insides.

Finally.

"I won't, baby."

Hope had cracked the door open. Now he was blowing the motherfucker off its hinges so she could never close it.

CHAPTER 11

"So..." Gwen smiled. "How long have you two been sneakin' around?"

Hope was startled by Gwen's question and it must've shown because the other woman's giggle rang out in the empty office.

They'd finished shooting and Jangles and Merlin were cleaning up the empty brass from the lanes and Gwen and Hope had gone to her office to retrieve their purses.

"Sorry, too personal?" Gwen asked, but if the wide smile was anything to go by, she wasn't sorry.

Of course, Hope knew Gwen. She was with Merlin so she'd been to the Ugly Mug plenty of times, and she and Merlin had been to the range while Hope had been working there, too. But Hope didn't *know* her, know her. It wasn't like they had weekly mani-pedis or anything.

Hope liked Gwen. If she was being honest, she liked Nori, Destiny, and Ivy, too. But she'd always kept her distance and never allowed herself more than a brief chat with the women. She didn't want to get attached. Actually, she didn't think it was her place to become friends with the women who belonged to Jangles' teammates.

They were together but not like that. Their lives didn't cross outside of his house.

Until now.

And Hope was at a loss for how to handle the situation.

Damn Jangles.

"Um..."

"Forget it." Gwen shook her head. "I shouldn't have asked."

"I don't know what to say," Hope blurted.

"What do you mean?"

"I don't have girlfriends," Hope sighed, and Gwen's eyes widened before they went soft. She didn't want to process what Gwen's look meant so she rushed on. "I also don't know what Beau would want me to say. But since he's the one that thought this would be a good idea...not that I didn't want to hang out with you and Merlin...just that... gah. I'm screwing this up so bad."

"I get it." Gwen laughed.

"Months," Hope admitted. "Since right after he moved to Killeen."

"That long?" Gwen gasped.

"Yeah. But we weren't really *together,* together. You know, more like...friends who had sex."

Gwen's face turned beet-red before she busted out laughing.

"TMI?"

"No. Not at all. I just can't believe I didn't see it. Geez, I need to pay more attention to what's going on around me."

Gwen was still smiling and Hope was struggling with what to make of the friendliness that was rolling off Gwen.

Then Gwen shocked the hell out of her and said, "But

now that the cat's out of the bag, you have to come to one of our girls' nights."

"I don't think the cat's out of the bag, Gwen. I think you just happened to show up at Beau's house while I was there and he's too nice of a guy to make me hide."

"You're kidding?"

"Not even a little bit."

Gwen stopped smiling and started studying her. The scrutiny made Hope want to squirm. She didn't like attention and something told her Gwen saw way more than she wanted her to.

"I agree with you, Jangles is a nice guy. But, Hope, if he didn't want you here, he wouldn't have invited you. And he went out of his way to point out not only had he cooked you breakfast before, but he also planned to in the future."

Hope hated how insecure she felt, hated that she was in an unknown situation, where she didn't know what to say or how to act. This was why she didn't have girlfriends, or any friends actually. The men she surrounded herself with were grumpy, old, and would never dream of talking to her about anything remotely personal, like who was making her breakfast.

"May I be honest with you?" Hope found herself asking Gwen.

"Of course."

Gwen was back to grinning so she hoped that meant the woman didn't think she was a total basket case. Or maybe she was grinning because she thought Hope was a little loopy.

Whatever.

She couldn't think about that now.

"I'm scared. I don't know what to do, and I don't have anyone to talk to. BF's my only friend, if you could call him that, and he'd run me over with his chair if I tried to talk to him about Beau."

Gwen giggled again and it hit her why Merlin was so smitten. It wasn't because she was positively beautiful, which she was, but she was genuine, friendly, and so damn sweet, Hope didn't know what to do with her. She wasn't used to anyone being kind to her. Sure, people were polite, and both Lefty's and Jangles' teams were nice to her in a bartender-patron kind of way. And Beau was…Beau. But that was different, they were…doing whatever it was they were doing. But on the regular, people were not kind and sweet to Hope. And Gwen barely knew her and she was being both.

"How about this?" Gwen started. "Since we only have a few minutes until Merlin and Jangles come looking for us, I'll give you my number and we'll make plans, just the two of us. But I'll say this now; love's scary. It's hard. But so worth it."

"Are you sure you wouldn't mind?"

"Girl…" Gwen bumped her shoulder and continued, "I'd mind if you didn't. Us girls need to stick together."

Welp, it seemed that after living in Killeen for eight years, Hope had made her first girlfriend. She was sure that made her pathetic, but she was floating on a cloud of goodness so she shoved the self-pity aside and decided to focus on the fact that she now had someone to talk to.

Hope didn't know what woke her, but when she opened her eyes, she was alone in Beau's bed. A quick glance at the clock told her it was four in the morning, and a touch to Beau's cold pillow told her he'd been up a while.

She tossed her legs over the side of the bed, got up, and

rooted around in the dark until she found the tee she'd torn off Beau earlier. Once she pulled it over her head, she went in search of her man.

Her man.

That's what he'd called himself earlier. Or actually, he'd called her his woman. So, if that was the case, then the reverse was true. And sometime over the last week since the flood gates had opened and he'd wormed his way deeper into her life, she tentatively decided to try this 'more' stuff on for size. It was scary as hell, but she found she liked it, which was a new kind of scary. The big kind that would tear her apart when Beau figured out she wasn't worthy of a man like him, or her constant fear of moving forward would get old.

The hallway was dark as she made her way to the dining room, but when she looked left, there he was in the living room sitting on the couch with only a dim lamp and his laptop to illuminate his form. His head came up as she approached but he didn't say anything.

Apprehension started to tickle the back of her throat. Something felt off. In all the months she'd stayed over, never had she woken up alone in the middle of the night.

"Everything all right?" she whispered.

Beau closed his laptop and set it aside before he answered, "Everything's fine."

"You sure?"

"Yeah, baby, come here."

She didn't go there. Instead, she stood rooted in place thinking over their day. After the shooting range, they'd gone to lunch. Hope thought it went well, but now she wasn't so sure. The four of them had joked and laughed, the conversation was light and fun, mostly poking fun at Merlin and his demand that Gwen continued to practice shooting even after she'd demonstrated she was a damn good shot and was totally safe with her gun. No one had brought up why Hope was at Jangles' house, wearing his shirt, so she figured that was good.

They shopped for new pots and pans. That was easy because neither of them liked to shop so they walked in, grabbed the first set that looked decent, and left.

During their quick trip to Hope's RV so she could pick up clothes, there was a small hiccup when Beau told her to grab a few days' worth and she didn't think that was necessary. They'd argued, but Beau had gotten his way, mainly because he was bossy and packed her a bag. She bitched loudly, then mentally scratched 'bossy' onto the top of the list of things Beau did that annoyed the shit out of her, even though secretly, she loved that he wanted her to pack a bag.

See? Basket case.

Dinner had been great. They'd always had a good time together though they'd never done it in public before. But Hope couldn't imagine that was what would be bothering him.

They'd come home, torn each other's clothes off, and had fantastic sex. That was not new, they did that all the time.

So the harder she thought, the more confused she became. Unless he'd changed his mind. And he'd gotten out of bed because he was trying to find a way to let her down easy.

"Something's wrong, Beau. Something bad enough that it took you from your bed and now you're sitting out here alone. Just tell me if you've—"

"Hope." Her name was a warning.

"Seriously, stop cutting me off."

"How 'bout this—I'll stop when you stop thinking the worst. I swear to you, I'll never do it again when you stop saying shit that pisses me off. And, Hope, it pisses me off, because I've given you no indication I've changed my mind."

God, it was annoying when he knew what she was going to say.

"Please come here."

It was the *please* that made her feet move. Beau reached out, tagged her hand, and pulled her forward. Hope's hands went to his shoulders, his went to her hips, and he yanked her down so she was straddling his lap.

"Nothing's wrong, baby. At least nothing worth you worrying about."

That didn't make her feel better.

"But it's worth *you* worrying about?"

Beau was quiet for a long time. So long, it started to freak her out. But she didn't break the silence because as freaked out as Hope was, she liked the way he was looking at her. It was mostly dark, so she couldn't see the blue of his eyes, but she saw they were gentle, introspective. His hands on her hips started moving, slow glides of his palms, featherlight. His touches were so different from their normal frenzied rush.

Hope felt some of the tension recede and she whispered, "What's wrong, handsome?"

"I'm trying to go slow. Give you time to adjust. But I'm not sure I can do it."

Hope's teeth sank into her bottom lip in an effort not to say what she was thinking, but it was hard. So difficult, she bit down harder to keep her runaway thoughts to herself. He told her to stop thinking the worst, but it was damn impossible when he said stuff like that.

Beau's hand left her hip and went to her jaw. His thumb grazed her lip and pulled the abused flesh free. "Thank you, baby."

"For what?"

"For keeping your thoughts in check. For trusting me." His palm slid across her cheek, then down until he cupped the back of her neck. "You are so beautiful. All of you, Hope. You have no idea how hard it is for me to control my need to protect you. To pack up that RV and move you in here. Don't twist that into something ugly. I know you're strong, I know you can take care of yourself, and you've made that RV into a home. But it's still an RV. You've lived there eight years. You deserve someplace better. I want to give you better. I want to move you in here, so I know you're safe. I want you here so I know you're coming home to me after work. I want you here so when I'm out on an assignment, I know you're in our bed. I want more, so much more, but I'm trying to have a mind to what you need.

"So, you see, I'm at war with myself. Half of me wants to push hard, completely take over, force you to see how special you are. I don't want us to hide from my team, their women, BF, or his cronies. I want them to know you're mine. I want to walk into the bar and not have to pretend you're just the bartender and not who you really are, the woman I love.

"But the other half of me knows I need to go gentle, handle you with care. Ease you into my life. I'm torn. And after the day we had today, I don't know if I can go back to hiding who we are. Hell, baby, I don't think we should. You're not a secret, and it feels like shit we've been hiding as long as we have."

Hope sat perched on Beau's lap and struggled to get enough oxygen. The air around her felt thin, her head was fuzzy, and her vision went blurry. Her eyes hadn't left his, but she couldn't make out more than a shadowy figure.

"Baby?"

"Bulldoze," Hope found herself muttering. "Please, don't let up."

Unconsciously, without thought, consideration, and on impulse alone, her nails dug into Beau's shoulders until he hissed in pain. "Promise me, Beau. Swear it. You won't let me go."

"Swear, Hope, I won't let you go, baby."

"Push hard, Beau. Even when I fight you, push. Don't let me leave you."

"Look at me."

"I am."

"You're looking, but you're not seeing me. I'm not gonna let you go."

A tidal wave of emotions crashed over her, bringing with it a surge of adrenaline. She was doing this. She'd given him permission to push, she wasn't completely sure what that meant, but she was sure Beau wouldn't allow her to change her mind.

Not that she wanted to.

She wanted more.

"We got this," Beau told her.

"Got what?"

"This. All of it. We'll see you through."

"Okay," she agreed, even though she wasn't a hundred percent convinced.

"Relax, baby."

"I don't think I can."

Beau's hand on her hip moved, taking with it the cotton of her tee until he hit bare skin.

"We got this," he repeated and trailed his fingers across Hope's belly. "Now relax and kiss me."

"I'm not sure kissing you will help me relax," she told Beau as she leaned forward.

Just as her lips touched his, he muttered, "But the orgasm will."

Beau put pressure on the back of her neck, their mouths collided, he gave her approximately three seconds of control, then he took over.

Hope trembled as his hand skimmed up her torso. His fingers glided under her breast before he lifted it, his thumb brushed over her nipple, and she moaned.

Beau growled and Hope twitched.

She became acutely aware she was on his lap sans panties—wet and ready with only a few swipes of his tongue against hers and his hand on her breast. His hands moved again and the tee was gone. Beau tossed it to the side, then his hands were back, this time on her ass. He shifted Hope forward without breaking the kiss, maneuvering her so he could yank his shorts down.

Skin to skin.

With his cock free, his hands went back to her ass and he moved her again. This time, her wetness coated his erection and he groaned. The sound vibrated against her chest, slid down her throat, and set her on fire. Every inch of her heated, from her pussy, to her tits, to her sensitive nipples rubbing against his muscled chest.

Beau stopped kissing her long enough to demand, "Put me inside you, baby."

Hot.

Hope shifted, lifted her hips, reached between them, and without delay sank down the length of his cock.

Heaven.

She mewed. He grunted and she tasted that, too, the sound of his pleasure as his fingers curled harder on her bottom as he thrust up.

Hope rocked her hips and Beau tore his mouth from hers. Before she could protest, his head dipped and he latched onto her nipple, swirling his tongue around the hard peak.

"Beau."

"Harder, Hope, take me deeper."

He was as deep as he could go. She felt him everywhere —womb, clit, tits—hell, her toes tingled with excitement. But Beau wouldn't be denied. He thrust up as he pulled her down until Hope shuddered and desire flooded between her thighs.

Beau's palms slid up her back and his arms went around her, cocooning her close. His face shoved into her neck and his tongue swept the skin there before he muttered, "You feel like heaven, baby. Your pussy snug around my cock, grinding down, your tits on my chest, all of it sweet, all of it feels good. But when you lose yourself and I hear you moan *my* name, knowing the only thing you're feeling, the only thing you're thinking about, is *me*, Christ, nothing better."

Hope's head dropped forward. Heat seared through her and her hands clutched his shoulders as she rocked harder, reaching for her orgasm. It was right there, dancing at the surface, ready to break and crash over her, but she wanted him with her.

"Beau, baby, come with me."

"Fuck," he snarled and tightened his arms around her, leaving her fighting for oxygen. But she didn't care about breathing. She was lost in him. He was right—all she could think about, feel, smell, was him. "Now, baby. Come."

And on his command, she flew apart. But she needn't have worried, Beau was there. He'd hold her together.

CHAPTER 12

"So," Woof drawled. "You and Hope finally decided to come out, huh?"

Jangles glanced up from the intel report across the table to his friend. "Come again?"

"We see how it is, friend," Zip put in, and Jangles' gaze sliced to him in time to watch Zip smile. "For months, you keep Hope hidden away in your Palace of Pleasure, then one day you decide to let her come up for air and you go out with Merlin and don't bother to call the rest of us."

"Palace of Pleasure? Where do you come up with that shit?" Jangles laughed.

"It just pops into my head." Zip shrugged. "It's a gift."

"It's really not."

As amusing as Zip's comment was, Jangles' smile waned. Then something ugly hit him square in the chest. Just last night, he'd told Hope she wasn't a secret, and he'd been feeling no small amount of guilt for keeping their relationship quiet for as long as he had.

"Right place, right time," Merlin joined in. "We caught them as they were both coming up for air."

Jesus.

"Does this mean you're done keeping her sequestered? Or was shooting and lunch a one-off?" Woof jabbed.

"They looked pretty cozy—"

"You done?" Jangles cut off Merlin, deciding he'd heard enough of the good-natured ribbing. It was no more than what he'd done to them when they'd hooked up with their women, but their commander would be walking in any minute, and Jangles had barely gone over the report in front of him. "Yes, I'm with Hope. No, I'm not hiding her. And, yes, you'll be seeing more of her."

"That's it? That's all you're gonna give us?" Zip asked.

"Yep."

"Well, that was short and succinct. I've heard Duff give more of an explanation than that," Woof complained.

Duff grunted. He was a man of few words so this was not surprising.

"There's nothing to explain," Jangles told him.

"Seriously?" Woof pushed. "You don't tell anyone. You don't bring her around. At least tell us how long you've been seeing her."

"How long have we lived here?" Jangles answered.

"Damn. That long?" Zip asked.

"Yep. Asked her out the first night we went to the Ugly Mug."

Duff snorted but wisely didn't call Jangles on his loose use of the term 'ask out'. And in an effort to ward off further comments, Jangles went back to the file in front of him and three out of the four men in the conference room busted a gut laughing at him. They did this loud and long. Duff chuckled, but being as Duff was stingy with his words, he was more so with his smiles and showing emotion—even happiness wasn't something he did regularly.

Thankfully, the door opened and Commander Rouvin "Roe" Turano walked in.

"One of you idiots forgot to turn your phone off before you tossed it in the box," Roe announced. "Merlin, go see whose it is."

Wordlessly, Merlin made his way to the door and slipped out, he did this while Roe was still muttering, "Goddamned fuckin' phones. Still hearing it clatter away even when they're in the—"

Roe stopped bitching because Merlin came back in with a ringing phone in his hand and a tight scowl. Jangles hoped like hell the phone was not his. A midday smoke session didn't sound like fun. Roe was normally level-headed but that didn't mean he couldn't and wouldn't crawl up your ass if you crossed him. And his mood suggested someone hadn't crossed him—they'd pissed in his Wheaties and he was looking to release some hostility.

All eyes sliced to Merlin, but Merlin's eyes were on Zip.

"Fuck," Zip muttered and stepped forward to take his phone. He quickly declined the call, but before Roe could rip him a new one, it started ringing again.

"Answer it," Roe snarled.

Zip brought the phone to his ear, and with supreme impatience, he answered, "Yeah?" Zip's torso jerked, then he stood frozen. "Come again?" Another pause, this one longer, and frozen turned to vibrating fury. "Exactly when and where was the last time you saw her?"

No sooner did the words leave Zip's mouth, Roe went on alert.

What the fuck is going on?

"When does the flight leave?" Zip continued. "What's the protocol? Do you leave without her?"

A string of curse words came from Roe, and Zip's narrowed eyes hit the commander.

"Right. Then text me the number to the TSA agent and call me when you land." Zip disconnected and flinched before he announced. "Destiny didn't make the flight."

"What does that mean, exactly?" Jangles asked.

"It means, no one's seen her. They landed twenty-five minutes ago. She got off the plane to go grab lunch for her and Libby and never made it back to the plane. At first, Libby thought there was a long line and that's why she was late, but the aircraft doors are getting ready to close and they're leaving without her. The airline alerted TSA and they're looking for her."

"Cell phone?" Duff inquired.

"On the plane."

"Did they call her over the airport PA?" Woof asked.

"Yep." Zip's phone chimed in his hand and he looked down at the message. "Libby texted me the number to TSA and the airline."

Roe cleared his throat and Jangles turned his attention back to his commanding officer. The man looked positively irate *and* guilty as fuck.

"What aren't you telling us?" Jangles questioned. He'd kept his eyes locked to Roe's so he didn't miss the flinch.

"Fuck," he repeated on a tight growl. "Fucking hell. Shut the door."

"Roe—"

"I know what you're gonna say, Zip, but before you tear out of here, I need a word. Merlin, shut the door. Zip, power off your phone."

Both men did as instructed while Jangles, Woof, and Duff remained where they were.

"Last night we received new intel that Onur Demir is alive," Roe announced, and the air around him charged.

Jangles heard Woof suck in a breath and his gaze snapped to his friend.

"Did you just say Demir is alive?" Zip sneered.

"Affirmative," Roe said.

"How is that possible?" Woof scoffed. "Demir was taken out by an airstrike."

"Bad intel."

"And *this* intel is good?"

Roe went to his laptop, and a few seconds later, an image flashed on the big screen mounted on the wall.

Onur Demir alive and well.

Jangles would never forget his face. The team had spent every day for a week in the man's compound while Eleanor "Nori" Bonham tried to negotiate a treaty of sorts. The U.S. wanted Demir's help stopping new shipments of guns and munitions from getting into the hands of ISIS, something the dictator of Kazarus happily provided. Nori was on the cuff of brokering the deal when the U.S. got impatient. A secondary Delta Team was sent in to rescue the hostages Demir was holding—doctors and nurses he'd kidnapped but had not ransomed. Nori wanted one more shot at negotiating the hostages' freedom, Woof had unequivocally disagreed, but Nori's boss made the call and sent her in.

It was a mistake. One that almost killed her.

A mistake Woof had not forgotten and likely never would, seeing as Nori had taken a bullet to the stomach and hip and now bore Onur's marks.

Zip had also paid a price. The hostage rescue was a shitshow, not because the team hadn't executed their mission and the hostages survived, but in the shootout, a stray bullet had hit a life-support machine. And that medical device had been the only thing keeping Onur's young son alive. To make matters worse, Zip's face mask had been pulled off. With facial recognition readily available, Demir had Zip's identity. And the man didn't delay setting about to exact retribution, sending his brother Farid to the U.S. to kill Zip.

Zip spent weeks in hiding. But in the end, to flush out Farid, Zip now had a new scar courtesy of the asshole.

But they'd all thought Onur Demir was dead. During Zip's ordeal, they'd been told Demir had been taken out by a coalition airstrike along with his top commanders.

"Please tell me that photo wasn't taken at SeaTac," Zip snapped.

"Wish I could."

Jesus fuck.

Jangles felt his body go tight and his anger swelled. His gaze slid to Zip and he knew his brother was feeling much of the same, only his was tenfold. A maniac hellbent on revenge happened to be at the same airport as his missing woman.

Three loud raps on the door sounded before it flew open and Trigger's large frame filled the doorframe. If his harried entrance didn't put Jangles on high alert, the deep, menacing scowl would've.

"Sorry to interrupt but..." Trigger trailed off, glanced around the room, and his frown landed on Woof before it slid back to Roe and he continued. "I need a word."

"Trigger." Woof's low rumble left no doubt—that one word was a warning.

Trigger cringed and Woof's eyes drifted closed. "Say it," he demanded.

"The State Department called." That was all Trigger got out before Woof moved.

"Out of my way," Woof shouted.

"Lock it down, Woof. You need this intel before you blow out of here halfcocked."

"Yeah? And would you stick around for an intel briefing if it was Gillian?" Woof shot back.

"I would. Nothing's been confirmed. You need—"

"Fuck," Roe clipped. "Fucking shit."

Well, that wasn't reassuring.

"What'd the State Department send over?" Jangles asked.

"The British intelligence officer Nori was working with in Cairo was found dead at seven this morning local time."

He quickly calculated the time difference. "It's four p.m. there. They waited nine hours to call it in?"

"State Department and the SIS have had men on the ground looking. But there's been no sign of Nori," Trigger hesitantly said.

"When was the last time you talked to Nori?" Jangles inquired.

"Yesterday, early afternoon our time. She was getting ready to sit down with her team so the conversation was short."

"She tell you who she was meeting with?" Roe asked.

"No. Unsecured line, and beyond that, we don't discuss work. We respect the boundaries." Woof's voice was strong and steady, and if Jangles hadn't been looking at him, he wouldn't have known how hard Woof was working to keep his control. But Jangles saw it, the tremor that shook his hands, the tic that jumped on his cheek. Woof was doing everything he could to lock it down, but that thread would snap, and when it did, there'd be hell to pay.

"When was the last time you talked to Destiny?" Jangles looked at Zip.

"This morning, early, before her flight left Dallas."

Zip was tossing his phone back and forth between his hands, looking like he was ready to throw it against the wall while hoping there was an explanation other than the obvious why his woman missed her flight.

"Call Gwen and Ivy," Roe boomed. "They have two

choices and it's up to you. They go home and lock themselves in or they come here to post. And you…" Roe turned to Jangles. "If you've been seen anywhere in public with that bartender, lock her ass down, too."

Jangles' body went solid. He chose to ignore the fact his commander knew about Hope and they hadn't been as secretive as he'd thought, and instead focused on the implication.

"You think the women are—"

"I think I don't like this," Roe started. "Bad intel. Two women missing. And a team that's compromised. I want the women locked the fuck down before I have three more men I can't control."

No one had to tell Merlin and Duff twice. Both were out of their chairs and out the door to retrieve their phones from the wall-mounted lockbox.

Jangles slowly made his way to Woof and Zip. Both with identical grimaces, neither trying to hide the worry.

"You know, right?" Jangles asked. "We have this, we're gonna bring them home."

Woof nodded. Zip stared off into space.

"Brother?" Jangles called and waited for Zip to look at him. "You know we have your back and Destiny's."

"Right," Zip mumbled, and Jangles knew he wouldn't get more from his friend so he left it alone and went to call Hope.

He grabbed his phone from the box, and while he waited for it to power up, he glanced around the wide hallway. He didn't see Duff or Merlin.

Jangles quickly scrolled to Hope's name, hit the call button, and put it to his ear. Five rings later, it went to voice mail.

"Hey, baby, when you get this, call me."

Jangles disconnected as Trigger exited the room and waited for him to disconnect. "No answer?"

Jangles inhaled deeply and tried to force himself to remember it was not uncommon for Hope to sleep in, and after they'd been up half the night, she'd barely lifted her head off the pillow to kiss him goodbye before he'd left for work.

There could be a hundred reasons why Hope didn't answer, all of them benign, yet he couldn't stop his stomach from tightening.

"No."

"Shit. Keep trying her. I gotta go call Gillian, we're wheels up this afternoon." Trigger didn't wait for a response before he took off at a jog down the hall.

Jangles dialed Hope again and he made his way back into the conference room. Roe was across the room on the phone, and when Hope didn't answer for the second time, he stabbed the end button and turned to Woof.

"Who's he talking to?"

"Major General Downing," Woof told him.

Fuck.

"Downing call Roe?" Jangles pushed.

"Yep."

"Christ."

"'Bout sums it up," Zip grunted.

It was not a good sign when the Commander of the Joint Special Operations Command personally called.

Someone knew more than they were saying.

"There's something we don't know," Woof voiced Jangles' thoughts.

"Did you try Nori?"

"Don't need to, he has her."

"Woof, brother, you don't know that."

Woof turned his hard eyes to Jangles and pinned him

with a deadly stare. "I know. And so do you. Demir left her for dead in that tunnel. He believes Zip killed his son. He knows we killed his brother. So don't bullshit me. He might not personally have his filthy hands on her since he's here in the U.S. but he *has* her. And we both fuckin' know she's got limited hours, so let's not pretend my woman's not on a goddamn clock."

Fuck.

"I can't get Ivy on the phone," Duff announced, unchecked fear clear on his face.

"Hold up," Roe called.

Duff jerked to a halt and narrowed his eyes but didn't say what was very obviously on his mind. The man had no intention of waiting long and he gave zero fucks what Roe had to say about it. Out of all the men, Duff would be the second hardest to contain. That was, second to Jangles if Hope didn't answer her goddamn phone.

He dialed Hope again as Merlin entered, a harassed expression visible, and Jangles swallowed the lump in his throat.

"No answer, and she's not at the bookstore." Merlin's rough, thick voice hit Jangles like a sledgehammer.

Five women unaccounted for.

Five women who belonged to the men who Onur Demir wanted to seek revenge on.

"Is there a snowball's chance any of you will follow my order to stand down and allow Team Two to handle this?"

Five resounding 'nos' rang out in the room.

"We are in-country. Do not turn Killeen, Texas, into a war zone. Go get your women and bring them back here. Zip and Woof, you're with me, JSOC and the State Department are feeling generous, intel's coming our way."

Jangles didn't spare his team a second glance as he shot out of the room and sprinted through the building.

CHAPTER 13

Hope's body swayed, her stomach recoiled from the motion, and her head swam in confusion. And the more alert she became, the more aware she was that her body ached. No, that wasn't right, her body *hurt*—all over, from the soles of her feet to her scalp and every part in between. But mostly her head pounded and her shoulders throbbed.

She tried to roll to her back and moaned in pain.

"Is someone there?"

Wait, what?

"Huh?" Hope croaked, and when she swallowed, it felt like sand was clogging her throat.

"Who's there?"

Hope fought to open her eyes but was unsure if she'd succeeded in this endeavor because it was pitch black. Something tickled the bridge of her nose but she couldn't move her hand.

What in the world?

"What's going on?"

"Oh, God. Hope?"

It was the fear in the other woman's voice that jolted

Hope from semi-consciousness to fully awake. She struggled to move her arms, sit up, bend her legs—something, anything—but she was stuck. Unable to move any part of her body. And she realized she was blindfolded.

"Gwen?"

"Yeah. Oh, shit. They got you, too."

"Got me, too? Who? What are you talking about? I can't move."

"Neither can I. I thought I was alone." Gwen's voice hitched before it broke into a sob.

"Who, Gwen? Where are we?"

"I don't know."

A cold detachment washed over Hope. It was almost as if she were back in Beau's bed, warm and cuddled under the mound of blankets he'd pulled up and over her before he'd kissed her forehead, then brushed her hair over her shoulder.

"I was in Beau's bed," Hope muttered. "That's the last thing I remember."

"I was behind the bookstore, setting out the boxes for recycling," Gwen told her. "Then someone grabbed me from behind. I felt something prick my neck and I didn't wake up until…until a little while ago."

"Are we moving?"

"Yeah."

Hope became aware of a mechanical roaring sound. She sniffed but couldn't place a single smell. She rocked side to side the best she could and realized her hands were tied behind her back. She felt around with the tips of her fingers—something hard, kind of scratchy but not abrasive. When she rubbed her palms against it, she was no closer to figuring it out.

They were definitely moving, but it was smooth motion.

"I think we're in a plane," Gwen said.

"I think you're right. Are we alone? I can't see anything."

"I can't either, remember?" Gwen hissed. "I thought I was alone until I heard you."

"Shit. I forgot. I'm not used to being tied up, blindfolded, and kidnapped," Hope snapped back.

"Sorry," Gwen mumbled. "I'm a little freaked out."

Freaked out, that's all?

Hope was on the verge of a panic attack. But before she freaked the fuck out, she wanted to know where she was.

"They'll know, right?" Gwen whispered. "They'll know and find us."

Jangles.

Jangles and Merlin.

Of course, they'll know and find us.

"Yeah. They'll find us." Hope nodded even though she knew Gwen couldn't see her. "Can you move at all?"

"No. My hands are behind my back and my legs are attached to something."

"Yeah, mine, too."

"What are we gonna do?"

Hope didn't want to think it, much less feel it, but she couldn't help it—the relief she felt knowing Gwen was with her was overwhelming. She didn't want to believe that Jangles wouldn't look for her, but the truth was, she'd dodged him in the past, and if Gwen hadn't been taken, too, Jangles might've thought Hope had ghosted him. But there was no chance Merlin would think Gwen would leave him. With them both gone, they'd look, and they wouldn't delay.

"We wait and we keep our mouths shut until we can see. Someone could be watching."

"Yeah. That's smart."

That wasn't smart.

Smart would be knowing what to do while you were blindfolded, tied up, and kidnapped. But Hope only pretended to be strong. She perfected the tough-chick act —at the bar, the shooting range, with BF and his cronies, with the guys who came into the Ugly Mug. They all thought she was carefree and sassy. She threw attitude their way and they believed it.

The truth was, Hope was none of those things.

She'd been scared most of her life, therefore she knew fear. She'd felt it the first time Went had grabbed her bicep too hard and left bruises. She knew it when her parents had demanded she break up with him and she'd stupidly told Went and he yanked her by her ponytail and yelled in her face that was never going to happen. And she'd been scared out of her mind when Went charged her dad with a knife and started to stab him. Then her world went black —darkness seeped into her, unconscionable evil soaked her soul, and that was when she'd learned there was something beyond fear. It didn't have a name, it couldn't be described, it was a feeling that coursed through your veins. It coiled in your stomach, a cancer that fed until it consumed you.

But right then, blinded and unable to move, Hope knew a new kind of fear—dread. The feeling one had when they were paralyzed. She couldn't do anything, even if she knew what to do, she wouldn't have been able to do it, because she couldn't move.

And sweet, funny, pretty Gwen was somewhere close and she could help her.

Hope lay there in the darkness, her hands trapped and digging into the small of her back, her shoulders cocked at a painful angle, her head fuzzy and pounding, her nose tingling with emotion she was trying not to show, and her ankles bound and secured to something so she couldn't even bend her knees. Gwen was beside her, and she decided that no matter what, she'd protect Gwen.

When they got to where they were going, Hope would beg their captors to let Gwen go. She'd do anything they wanted. Sweet, pretty Gwen didn't deserve this. Nope, whatever this was, Gwen absolutely didn't deserve it.

"Gwen?"

"Yeah?"

"You're gonna be all right."

"So will you."

Before Hope could explain that her life didn't matter, a moan filled the room, or the cabin, or the train car, or the ship hull—whatever kind of space they were locked in—the painful groan filled it and Hope froze.

"What...where...oh, God." The panicked voice sounded familiar but Hope couldn't place it. She was reeling from the knowledge she and Gwen weren't alone.

"Ivy?" Gwen asked.

Oh, shit.

"Gwen?"

Oh, fucking *shit.*

"Yeah, it's me. Hope's here, too."

CHAPTER 14

JANGLES DIDN'T BOTHER with his driveway. He pulled to the curb and slammed his truck in park. Not bothering to take the time to kill the ignition, he jumped out and looked at his house.

Front door open.

In one smooth motion, he brushed his shirt aside and pulled his Glock free from the concealed carry holster and racked the slide. His feet hadn't slowed taking him to the porch. He listened. Nothing. Jangles cleared the front rooms and made his way to the bedroom.

Empty.

He went to the bed, touched the sheets, and found them cold. Fury engulfed his system and took him to his knees. His forehead hit Hope's pillow that was sideways, mostly hanging off the bed, and he breathed in her scent.

Fuck.

Jangles got to his feet and looked around the room. The sheets and comforter he'd tucked around Hope before he'd left were tangled on the floor, the lamp on the nightstand broken and on its side. Her jeans, T-shirt, and shoes were still laying where she'd tossed them the night before.

Which meant Hope had been taken from his bed, wearing only his tee and a pair of fucking panties.

"Fuck!" he roared.

A burn ignited—so hot, so deep, it scorched his chest.

"I'm gonna find you," he whispered to an empty room. "I'm gonna find you and bring you home."

Jangles turned on his heel and left.

THE WAR ROOM was filled to capacity.

Grover, Doc, Lucky, Trigger, Lefty, Brain, and Oz were huddled together on one side of the room, Roe was front and center, and Jangles and his team were squared off on the other side.

"We're playing this smart," Roe repeated his earlier statement, the one that had started the standoff, and the air around them went from simmering to sizzling.

"Smart would be sending us in," Woof also repeated his earlier response.

"If I send you in, I'm giving him what he wants, and you'd be walking into a trap."

"It's not a trap if we know he's laid it. Besides, you sending in Team Two is no different. They'd be walking into the same snare," Zip added.

"They'll have backup. I'll call in—"

"Waste of time," Jangles cut the commander off. "We've been there. We know the compound. We know Demir. We know the tunnels. We're up to speed. It'd take hours to get another team up to speed. Hours they don't have."

Roe clenched his jaw, his face paled, but he didn't relent. "I can't allow a bloodbath."

Jangles felt it, his control was dangerously close to snapping. Pain shafted through his heart thinking about Hope—how scared she was, if she was injured, being tortured—ugly images that plagued his thoughts until he couldn't tamp them down. Couldn't keep them locked inside.

"My woman was taken from my home." The words blistered Jangles' throat as he said them. "From my *bed*. A place she should be safe. She was torn from the sheets I'd tucked around her just hours before, taken in nothing but my shirt and a pair of fucking *panties*. So, you're goddamn right there's gonna be a bloodbath. And if you think by sending in Team Two there will be any less blood spilled, you're kidding yourself and you know it, Roe. Look at them, they're itching to get their hands on Demir. Luckily for you, when we're done the world will be a better place, one less piece of shit breathing. Now we're wasting fucking time. Five women are being held hostage. *Five civilians*. And let's not forget one of those civilians is Senator Fremont's daughter. The media catches wind of this, the clusterfuck we'll have on our hands—"

Jangles clamped his mouth shut when a low menacing sound emanated from Duff at the reminder his fiancée, Ivy, was kidnapped—*again*. It hadn't been too long ago they'd gone down to Costa Rica to get her. An operation that had ended with Ivy recovering from a gunshot wound.

Roe glanced around the room, knowing Jangles was right. Even if by some miracle he managed to lock down Jangles and his team, Trigger and Team Two would not go in easy. They'd spill blood and they'd do it the same way Jangles, Woof, Zip, Duff, and Merlin would—with precision, with extreme violence—and they'd do it for the brotherhood.

The commander walked to Jangles, shoved a piece of

paper at him, and said, "Call this number. The man's name is Tex. He can get you everything I can't." Roe paused, held Jangles' gaze, and finally dropped the mask of Delta commander. Anger glittered in Rouvin Turano's eyes, his face set to fury, and then he continued. "Go. Be smart. And whatever you do, don't get dead."

Fucking *finally* they had the green light.

Roe prowled to the door, turned to face the room, looked to each man with his gaze still hard, jaw tight, trying to keep his own emotions in check.

"Transport's fueled and ready. Good luck, men."

HOPE WAS FREEZING her ass off, had been since she'd been carried off the plane. And the only way she'd known it was an aircraft was because when the wheels had touched the tarmac, she bounced and landed so hard she would've thrown up from the pain had she not been so scared. And she knew Gwen and Ivy had hit hard, too, because they'd both cried out in pain. Then she was carried off the plane, this was done in silence. Total and utter deafening silence. For her part, she hadn't said a word because she couldn't see, and that was so frightening any thoughts of protest died on her tongue. She also hadn't struggled to get free because she didn't know where she was, and without sight or the use of her limbs, she was literally at the mercy of whoever had been carrying her.

The bumpy car ride had been the same.

No one spoke. She couldn't see or move but she could smell. And for some reason, the musky scent of cologne and leather freaked her out. In her mind, she'd pictured herself sitting next to an unbathed monster in a piece of shit junker car. Not a luxury ride next to a man who bathed and wore aftershave. Between the leather and the smooth ride even though they were cruising on what she'd assumed was a dirt road or one that was full of potholes, the drive hadn't been as bumpy as it could've been.

It wasn't until she was carried from the car and set on her feet that the man spoke, and his only words were not to move. Therefore Hope didn't move. She stood rooted, frozen in fear. She needed to play it smart and wait until she could see before she came up with a plan.

And she prayed for the first time since her parents died.

She prayed Ivy and Gwen were still with her and they hadn't been separated and taken to different locations.

So there she was, standing statue-still, like a coward, too afraid to move, while someone was working the ties around her ankles. She felt the rope loosen and finally drop around her feet. She bit back a cry of pain but only because the hands that had untied her were now on her calves, and they slowly inched their way up to the backs of her knees. When they got to her thighs with no signs of stopping, self-preservation kicked in and she jerked her body forward while taking a step and slammed into something hard. Her face took the brunt of the impact and she cried out.

"Stop!"

A decidedly male chuckle rang out close to her ear and she lurched away, smacking her face a second time.

"Don't touch me!"

No answer. But the hands were back, this time at her wrists. Seconds later, the rope cruelly slid over her chafed flesh until finally it unwound and her arms fell useless to her sides.

Pins and needles raced up her arms, her shoulders cramped, and bile pooled in her mouth. So much pain, just from her arms being freed. Scratchy material brushed her bare arm, and she felt the man press close to her back. Her mind raced, trying to find a way to escape. Her legs were jelly but freed, her arms useless, and something was blocking the path directly in front of her, but if she could turn and body slam—

Hope couldn't finish her thought before the blindfold was ripped free and the blazing light pierced through the darkness. Before she could blink away sharp pain, a hand between her shoulder blades shoved her so hard she stumbled forward. Unable to get her balance or her arms to work, she could only twist at the last second so she landed with an agonizing thud mostly on her shoulder and hip, but the side of her head still slammed onto the concrete floor.

"Holy fuck." The voice was female, but with multiple blows to her head, Hope couldn't stop her eyes from closing.

"No, Hope, stay awake. Open your eyes."

"Hurts," Hope mumbled.

"Ivy, get her some water."

Suddenly, water sounded spectacular.

"Open your eyes, honey, I'll help you up."

Hope pried her lids open and immediately slammed them closed again, but not before she'd caught a glimpse of Destiny.

Oh, no.

"Destiny?"

"Yeah, it's me."

"Is Nori here, too?"

"Right here," Nori snapped, sounding more pissed-off than scared.

Oh, shit.

This was bad, way worse than she'd imagined.

Gwen. Ivy. Destiny. Nori. Hope.

All of them together. All of them taken.

Hope's head hurt, literally hurt. It thumped to the beat of her pounding heart. But figuratively, it swam with possibilities.

"We're bait," Hope mumbled.

"Yep," Nori once again snapped.

"They'll come."

"Yep."

"Shit."

"You can say that again," Destiny muttered.

CHAPTER 15

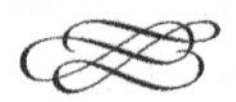

JANGLES PULLED HIS SHADES DOWN, blocking out the blinding rays while keeping his phone to his ear.

"Yeah, we just landed."

He hitched his backpack higher on his shoulder and glanced around Adana airport, a place he decided he never wanted to see again. Jangles' eyes landed on Woof and he knew he was having the same thoughts.

The last time they'd been in Turkey hadn't been pleasant for any of them, but especially Woof. The shit-show had started with a kidnapping attempt and had ended with Nori being shot.

Now they were back.

This time, because Onur Demir, a man who was supposed to be dead, had made a grave error in judgment. There would be no covert negotiations this time. There'd be no talks of exchanging hostages for satellite images. There'd be no bad intel and assumption of death.

There'd be no question about whether or not Onur Demir was breathing because Jangles was going to make sure he wasn't left alive.

Panties.

Jesus fuck.

Jangles couldn't stop thinking about Hope being exposed. The thought clawed at him—it had been over twenty-four hours and his woman was in a tee and panties with a man who wanted revenge.

Fuck.

"There's a black 4Runner waiting for you," a man called Tex told him.

"Black 4Runner," Jangles relayed to Duff.

Duff's normal quiet had turned deadly, and over the last few hours, he hadn't said more than a handful of words. So when he jerked his chin in acknowledgment, Jangles wasn't surprised. As a matter of fact, none of them had said more than necessary. All talk had dwindled to mission specifics.

"See it," Jangles returned.

"Good. I arranged for Drake to load you up with some extra firepower. Take a look and let me know if there's anything else you need."

"Not sure Uncle Sam's gonna reimburse you for any extra line items on your expense report," Jangles noted.

"Right. We'll call it a gift then. Drake's your man, anything you need, it's yours. I'll be in touch." Tex disconnected and Jangles pocketed his phone and followed Duff to the awaiting SUV.

"Which one of you is Merlin?" the man Jangles assumed was Drake asked.

"Me." Merlin stepped forward and his hand shot out and nabbed a set of keys Drake tossed.

"Drake." The man introduced himself. "Don't know if Tex told you or not but you got new toys in the back." Drake jerked his head in the direction of the SUV. "Lots of fun shit that goes bang. There's also tracking devices back there. Do us a favor and wear them, yeah? It'll save us time having to hack into the shit the Army's outfitted you with. I'll be your shadow, Tex will be our eyes. Brady's on Team Two, he'll meet up with Trigger when they land and take them to a different border crossing."

At first, Jangles had been unsure about working with the unknown Tex, even after Roe had boasted about the man. It wasn't until his mentor Ghost called him and told him not only was Tex to be trusted, but he was the best at what he did. What Tex *did* exactly, Ghost didn't elaborate, he'd simply said that Tex could get them anything, anywhere, and when shit hit the fan, Tex was their best option. So far, Tex had been precisely who Ghost had said he was—efficient, to the point, and damn helpful.

Good to know.

"Which one of you is Eleanor Bonham's?" Drake asked.

"If by hers, you mean which one of us is her man, that'd be me." Woof scowled.

To say that none of them was in the mood for a stop-and-chat would be the understatement of the year.

"Got word while you were in the air, her phone was located. She was trying to get word to you when she was taken. Not that we need the confirmation, but it's still good to have. Part of the message she'd gotten tapped out was telling you Demir was alive. She saw the Brit taken out and was trying to get to safety. Tex pulled the hotel's footage. Facial rec confirmed the man who took her is a general in Demir's KFA."

The Kazarus Freedom Army. What a fucking joke. Demir wasn't as bad as some terrorists in that he didn't bomb and kill innocent civilians, but he was still a fucking terrorist. A rebel against the current leadership in Kazarus. Jangles didn't give the first fuck Demir was fighting for what he thought was the betterment of his country—all he cared about was getting Hope and the other women home safely and burying the asshole.

"What else did the footage show?" Woof inquired with an enthusiasm that he'd lacked since they'd gotten word Nori had been taken.

"Didn't see it, but Tex said she put up one helluva fight and looked to be uninjured when they got her into the car."

That was good news, and as happy as Jangles was for Woof and Nori, it was time to get this show on the road.

"You know where we're going?" Jangles asked Drake.

The man didn't bother to answer, he just turned on his heel and stalked away, which was the answer.

"Let's roll," Merlin impatiently announced and went to the driver's side of the SUV.

The rest of the team piled in, and before they could buckle their seat belts, Merlin was pulling out of the airport.

"THIS IS MY FAULT," Nori announced, pulling Hope from her thoughts.

For the last few hours, Nori had quietly paced.

Hope conducted a lengthy search of the room, one that was useless because it was mostly empty except for five cots and a primitive bathroom in the farthest corner of their prison. There was a toilet, a sink like you'd find in a dirty gas station, and a white fabric partition for privacy. No sheets or pillows, just metal-framed, camping-style cots.

No windows and one sturdy—Hope's face had found that out the hard way, twice—locked metal door. Fluorescent overhead lights that illumined the space with a sickly, flickering light, and stone walls. Hope had used her time wondering if they could Shawshank their way out, alternately wondering if they were underground. Then she tried to remember how long it had taken Andy Dufresne to tunnel his way out. To the best of her recollection, it had taken Andy nineteen years. She didn't figure they had nineteen years before Beau and the guys came looking for them. Probably not even nineteen hours.

That both elated and scared the hell out of her. She didn't want them getting hurt or worse—killed.

So hearing Nori's proclamation didn't give Hope warm and fuzzy feelings.

"It could be because of me instead," Ivy said, and Hope looked at her.

Destiny and Gwen were sitting close to Ivy on one cot and their eyes went to her, too. And there Hope was like she'd been most of her life, sitting alone, mostly removed from everyone else. Ugly jealousy she had no right feeling started to blossom. The others had always been nice to her when they'd come into the bar, and recently she'd struck up a friendship with Gwen, but still, it was no match for the bonds Gwen had with Ivy and Destiny.

Feeling sorry for herself wasn't going to help, and really, Hope only had herself to blame for the disconnect and she knew it.

"Why would you say that?" Hope asked.

"This wouldn't be the first time I was taken because someone didn't like my mother's policies," Ivy explained.

"What? Who's your mother?"

"Senator Madeline Fremont."

"Holy shit."

"No. We're in Kazarus, at a compound a man named Onur Demir uses as a base of operations for his Freedom Army," Nori told them.

Destiny's eyes got big and they flared with concern.

Then she whispered, "Kazarus? The mission where you were shot?"

"Yes," Nori confirmed and straightened her shoulders as if she were waiting for one of them to lash out, or maybe agree with her.

"Zip didn't tell me the details, not even when Farid was after him. I didn't know until after it all went down. But, Nori, none of this is your fault," Destiny told her.

"Wait, who's Farid?" Hope asked, confused.

"Farid Demir is Onur's brother. He was sent to the U.S. to kill Zip." Hope's eyes widened at Destiny's calm clarification.

"You don't understand," Nori cut in. "They were here protecting me. We're all in this mess because—"

"Because some asshole kidnapped us," Hope cut Nori off. "Is Onur the one who shot you? And I remember when someone was looking for Zip, I just didn't know his name. That wasn't on you, either. None of this is your fault."

"Jangles talks to you about his missions?"

Hope sat up straight at Destiny's tone.

"He doesn't give me specifics. But he was worried about Woof after Nori was shot. I mean, he was worried about Nori, too, but he said Woof was around-the-bend crazy." Destiny and Gwen were giving each other a knowing look that put Hope on edge. "What? Why are you looking at each other like that?"

"They don't talk about their work," Gwen told her.

"He doesn't—" Hope started to defend herself, but Gwen spoke over her.

"What I'm saying is, they don't talk about it with outsiders. You mean something to Jangles or he never would've told you about what happened to Nori."

Hope thought about what Gwen said and reckoned she was right. She still sat on her cot removed from the other women but suddenly she didn't feel so alone. She meant something to Beau and she had for a long time.

"If you knew the whole story, you'd understand," Nori interrupted Hope's musings.

"Then tell us," Hope invited. Nori's torso jerked and she started to shake her head. "We're locked in a room with no way out, we literally have nothing better to do than sort your head. You're blaming yourself for something that is not your fault. I have lots of experience with that, twelve years of it actually. And it was just last night that Beau finally convinced me that maybe I've been holding onto some stuff that I shouldn't have been. Don't wait twelve years, Nori. Spit it out and unpack it. We'll sit and listen, because hello, we got nowhere to go. Then we'll take some time and convince you that we're sitting here because some asshole has a vendetta against our men and you are not to blame for *anything*."

Nori continued to stare at Hope. When a second turned into five, Hope started to worry she'd overstepped. Hope didn't have the first clue about being friends with women. She was used to men—they were easy, you said what you had to say, and that was it. Straight out, no bullshit, simple. But the way Nori was looking at Hope, she figured Nori didn't appreciate her straightforward approach.

"How's your head?" Nori asked.

"Um...better."

Nori's lips twitched before she smiled outright and moved toward Hope. "Good. Scoot over, will you?"

Hope skooched over and Nori sat down.

"These are the highlights. I was sent in to negotiate..."

Over the next little while, Hope hung on to Nori's every word. She couldn't believe what she was hearing. Hope had no idea Nori's job was so interesting, but why would she—negotiating covert agreements with a rebel leader isn't something you talk about to the woman serving you drinks. Beau had told her that Nori worked for the State Department, but nothing more.

Hope also had no idea Nori's job was so dangerous it necessitated armed guards all of the time, and a Delta team some of the time.

"During our meetings, I couldn't get a read on Onur. I felt like he wanted to do the right thing. He loves his country, but his love for his son outweighed everything else. Family is everything to him. His son had leukemia, he was dying, there was nothing anyone could do. I think deep down, Onur knew it, but he still kept those doctors and nurses hostage because he couldn't bear to lose him. Then everything went to shit. And now, we have the perfect storm. Onur blames Zip for killing his son, he blames the rest of the team for killing his brother, and he wants them to pay. This isn't about his country, freedom, or money. It's about family."

Nori stopped speaking and closed her eyes. She wrung her clasped hands on her lap.

"This is *the* room," Nori muttered. "The room where Onur's son died. The room where he held the doctors and nurses hostage."

Hope heard someone suck in a breath but her gaze hadn't lifted from Nori's hands. Her short, neatly manicured nails dug into her flesh, leaving little half-moon shapes as Nori clutched her hands together.

"I'm sorry you were shot," Hope lamely said and reached over to grab Nori's hand. "I'm even sorry his son died. But it wasn't Zip's fault the boy had leukemia. It's not their fault he kidnapped people. It's not their fault that Onur's brother died. And none of that is your fault. All of it is Onur's. Except for the leukemia, that part's not anyone's fault."

"I agree," Gwen said.

"Me, too," Ivy put in.

"I'll tell you what I think," Destiny started. "I'm tired of men with the last name Demir fucking with my life. First, I finally reconnected with Trent after twelve years of avoiding him, only to have Onur send Farid to the U.S. to kill him. Then he had to go into hiding after we only had one date. Just one. And it was the best first date ever, but we hadn't gotten to the good stuff before he was called back to Killeen. Then, Trent decided not to tell me there was someone after him. Then he got shot by a Demir. Then we broke up. It was bad, really bad, so bad I cried into my cookie dough ice cream, and Libby, my roommate, was getting ready to stage an intervention. So when I say I'm tired, I really mean I am *done*." By the time Destiny was done with her rant, all eyes were on her and she looked positively pissed.

"I've got a few years on you," Nori said. "I lost fifteen with Heath."

"I didn't know that," Gwen gasped.

"I did," Destiny chirped. "They went to high school together like Trent and me."

"Well, I didn't know either of those things," Hope put in, and Nori squeezed her hand.

"I was kidnapped on my first date with Duff," Ivy chimed in.

"It was more like your second date," Gwen corrected. "Though your first date wasn't all that great."

"Actually, some parts of that night were great," Ivy rallied.

"Blind date, right?" Hope recalled serving drinks to Ivy and Duff at the Ugly Mug on their first date.

"Yeah. Gwen set us up."

"That was the first time I'd ever seen Duff smile," Hope told her.

Ivy looked like she was struggling with something before she said, "He didn't have a lot to smile about. He was holding on to a lot of guilt about his wife dying."

"Duff was married?" Nori gasped.

"Yeah. He married his high school sweetheart. She died on their honeymoon. Duff couldn't save her and he let it tear him up for eight years."

"Oh my God. That's horrible," Destiny whispered.

Hope fully understood holding onto guilt and pain. She knew what it was like to let the past tear you apart. Then she thought about Duff and how since he'd met Ivy she'd seen him smile more, and suddenly Hope felt lighter. If a man like Duff could let go of some of the pain to find happiness, maybe she could, too.

CHAPTER 16

JANGLES TOOK a breath in through his nose and exhaled. He couldn't say his patience was waning because he had none left. He wanted to get to his woman and get her safe. And while sitting his ass in the SUV for the last five-plus hours had gotten him closer to that goal, it wasn't close enough and wouldn't be until he had his hands on Hope.

"Call it in," Merlin barked, and Jangles knew he wasn't the only impatient one.

With each minute that ticked by, all of them were feeling the air thin. Every extra minute the women were with Demir, their chances of survival diminished. None of them were wet-behind-the-ears rookies. They knew the game, were intimately familiar with it, this wasn't their first hostage extraction, it wasn't even their first high-value rescue. But it was the first time the outcome would make or break them.

One wrong move, one second too late, and one or all of their lives would forever be changed.

Jangles sucked in another breath and exhaled, and

much like the first, it did nothing to calm his nerves. They were close to the border-crossing, but not close enough.

He grabbed his phone and made the call Merlin requested.

"I see you," Tex said by way of greeting. "The sheepherder's clean—you're good to go. But I've got concerns about that tunnel."

"What kind of concerns?"

"Mainly, I don't like that you're coming out of it wide open. You got patrols on the other side. Before you exit, you need to check-in. The other issue I have is communication. Once you're down there, we got dead air."

"Not the first time we've used this tunnel. Not even the second," Jangles returned.

"Right, which means the crossing isn't a secret. You boys go underground, one of those patrols feels like getting nosy and enters from the other side, I've got no way to communicate that to you. Be smart and watch your asses down there. You're clear to enter and call when you get to the other side. But do not come out without calling in first and let's hope you get service." Tex disconnected and Jangles quickly briefed the team.

"Once we surface on the other side, comms will work," Merlin assured the group. "And if they don't…" His right shoulder shrugged and he continued, "I'm not waiting around for some satellite to pass by which means Gwen's waiting even longer."

"Agreed," Duff grunted.

No one else verbalized their answer, it was unnecessary. None of them planned on sitting around with their thumbs up their asses while their women were in danger.

Merlin took the turnoff to Aksan's farm. Jangles couldn't say if the sheepherder was a good man, but he was a peaceful man. He didn't want trouble and he didn't invite it. His cousin, Hazan, was the same way. The tunnel to cross into Kazarus started on Aksan's land and ended on Hazan's. Jangles didn't know if they split the money they handed off to Aksan or how that worked, only that the men provided safe passage if you could afford it. Admission wasn't cheap but it was well worth it.

A light came on, signaling it was safe to continue to the barn where they'd hide the SUV. The rest of the journey would be done on foot. Merlin slowed as Aksan opened the barn doors and then he pulled in. The men piled out as a second SUV pulled up into the lane.

Merlin turned to their host and quickly explained. "He's with us and will wait here with the vehicles."

Aksan's brows pinched, unhappy at the unusual turn. They normally worked alone and they'd never left a vehicle exposed.

Merlin held out a wad of cash; by the look of it, double the amount they normally handed over.

"For your trouble, friend."

The other man bowed his head before he silently took the cash and walked farther into the loafing shed. A small flock of lambs bleated as he passed by their enclosures. The man paused to give one of the baby sheep a gentle touch before he continued to the large tarp piled on the ground. Said a lot about a man how he treated his animals, so Jangles figured the old man had a lot of good in him along with his peaceful nature.

Once Drake parked his SUV next to the 4Runner, he didn't delay laying it out.

"I'm staying on this side. I got you covered on this end. You run into any problems, Tex first, me second," Drake instructed.

"You do know this is a fully sanctioned op and we have the assets in the area at our disposal," Zip told him.

Drake nodded. "Indeed you do. However, what we got is better. When shit goes sideways as it always does, you want Tex at your back. You need references on that, talk to Ghost. You need more, call a man by the name of Wolf. He's a SEAL, though not sure you'd take his word. Though don't mention I said that part to Tex, he gets salty when I make seaman jokes, considering he was one."

"No shit?" Zip mumbled.

"Story for another day. All you need to know right now is, Tex answers to no one, therefore he's got no red tape to cut through. His only objective is getting your women out alive and you home in one piece. I'll be here, you need something."

Under normal circumstances, Jangles would have more than a few questions about Tex and who exactly Drake was and who he worked for. But right then, he didn't give the first fuck who they were if it meant he got to Hope.

However, Jangles needed to know one thing before he left the stranger to watch his six.

"And you?" Jangles inquired.

"Me what?"

"How do you know Tex?"

"Once a Team Guy, always a Team Guy."

"You're a SEAL?"

"Only a SEAL can make seaman jokes to another Team Guy without swallowing lead."

"Right." Jangles offered Drake his hand. "'Preciate your help."

"Anything you need." Drake took Jangles' hand and held on to it. "Word of advice from a man who knows what you're walking into—keep your shit. When you get to her, she's gonna need you. Bury that fire you got in you, and remember it's all about her and what she went through. You need to unload, you do it with your team. You can't do it with them, you call me. But no matter how strong she is, you keep your shit tight. She's gonna need you more than you think."

"You know this how?"

"My woman was held as a POW for a week, was treated to torture that would've broken a man three times her size. She didn't break, not when she was being waterboarded, beaten, or humiliated. I still have nightmares about how I found her. But she's got it worse, it happened to her. That's how I know. Luckily for you, Demir's not known for torture, and he's never hurt women. This is about you and your team and getting you on his turf. He's got you here, now all you gotta do is take him out and get your girl."

Right. Easier said than done.

"You put the motherfucker down that took her?"

"Nope. She did."

With a jerk of his chin, Jangles made his way around the parked SUVs to where his team was already filing down the ramp into the tunnel.

Drake had sound advice, however, Jangles didn't think he had it in him to hold his shit together if he got to Hope and she'd been tortured. It had been a miracle Woof didn't lose his mind and slaughter his way through Kazarus looking for Demir after Nori had been shot. Then again, Nori had been bleeding out and all Woof could think about was saving her life.

There wasn't a chance in hell Onur was getting that lucky this time. Jangles wasn't leaving Kazarus until Onur Demir was under dirt.

~

"I FEEL like we should be doing something," Ivy complained.

"We talked about this," Gwen reminded her.

"I know. But we're just sitting here."

"We're not just sitting here," Hope said. "Nori's right. There's no way out of this room. The best way for us to help is to not cause any trouble and wait."

At first, Hope had balked at Nori's advice. Now that her arms and legs weren't bound and she could see, her first instinct was to escape. Shout, fight, claw, scratch, whatever she could do if that stupid door ever opened. But Nori had made a compelling argument. If one of them did that and was injured, they had no medical supplies, and since they didn't know how long it would be until the guys came, infection could set in if they weren't killed outright. So the best way to keep themselves safe was to wait. That way when the guys did come, they had five able-bodied women making the rescue easier.

Ivy didn't look happy, and Hope understood why. Being kidnapped a second time had to suck. Hope knew, being as this was her first time and it *sucked*.

They were powerless to help themselves, and sitting around chitchatting felt wrong. But attempting to hatch a plan to break free wasn't smart. They had to wait. Beau, Woof, Zip, Merlin, and Duff would be there soon, they had to be. Hope refused to believe anything else.

"What's Duff's real name?" Hope asked. "I know Heath, Trent, and Luke's names but I've never heard Duff's."

Gwen started to giggle and knocked her shoulder into Ivy's. Finally, a big broad, playful smile stretched across her pretty face.

"How bad do you wanna know?" Ivy teased.

"Well, before you asked that, I was just mildly curious. Now I *have* to know."

"I don't know if I should tell." Ivy winked and Gwen burst out laughing.

"Do you know?" Hope asked Gwen.

"Yep."

"Does everyone know?"

"I just found out recently." Destiny smiled.

"I've known a while. After I was shot, Ma—I mean, Duff, flew to D.C. to see me in the rehab center. We had lunch and he shared," Nori added.

"You did that on purpose," Hope complained. "Come on, what's his name?"

"Magnus."

"*Magnus*?" Hope repeated. "Seriously?"

Ivy nodded and Hope felt her eyes go round and her body started to shake.

"Oh my God." She lost the battle and started to laugh. "That's perfect. He's totally a Magnus. If he didn't scare the hell out of me, I'd call him that instead of Duff."

"Duff isn't scary," Ivy defended her man. "He's like a big teddy bear."

At that, all the women dissolved into fits of hilarity. The last thing Duff was, was a teddy bear. He was more like a large, snarly grizzly bear, with very large teeth.

"Maybe a grizzly." Hope voiced her thoughts.

Ivy smiled and Hope's chest tightened. Of course, it was just her luck that the first time she was bonding with a great group of women it was while she was kidnapped, sitting in a windowless room in a foreign country.

CHAPTER 17

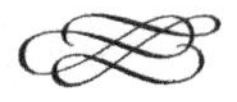

LAST TIME JANGLES and the team made the mile-long journey, Nori had been with them. This go-around, the trek took half the time. Mostly because the men wanted to get to the other side and partly because without Nori with them, the men went at a much faster clip.

"You good?" Jangles asked Woof as they approached the end.

"Nope. You?"

"Not even a little bit."

"You think they're coming up with a way to escape?" Zip questioned.

God, I hope not.

"No. And if they were planning something, Nori would've eighty-sixed it. She knows where she is, she knows Demir, and she knows their best play is waiting for us. The five of them loose in that compound would be a nightmare," Woof answered.

Jangles' gut tightened at the thought of them out in the open. The possibility of one of them getting hit in the crossfire made him want to hurl.

Another ten feet and they'd be out of this goddamn tunnel. Then they had two miles to Demir's compound.

Hold on, baby, I'm almost there.

"Duff?" Merlin called.

"Don't." That was all Duff said, and Jangles turned back to look at his teammate. Duff's features were tinged green from Jangles' night vision goggles, but green or not, Jangles couldn't miss the hard set of his jaw.

"They're—"

"Don't fucking talk to me. Don't make promises. Don't spew platitudes. I get that we're all in this together. I know you're feeling it just like me. But don't fucking say a word. I just got Ivy back. And the last time this happened to her, I swore she was safe. So, not a goddamn word. We get in, we secure the women, and I don't care who does it, as long as it's done. But that fucker is not being left breathin'."

Duff's angry words echoed in the tunnel, reverberated, and hit Jangles square in the chest. When they'd gotten Ivy back, she'd been shot before they could get out of Costa Rica. That had sent Duff into a tailspin and he'd finally told the team about losing his wife, Katie. The fact he'd held onto that secret for years, only telling them when he was worried about losing Ivy, too, told Jangles how much he loved Ivy.

"Copy that," Merlin acknowledged and dropped it.

Jangles pulled his phone from his vest, was happy to see he had service, and called Tex.

"You at the end?" Tex answered, and Jangles wondered if the man ever greeted with a hello.

"Yeah."

"Good news is, patrol passed by five minutes ago. Bad news is, even though I was able to take the airport cameras offline when you landed, Demir must've had a scout there looking for you. His men are assembling fifteen miles to the east. Bravo Team is on standby and waiting, two miles west of the compound. When you leave the tunnel, you switch to direct communication with me. Roe's called in an airstrike. We need to time that just right."

"Copy." Jangles pointed to the door and Merlin slowly pushed it open. "Tangos fifteen mikes east. Bravo at the ready two mikes west. Let's roll." To his team, then back to Tex, "Going to comms."

Jangles disconnected the phone, stowed it back in his vest, and put in his earpiece. Before he turned on his radio, he informed the team, "Gunship on station."

"Let's get it on," Merlin muttered, and rifle up and at the ready, he scanned right then left and led the way.

~

"I WISH I HAD ON PANTS," Hope quietly mumbled to Nori.

Ivy and Gwen had both fallen asleep, Destiny was lying in her cot but awake. Every once in a while, Hope caught her opening her eyes and staring at the ceiling, then she'd close them again.

"If you wanna try to sleep, I'll stay awake," Nori told her.

"I should be tired, I feel like I've been awake a million years, but I can't sleep."

Nori gave her a sympathetic smile and looked down at her skirt. "Yeah, I'm not exactly dressed for a kidnapping, either."

Hope's gaze followed Nori's, taking in her fancy navy blue pencil skirt, nude spiked heels—complete with a pointed toe and sexy ankle strap, then her eyes traveled up to the taupe blouse and she asked, "Is that silk?"

"Yep."

Then suddenly Hope lost it—exhausted, half-delirious,

scared, along with a huge helping of anger, she burst out in hysterics. Her body shook with it, and by the time she was done, her belly hurt and there were tears in her eyes.

"You didn't even break a heel?" Hope giggled. "You said they pulled you into a car in your fancy get-up and you didn't even break a heel."

Nori looked at her like she'd lost her mind, then smiled. "Well, they are my favorite pair."

"Right." Hope giggled again.

"At least you're not in your work uniform," Destiny grumbled. "My heels aren't even sexy. They're low and sturdy. Totally ugly. I don't get why we can't just wear flats."

"Hate to agree, but they're totally ugly," Nori observed.

"*Hello*. I'm in Beau's tee and panties. I don't even have on a bra. As far as the worst kidnapping outfit goes, I win."

"You totally win," Destiny agreed. "Though right about now, I'd give up my skirt and shoes to have something that smelled like Trent."

Why hadn't I thought about that? Her hands went to the collar and she pulled the fabric over her nose and inhaled. A faint trace of Beau's bodywash lingered.

Heaven.

Come on, Beau, where are you?

But just as quickly as the thought flitted through her head, guilt followed. Beau coming to get her meant he was putting himself in harm's way. Her thoughts turned to her parents and witnessing the horrors that had played out in front of her. She'd been powerless then, too. Paralyzed with fear as Went had stabbed her father. Overcome with blinding rage when he'd turned to her mother. But she couldn't stop him. Hope's hand went to the long raised scar on her forearm and her finger traced the line. The physical reminder that one bad decision could forever change your life. She hated herself for bringing Went into their lives. Hated that she was so selfish. And there she was again, helpless.

Her mind shifted back to the morning she was taken. Raking through the memories, she wondered if there was something she could've done differently. Something that would've stopped her abduction. Everything had happened in the blink of an eye. The sound of the bedroom door creaking made her open her eyes. After that, she couldn't remember. Had she fought, screamed, anything?

Then suddenly she was pulled from her musing and the lights went out and Hope's world turned black.

"They're here," Nori whispered.

Hope closed her eyes and prayed for the third time that day, something she hadn't done since she'd gotten her parents killed. Something she didn't do because she didn't deserve anything. But Beau did, he was a good man and so were his teammates. And the four other women with Hope, they deserved to be saved.

CHAPTER 18

JANGLES FELT the bead of sweat as it slowly rolled down his temple, along his cheek, and finally dripped off his chin. As soon as one fell, another took its place. The wait was killing him. They were so close, the building where Tex had confirmed Demir was holding Hope and the others was in sight.

So fucking close, but so goddamn far away. Jangles was bouncing on the balls of his feet, itching for the go-ahead.

"What's taking so goddamn long?" Jangles asked over the radio.

"Short approach now," Tex answered. "Trigger's in place and ready."

Static came over Jangles' radio, then he could hear the Apache pilot's voice crackle over the line. "We're inbound with a thirty mike-mike." There was more static and finally, Jangles heard the words he'd been waiting for. "Target acquired. Standby for full cycle." Then finally the sound of heavy automatic artillery raining down. Jangles heard it twofold—through his earpiece and off in the distance. "Left break and come around with a hellfire."

"Coming back around with a hellfire," Jangles relayed to the team. He saw Merlin jerk his head, Zip and Woof both continued to scan the area, and Duff didn't move his gaze from the building the women were in.

"Ready to engage," the pilot announced. "Rifle." There was a thump and Jangles waited two beats before he received the confirmation. "Good splash. Repeat, good splash."

"Good to go," Tex cut in and the static disappeared. "Bravo two is on the move."

"Copy that."

"We're good to go. Trigger's on the move."

No sooner did the words leave Jangles' mouth, than the compound went black.

"Was that you?" Trigger asked Tex.

"Negative."

Jangles shook his head when Merlin glanced over his shoulder.

"No change," Merlin instructed. "We stay on course."

The power being cut made no difference to them. As a matter of fact, it made it easier. Demir had to know they'd come in with NVGs, and plunging the compound in total blackout wouldn't affect them.

"What's his game?" Zip asked.

"No clue," Merlin returned.

"I don't like it," Duff grunted.

Duff didn't like much of anything, but Jangles had to agree in this situation. He didn't like not knowing what Demir was doing. From a tactical standpoint, he'd just given the team the advantage.

"Stay to the shadows." Jangles glanced around the sparsely treed landscape. "He wants us in the open. In two minutes, those lights are coming back online and he's hoping we took advantage of the darkness and made a straight cut through the field. We'd be sitting ducks out in the open."

"We cut across, we cut two minutes off our time," Duff pointed out.

"And he'll turn the lights back on and pick us off. No change," Jangles reminded him.

Quickly and silently, they made their way across the stretch of land that separated them from the women.

Almost there, baby.

Less than two hundred yards to go and the lights came back on. Men charged from the courtyard.

Jangles cleared his mind until there was nothing but the approaching enemy. The mission, his targets, his team. This was what they did. They were five men, but one element.

One team that moved seamlessly.

Gunfire sounded off in the distance—Trigger and his team were under fire. But Jangles didn't think about that, either. They were waiting, drawing the enemy out into the open. His gaze slid to the building the women were in—unguarded. Though he couldn't be sure Demir didn't have people in there with them. The building was windowless and stone, their thermal devices wouldn't penetrate and pick up heat signatures, leaving them blind.

"Now," Merlin snapped, and Jangles' gaze sliced back to the wave of insurgents and took aim.

Time slowed.

His focus narrowed.

Through his night-vision goggles, he could make out green-hued faces. But as his finger pressed the trigger, their features melted away and the men running at him became nothing more than targets.

Moving, shooting targets that stood between him and Hope.

"Bravo's taking heavy fire," Tex sounded over Jangles' earpiece.

Fuck.

Jangles shifted to his right and started to move, firing his rifle with every step. He didn't need a verbal confirmation his team was falling into formation. They'd done this countless times, each of them knew what to do, where to go, and how to eliminate the enemy with deadly precision.

Less than a hundred yards to go.

Almost, baby.

"Rocket—" Tex's warning was cut off when Jangles' world exploded.

Like a rag doll, Jangles' body flew through the air. At the last second, he forced himself to relax and hit the dirt with a bone-jarring thud.

"Overshot," Zip shouted.

"Check-in," Merlin demanded.

Jangles heard Duff and Woof call out, then he did the same and rolled to his feet.

"You have eyes on the shooter?" Jangles asked Tex.

"Courtyard. To your ten o'clock. Three men covering him."

"Ten o'clock," Jangles shouted and popped off more rounds at the advancing men.

Jangles scanned the area. Ten bodies on the ground, ten more coming at them.

"How's bravo?"

"Holding their own," Tex sharply returned. "An airstrike—"

"We're not falling back," Jangles cut him off. "How many more we got?"

"Best guess, Demir brought in fifty men."

Fuck him. Best guess.

Christ.

"An airstrike—"

Jangles cut Tex off. "No. We don't have a visual on the women. There's a tunnel under that house." Jangles paused to fire on two more targets. "We didn't get to sweep the bunker, there could be a trap door like in Demir's office. No-go on the airstrike."

Jangles didn't want to think about the last time he'd been in that building. Someone had tipped off Demir that they were rescuing the hostages. They'd given Nori time to broker the deal for the doctors and nurses to be released, but the outcome of those negotiations didn't matter. Trigger's team had already been inserted along with Jangles, Woof, and Zip. But when shit hit the fan, their objective was to get the men and women out alive, not survey the room. Therefore, it was unknown where the tunnels under Onur's house led.

Five more down.

A second RPG flew over their heads, this time landing far left.

Thank Christ.

"Fuck this," Duff yelled. "Cover me."

"Don't—"

Merlin didn't get his order complete before Duff shot forward, leaving his cover behind a tree and small boulder.

Fucking, fuck!

"Goddammit," Tex growled in his ear.

Good to know Tex was watching from wherever the hell he was in real-time.

Zip and Woof followed Duff, laying cover fire, while Merlin hung back, picking off the men as they stood from behind the wall they hid behind. Jangles was moving slowly toward the bunker with one objective in mind—kill anyone who dared to stand in his way from getting to Hope.

Almost there.

Four more targets.

Jangles made his way around the bunker. The door was almost in sight when he felt searing pain slice the side of his neck. He took a deep breath and found oxygen still filled his lungs so he didn't bother to check where he'd been hit, then swung the barrel of his rifle to the right and took aim and fired.

He ignored the blood he felt dripping down his neck, likely soaking the front of his vest, and kept moving.

Rapid gunfire rang out all around him—quick bursts, then long volleys. The sound was relentless. The last twenty minutes felt like a lifetime.

"Door's clear," Tex unnecessarily told him. "Bravo has entered the main house."

Jangles didn't bother to alert the rest of the team, not that they needed him to. They had direct communication. Jangles was the only one who'd been cut off from intrateam communication.

"Copy."

Hang in there, Hope. Just one more minute, honey.

"CAN YOU RUN IN THOSE SHOES?" Nori whispered, and Hope assumed she was asking Destiny considering Hope was barefoot.

"Yeah, but I already took them off. I'll be faster without them."

Hope heard Nori's heels clatter, then a hand wrapped around her bicep.

"Who's this? Hope?" Gwen asked and squeezed.

"Yeah. Where's Ivy?"

"Here. I have Gwen's other hand."

"Destiny, make your way to us and we'll move together to the wall." Hope reached out and found Nori's hand midair as she blindly waved trying to find Hope. "That's me, Nori."

"Good. Hope's right. We need to stick close and get our backs to the wall farthest from the door. In case—"

Nori went silent. Her hand in Hope's squeezed so tight, pain shot up her arm.

"Is that..." Gwen started but trailed off as the unmistakable sound of gunfire vibrated all around them.

Hope's breath caught, panic seized her lungs, fear swirled in her belly as the reality of her situation slammed into her. Over the hours they'd been locked in the bunker, unharmed, left alone, she'd been able to go long stretches of time where she could pretend they weren't being held captive by a man who wanted to kill Beau, his team, and possibly them. They filled the time getting to know each other, each of them doing her part to keep the group calm.

But now it was real, there was no more pretending.

"Move," Nori barked, and Hope started to shuffle in the direction she was being pulled.

"I can feel the wall," Ivy said. She must've yanked Gwen in that direction because suddenly Gwen was pulling Hope. She'd barely regained her balance when the lights came back on.

"Ladies." A male voice filled the room.

Hope's heart lurched as she spun around and saw a man standing near the makeshift bathroom.

"Eleanor Bonham," the man sneered.

"Onur," Nori returned, using the same unfriendly tone.

Behind her, Hope heard someone whimper but she didn't dare turn and look.

There was something about Onur that went beyond evil, cruelty she'd never seen before shone on his face.

Hope was surprised to find the man spoke perfect English, and even though his hair was long, it was clean and tidy, the same as his beard. But it was the deep set of his eyes that captivated her, the determination she saw. He wasn't angry, and that scared the shit out of Hope.

The man looked resigned.

"I just need one of you," Onur said and raised the pistol in his hand.

Before anyone could ask, the building shook and the gunfire sounded louder, closer, the rapid succession neverending.

Please, God, don't let Beau get hurt.

"Yes, one of you will do." Onur smiled. "Any volunteers, or shall I choose?"

Hope felt Nori start to move, and in a split-second decision, Hope jolted forward.

"Me. I volunteer."

"Hope Mitchell. Now, this is a surprise. Though it shouldn't have been. You're not very smart."

Hope ignored Onur's comment and shrugged off Nori's hand as it curled around her shoulder trying to pull her back.

"That's me, the stupid one," Hope remarked, and stopped halfway between the women at her back and Onur.

"Shame, I thought Eleanor would come forward." Onur looked beyond Hope and narrowed his eyes. "Though, I'm sure you haven't forgotten me, have you, *Nori*? I was surprised to hear you were alive."

"No more than I was to hear the unfortunate news of your survival."

Onur smiled and Hope flinched. "Yes, your government is so easily fooled. Come." Onur looked back at Hope. "We're almost out of time."

Onur didn't wait for Hope to comply, he quickly closed the distance and grabbed Hope's arm.

"I can walk by myself." Hope tugged her arm but Onur's grip was relentless.

"There's still time for us to sit down and talk," Nori told him. "We can work something out."

"Always the negotiator." Onur clucked and shook his head. "Time for talking was when I welcomed you into my home. I extended you my courtesy, and you knifed me in my back. I'm no fool, I don't give second chances. My men have been instructed to kill only two of you. After all, I'm a reasonable man, but two of you will pay for my son and my brother. A life for a life."

Onur pulled Hope toward an open door in the wall that they hadn't discovered.

"Then leave Hope. You don't need her," Nori demanded.

Hope craned her neck and looked back at the women huddled by the wall. All the color had bleached from Gwen's face. Ivy's pretty features were arranged into an angry scowl. Destiny looked like she was debating whether she was going to do a running tackle or scream. But Nori looked calm, cool, and collected. As if she could talk their way out of this mess.

She couldn't. Hope knew it, and deep down Nori did, too, but she wasn't going to give up and Hope needed her to. Or her plan to get Onur out of the room so the others could find a way to escape would all be for naught. If there was one hidden door they'd missed, there might be more. There was a possibility they could get out or the guys would find them before it was too late. But that wouldn't happen while Onur was there waving a gun around. Not that he'd actually waved it, he'd pointed it directly at Nori, and Hope saw the hate on his face. He'd wanted Nori to volunteer, and she would've if Hope hadn't stepped forward first.

Now she needed to get Onur to take her.

Hope waited for Nori to look at her, then she smiled.

Onur yanked her through the door and slammed it closed.

The musky scent of dirt filled Hope's nostrils and she started to plan. She had no intention of getting out of there alive. That was freeing. As long as the others got to safety and Beau was okay, she'd gladly give up her life.

But she wouldn't be going alone—Onur Demir would die with her.

CHAPTER 19

THE LONG EXCHANGES of gunfire started to wane to short bursts and longer periods between, and by the sound, those lobs were coming from inside the house.

"At your six," Merlin said as he approached. "Duff and Zip are right behind me."

Jangles didn't stop picking the lock. He'd made the decision not to blast the door because there was no way for him to tell the women to get back and he wouldn't take the chance of injuring one of them.

The last tumbler clicked into place and he felt the lock click.

"Ready?" Jangles asked.

Merlin slapped his shoulder twice, telling him he was ready and he'd clear to the right.

Seamless.

With a nod, Jangles opened the door, kept his barrel low until the door was fully open, then he surged in, side-stepped to his right, and scanned the room.

Four women huddled with their backs to the wall. A quick glance told him they had no visible wounds.

Ivy. Gwen. Destiny. Nori.

No Hope.

"Where's Hope?"

Nori stepped forward, lifted a shaky hand, and pointed to the far wall. "He took her into the tunnels."

"Fuck," Jangles snapped.

"How long?"

"Maybe three minutes ago."

"Demir's got Hope in the tunnels," he told Tex.

"Bravo's clearing the house now. We'll find her."

Jangles turned to find Duff running into the bunker.

"Duff?"

He'd shoved his night-vision goggles up onto his helmet. Duff had done the same, so Jangles saw it—relief mixed with extreme fury. Ivy was already running to her man. Duff had his arms out prepared to catch her and Jangles' gut clenched.

It wasn't jealousy as such, but his heart throbbed with an ache so fucking deep he could barely keep his feet. He needed to find Hope.

"Duff!" he repeated and waited until he had his teammate's attention. "When you were in the tunnels, were there other exits?"

"Yes."

"Christ." Jangles stalked the wall Nori had pointed to and started to feel around. "Where is it?"

"I'll show you," Ivy said and jogged to his side, her hand going to the stones.

He felt Duff's presence behind him but didn't stop feeling for any abnormality.

He vaguely heard the reunions going on behind him, Merlin barking orders, women talking. But nothing penetrated. He just needed to find Hope.

"Here." Ivy pounded on the wall and Jangles followed her hand pointing to a tiny crack.

If you didn't know it was there, you'd miss it.

Thank fuck for Ivy.

"I'm going in with you," Woof said.

"No. You get Nori to—"

"He's going with you," Nori snapped. "She knew he wanted me. She knew and stepped forward. So shut up and take Heath with you."

Jangles felt every muscle tighten—she'd given herself up.

"And you're late," Nori continued to snap. "You need a new motto. 'On time, every time' no longer works."

He didn't have it in him to find her amusing, so instead, he pulled his knife from his pocket, and with a flick of his wrist, the blade sprang free and he shoved it into the crack.

"Duff and Zip, get them out of here," Merlin ordered. "Woof, you hit Demir's office and drop into the tunnel from there. Jangles and I will go in from this side."

Jangles kept at the wall, using the tip of his knife to try to find a way in.

"Princess, you stick close to Duff. I'll be right behind you."

"I got her," Nori said, and there was movement behind him.

Jangles clicked on his radio. "Zip and Duff are on the move."

"Got 'em," Tex returned. "They've got a clear path."

"I'm gonna tan her ass," Jangles mumbled and dug his knife in deeper.

After a few beats of silence, Merlin spoke softly. "She saved Nori's life."

"She gave herself up," Jangles angrily returned. "And we don't know if he would've killed Nori."

"He would've and you know it. Hope saved her life. So all I'm saying is, when we find her, check that anger."

Jangles decided to ignore Merlin and worked the wall.

~

"YOU'RE QUIET," Onur said.

"What?"

"You are quiet," Onur repeated slowly, like Hope was two and hadn't yet learned to comprehend words.

"I'm sorry, was there something specific I was supposed to talk to you about?"

"One of the many things I hate about American women is their attitudes."

"Is that so? Do you have experience with a vast array of American women or are you basing your opinion on what you've seen on the internet and TV? Or maybe it's just Nori you don't like since she outsmarted you."

Hope was talking out of her ass, she had no idea what had gone on, outside of what Nori had told them while they were sitting in that stupid bunker. But to Hope, it sounded like Onur had been played by Nori and the U.S. government.

"Eleanor did no such thing. And it was she who took my bullets."

"Right. So TV and the internet then. You know you can't believe everything you see on the boob tube."

"So crass, another reason American women are distasteful."

"I'm crass and distasteful? Bud, you kidnapped *me*. From my bed, no less. I don't even know you. That's not distasteful, that's in its own universe of fucked-up."

"Maybe you should stop speaking and we can go back to silence," Onur suggested.

"You're the one that wanted to talk. I'm not exactly sure what you thought you'd get, and you haven't begun to see my attitude yet. But if you think I'm sheepishly following you, you're more of a fool than I thought you were. And you have to know, I thought you were pretty fucking stupid."

Quick as lightning, Onur had Hope against the rocky tunnel wall, one hand around her neck, the muzzle of the gun pressed to her temple. He began to squeeze, making it hard for Hope to take a full breath. Her hands went up and circled his forearm but she didn't try to remove his grip on her throat.

"Who's the stupid one?" he shouted. Spittle hit her in the face.

That's it, asshole, get mad.

"You are if you think you're getting out of this alive," she wheezed. "They'll find you."

"Yeah?" Onur smiled.

Ugly.

Evil.

Cruel.

His face started to turn red—he was getting angrier and angrier. She needed him enraged, blinded, thoughtless. It was her only chance.

"Oh, yeah. And they'll kill you just like they did your brother."

Red turned to purple. The muzzle at her temple started to shake.

Almost there.

Then he gave her the opening she needed. The hand around her throat tightened but the hand holding the gun shook violently and the pressure at her temple lessened. He was more concerned with choking her to death; it was as if he'd forgotten all he had to do was pull the trigger and she'd be dead. Just as she had hoped, a man like Onur Demir would rather kill her with his bare hands. He'd find pleasure in it. But not Hope—the gun would work just fine.

And as quickly as Onur had moved to pin her to the wall, her hands left his forearm. She twisted her body, then threw all of her weight to the right, controlling his arm as they tumbled to the ground. Hope landed on top of him, and without giving Onur time to think, she elbowed him as hard as she could in his gut. He grunted and dropped his arm. Hope went for the gun with one hand while the other went to the inside of his bicep and found the sweet spot. She dug her nails in, pinching the soft tissue until he released the gun and she grabbed it while he struggled to free himself.

All of Hope's attention had been on getting the gun, therefore she wasn't prepared when he clipped her jaw with a left-handed punch. Thankfully, he was on his back and she was on top of him so there wasn't much power behind it. But it still hurt like a motherfucker, and it knocked her clean off him. She rolled to her side, back against the wall. He rolled the other way, reached out to grab her, and she pulled the trigger.

She pulled it again, and again, and again, until the magazine emptied and the slide locked open.

Then she closed her eyes, sealing herself off from the mangled, bloody mess that was left of Onur Demir.

"Did you hear that?" Jangles asked, not slowing his pace as he and Merlin made their way through the tunnel.

"Go!" Merlin shoved him and they both took off at a full sprint.

Jangles hadn't taken a full ten strides when he heard the final shot.

He counted fifteen in total.

Fifteen.

Jesus Christ.

A full magazine.

Then silence.

Deafening, chilling silence.

"Don't go there," Merlin ordered.

It was too late, Jangles was already there. His mind filled with rage, his heart full of hate, and his soul was bleeding.

In the dim light, Jangles could see two prone bodies up ahead.

"Fuck!" he roared and pushed his muscles harder than he ever had. His lungs burned with exertion, and his heart pounded in fear.

Blood pooled between Demir and Hope—an ocean of blood—so much it covered both bodies. It was splattered on her face, in her hair. She was covered.

Jesus fucking Christ.

"Fucking hell," Merlin muttered.

Jangles went down on his knees near her head and yanked his glove off. But before he could check for her pulse, she whispered, "I can't open my eyes and see it again."

"Thank God," Jangles breathed. "Are you hurt?"

"No."

Thank fuck.

"Okay. Keep your eyes closed. I'm gonna pick you up."

Hope nodded, and as gently as he could, he pulled her

through the blood until he had her far enough away from the slippery liquid he could safely lift her into his arms.

"Where're the others?"

"Safe. Everyone's safe," he told her.

"I want this off," she mumbled.

"What do you want off?"

"All of it. I can feel it all over me. He's seeping into my skin."

Jangles closed his eyes, tipped his head back, and took a moment to calm his racing heart.

Hope was alive. That was all that mattered.

Demir was dead and Hope was breathing.

"As soon as I can, baby, I promise we'll get it off."

"Now."

"Soon, Hope. Promise, baby. Just keep your eyes closed."

"Let's roll. Trigger and Lefty are waiting," Merlin said.

THE TWO-MILE TREK back to the tunnel was a blur. Jangles carried a silent Hope. Merlin and Woof kept communication with the rest of the team to a minimum. Just enough to give location updates. Jangles knew both men were eager to get back to their women and he didn't complain when they kept a fast clip. He wanted to get Hope the fuck out of there and find somewhere to clean her off.

"Tex arranged for rooms in the hotel we stayed at last time." Woof had taken over radio contact with Tex—Jangles was in no state to coherently speak to anybody.

"Trigger?" Jangles inquired.

"They're going straight through. Drake will stay with us."

Jangles adjusted Hope in his arms as he negotiated the tight tunnel.

"Almost there, Hope," he told her.

"I killed him."

Fuck. He wanted to comfort her. Kiss her. Run his hand over her face, smooth out the deep creases on her forehead, but he couldn't. Not until they were out of the tunnel and he could get her cleaned up. He tried to clear his mind, shut down the hatred and anger, but hearing Hope's tortured whisper brought everything swelling back to the surface.

"I'm not sorry," she continued. "He wanted to kill you. I'm not sorry. I'll never be sorry."

Christ. She was killing him.

"There's nothing to be sorry for, Hope."

She nodded against his vest and fell silent, so he did, too. He didn't want to discuss her killing Demir until he had his blood washed off her skin.

Nori stood at the end of the tunnel, a silhouette due to the light behind her. He couldn't make out her features but her hands were on her hips and he could swear he saw her tapping her foot in impatience. And he didn't think she was waiting on Woof.

No, Nori wanted to see for herself that Hope was okay.

As they neared and Jangles could make out her features, Nori opened her mouth to say something but quickly snapped it shut when she caught sight of Hope. Then her lips pinched together and her eyes turned bright with unshed tears.

"None of it's hers," Jangles assured her.

Woof stepped around Jangles, tagged his woman, and tucked her close.

"Let's get out of here," Woof said and steered Nori toward the SUVs.

By the time Jangles was up the ramp, Drake had the passenger door to the 4Runner open. With a lift of his chin, Jangles got in, situated Hope on his lap, and Drake closed the door.

Merlin, Gwen, Zip, and Destiny piled in with Merlin behind the wheel. The others got into Drake's vehicle and off they went.

Thank fuck.

CHAPTER 20

HOPE DIDN'T REMEMBER the drive to the hotel. She didn't remember Beau carrying her into the room. And she barely remembered him setting her on her feet in the shower.

"It's all gone, baby. You can open your eyes."

He'd washed her twice. She hadn't asked but he knew, so he'd soaped her head to toe, rinsed her, and started over scrubbing her skin clean.

When she was in that tunnel, she hadn't thought it possible. But the moment her eyes opened and Beau's blue eyes filled her vision, she no longer felt gritty and dirty. She didn't feel clean—she never would—not after what she'd done.

She just felt like Hope.

Like Beau's woman.

"Thank you," she whispered.

Beau's hand moved from where it'd been resting on her hip and his thumb brushed under her jaw and down her throat.

"Does it hurt?"

"No."

"You're bruised," he told her before she could ask.

That didn't surprise Hope. Onur had tried to squeeze the life out of her.

"I made him—"

"Not yet."

"Huh?"

"Not until I have you dried off, fed, and tucked into bed. Then you can tell me."

Hope nodded and her gaze dropped from his face. A large gash on the side of his neck caught her attention.

"You're hurt," she gasped. "Why didn't you tell me? I should've—"

"Shh. I'm fine."

"It's not fine, Beau. You're still bleeding."

Beau lifted his hand to his neck and hissed when his fingertips grazed the gash.

"Zip will stitch me up."

"He'll stitch you up?" Hope asked, appalled by his nonchalance.

Beau leaned forward and rested his forehead against hers.

"Hope, listen to me, I'm more than fine. You're standing here in my arms, I'm looking into your warm, pretty brown eyes, you're breathin', you're safe, and no one was hurt. Zip will stitch up the scratch on my neck. I'm gonna feed you, take you to bed, we'll talk, then I'm gonna hold you while you sleep, and then you're gonna wake up in my arms, and I'm gonna take you home. So, baby, I'm fucking great."

"I don't know if I can go—"

"We'll talk about that, too. After you eat."

Hope gave up trying to talk and just nodded. She was starving and was thirstier than she'd ever been in her life.

They got out of the shower. Beau had her dried off and in one of his tees and a pair of sweatpants that didn't belong to her, but she didn't ask where they came from. He called Zip and asked him to come to the room to stitch him up.

Two minutes later, the connecting door opened and in walked Zip followed by Destiny. She, too, was fresh out of the shower, her long brown curls still wet, and dressed the same as Hope. Destiny beelined it to Hope and their bodies collided with such force, Hope stumbled back.

Destiny followed her back, not letting go, and squeezed the breath right out of Hope.

"Thank God," Destiny breathed, then she pulled back and shook Hope. "Are you crazy? Don't ever do that again. You could've died."

The fierceness in Destiny's tone took Hope by surprise, and when the fog of that lifted, her gaze went to Beau's and found him staring at her. The icy look was so chilling Hope quivered. Never had she seen his beautiful blue eyes so stormy. No, not stormy—turbulent.

Violent.

Downright frightening.

So much so, Hope didn't answer Destiny, she simply let her eyes fall from Beau's and hugged her friend.

She sucked in a breath, then two. Neither helped to calm her racing thoughts.

Over the months she'd gotten to know Beau, she'd learned to read him. Most of the time, he didn't need words to communicate. She knew he was disappointed he was leaving her before he said he was leaving. When he was happy, his face was bright with it. When he was turned on, his blue eyes deepened.

But right then, the way he was looking at her, she realized she'd been wrong. Hope thought she'd seen Beau angry. She had not. She might have seen him mad, pissed, supremely ticked off, but never angry. Seeing it then, mixed with something else—maybe fear, maybe agony—it scared the bejeezus out of her.

Hope felt his look penetrate, it seeped into her bones, it knotted in her stomach. That didn't scare her, it terrified her. Something was happening, something she didn't like, something that didn't feel too good.

It was the beginning of the end.

She knew it. That one look told her everything she needed to know. He was letting her go. He promised he wouldn't, but he was going to break his promise and leave her broken.

Hope knew it like she knew she killed her parents.

Like she knew she didn't deserve a man like him.

She never should've believed Beau.

~

You could've died.

Jangles couldn't get those words out of his head. Zip had finished closing the gash on his neck and he hadn't felt a second of it. Destiny and Hope had sat on the bed quietly talking and he hadn't allowed himself to listen.

He stayed locked in his head, thinking back over the last thirty-six hours. Dissecting every minute, every move. Then he thought back further over the months since he'd moved to Texas. He remembered the first time he saw Hope behind the bar smiling—not at him, at someone ordering a drink—then he'd heard her laugh. The sound hit him square in the chest and he knew he was going to talk her into going home with him. He'd told himself it was because she was sexy as all get-out, but he knew that wasn't it. He wanted to witness that smile in private, he wanted that laugh all for himself. He wanted both directed his way with an unhealthy need.

Then he harkened back to a few hours ago. She wasn't smiling then. She was covered head to toe in blood. Onur Demir's blood. A man she shouldn't know, never even should've heard the name. Yet, she did. Because of him. He'd put her in danger and now she was stained, just like him—a mark on her soul that never should've been there, but now it was. She'd been forced to kill a man to save her life—again. The thought made acid churn in his gut.

Because of me.

By the time Zip and Destiny left the room, he knew what he had to do.

It was the only thing he could do.

He'd fucked up huge. He'd known better than to bring a woman into his life. He'd promised himself he never would. Then he'd found Hope. He never should've started it, never should've made promises to her he was going to break.

And that night, with Hope at his side, her arm resting across his gut, her palm over his heart, her scent filling his nostrils, he made a plan.

An exit strategy.

The fuck of it was, even though it made him a son of a bitch, he did this with Hope sleeping in his arms, taking more from her before he set her free.

He listened to her breathe, felt her warm body pressed against his, and he knew it wasn't right but he was giving himself one last night.

One last night to memorize every nuance, every sound, every quiet mew, her soft hair falling down her back, the way she fit tucked close.

One last night to feel everything he could, because tomorrow, he'd set her free.

CHAPTER 21

Numb.

Just numbness.

That was all that was left.

Beau had done all the right things, said all the right things. He'd held her when he told her what had happened, what she remembered about being taken. He soothed her when she cried. He'd held her hand when they left the hotel, guided her on the airplane, kept his arm around her the whole flight. He listened to every word she had to say, offered his support, told her she shouldn't feel guilty. But he never shared what he felt.

In other words, he was there for her, but he wasn't.

She'd lost Beau.

Jangles was in his place.

She didn't know how she knew exactly, but he'd made the shift. And thinking over everything, she realized she'd always had Beau, even way back when they first met. She might've called him Jangles, but with her, he'd always been just Beau. He'd given her the man, not the cold hard soldier.

Now she had Jangles. She was a mission to him. That was all.

They'd all been separated when they arrived at Fort Hood. At first, Jangles and the men had protested. Zip, Merlin, Woof, and Duff intensely so. Jangles mildly so. That was, until Commander Turano had stepped in and assured the men he would personally oversee the debriefs. At the time, Hope had no idea what a debrief was. Three hours later, she was well-acquainted with the term.

Hope had been questioned, re-questioned, and questioned some more. She went over every minute detail. When it was over, Commander Turano asked her to never speak of the *situation*. Though Hope knew it wasn't a request, it was a gentle command that wasn't really gentle. It was just a command to keep her mouth shut along with an offer to talk to a military counselor if she should need help dealing with her kidnapping and killing Onur.

Weirdly, she felt no remorse. Perhaps that would change when the shock wore off but she knew she'd never seek help. She'd shove it down where all the other junk lived.

Now she was done and all that was left was a hollowness she never thought possible. Commander Turano accompanied her down the long corridor to take her back to Jangles, the one person she didn't want to see.

"Ms. Mitchell," the commander called and brought them to a stop. "I know the last two days have been hard."

Yes, one could say they've been hard.

Not understanding where he was going with his statement, Hope nodded her agreement.

"When this starts to weigh on you, tell Jangles and I'll personally see to it that you get the help you need."

"I appreciate that, but it won't be necessary."

Besides, by the time the weight hits, I'll be nothing but a memory for Jangles.

"Ms. Mitchell—"

"Really, I appreciate the offer, I do. But when I tell you it won't be necessary, I'm telling you the truth. I know what guilt feels like, I live with it every day. I know how it feels to lose a part of yourself because of something you've done. I do not feel that now. I'm okay with what I did because I know it was my only option and it was the right thing. Onur was going to kill me, but before he did that, he was going to kill one of the guys. He wanted them to pay for a debt that was not theirs. I feel nothing but relief he's dead, and that Jangles, the team, and the women are alive."

"And you?"

"What about me?"

"Are you relieved you're alive?"

Hope shrugged. "I'm expendable. They're not."

"Hope—"

"Are you done?" Jangles came around the corner, effectively ending the conversation Hope didn't want to have. Especially when the commander's face had gentled and he'd said her name in a soft tone.

Numb, she reminded herself.

Just be numb.

"Yes," Hope answered. "If you still have stuff to do here, I can take a taxi home."

Jangles' torso jerked and his chin dipped. "Even if I wasn't done, you still wouldn't be taking a taxi home."

Right.

One of the others will give me a lift.

On that thought, she asked, "Where's everyone else?"

"They're already done."

"They left?"

"Yeah. Nori asked me to give you her number." Jangles

dug into his pocket, pulled out a folded piece of paper, and handed it to Hope.

Assuming it was a phone number she'd never use, Hope fisted the paper, uncaring it crumpled. Jangles' gaze dipped to her hand, then his eyes came back to hers, wearing a mask of indifference.

Oh, yeah, she'd now officially met Jangles. Badass soldier.

"Check-in," the commander instructed and left without sparing Hope another glance. He also looked unhappy, as in un-freaking-happy. Then again, Hope figured there was a lot to be unhappy about. Or maybe there wasn't and the man just had a bad attitude.

Hope didn't know, didn't care, and would never know because she'd never see him again.

Numb.

"You don't have to—"

"Let's go, Hope."

Hope. Not babe, baby, honey.

Just Hope and just Jangles. That was who they were.

So noted.

Once again, Jangles did the right thing, the nice thing, and held her hand through the building, the parking lot, and even helped her into his truck, though it was completely unnecessary.

The drive was quiet. Hope didn't ask where they were going and Jangles didn't offer the information. Though she didn't need him to—without looking, she knew he wasn't taking her back to his place. He'd said he was taking her home and home meant her RV at BF's.

Jangles rolled to a stop in front of her place and killed the engine.

"You don't have to get out," Hope said as she unbuckled her belt.

"Gonna get you inside."

"Really, you don't—"

"Baby, I'm gonna get you in and get you settled."

Hope's eyes slowly closed and pain scored through her.

Baby.

Good Lord, that hurt so damn bad.

Before the pain of that receded, Jangles had rounded the hood and opened her door. She took his offered hand and did it only because she wanted one last touch. And she knew it was the last she'd get—once she was steady on her feet, he pulled his hand free from hers.

When Jangles opened the door to the RV, she waited for him to complain that she didn't lock her door. She never had. As a matter of fact, she didn't think BF even had keys to the RV. She was far enough off the road but close enough to BF's house she'd always felt safe. And if that wasn't enough, she slept with a nine under her pillow and had multiple weapons hidden around the house—she wasn't a complete moron. She was, however, stupid enough to believe Jangles.

But the complaint never came. More evidence she didn't need to prove Jangles was done with her.

They entered and she became acutely aware of how small her RV was. But she loved it, she'd made it hers, and it was plenty big enough for what she needed, and that was a bed and a shower.

Jangles finished taking in the space and his eyes came back to her—tortured and stormy—blue and gray swirled together. She hated this new look worse than the angry one he'd given her yesterday in the hotel.

She hated it so bad, she wanted it gone. And there was no reason to prolong the pain.

"I get it," she told him.

"Get it?"

"Yeah. We both know what this is, there's no reason to make it ugly. You're a good guy so you're gonna want to let me down easy."

There it was, all the proof in the world she was right. With fascination, she watched the shutters lower and his brows crease, but the rest of his features remained impassive.

"What I'm trying to say is, you don't have to. I get it. Which also means you don't have to say anything."

"Hope, honey, this is about me doing the right thing," he voiced softly.

Translation: I don't want you.

"Okay."

"I never should've asked you to go there with me."

But you did. Then you promised not to let me go.

"What I do, my job." He shook his head. "You deserve better."

"Right."

No, I don't. I don't deserve anything.

But she wasn't going to argue.

"What happened was extreme. If that starts fuckin' with you, promise me you'll reach out."

"Sure."

"Hope, I'm serious. Promise me."

"I promise," she lied.

"Baby—"

"Jangles, stop." His back snapped straight and his eyes narrowed, but before he could attempt to correct her—because hearing him demand she call him Beau would make her lose what was left of her mind—she continued. "What we had was good. It was fun. Let's not ruin it by saying anything else."

"At least let me stay awhile. I need to know you're okay."

Is he serious? Fuck no, she wasn't okay, and she didn't think she ever would be again.

"I'm fine, Jangles, please leave."

"Will you call Nori then?"

She could've lied and told him she would but there was no point.

"You know I'm not going to call her. I'm glad that everyone's all right, and home safe and sound. But I'm gonna leave it at that."

"Hope—"

"Seriously," she snapped. "Just stop."

The numb started to slip and she needed him to leave before she broke down.

"I know, Jangles," she whispered because that was all she had left in her. "You know. It was good. Leave it at that and please just go."

Jangles clenched his jaw, fisted his hands, and woodenly left.

And that was it.

It was done.

Hope remained rooted staring at the door, praying for numb.

CHAPTER 22

JANGLES WASN'T certain how long his ass had been planted on his couch, but if the two empty bottles of Jack at his feet were anything to go by, he'd guess three, maybe four days. He lifted the third half-full bottle to his lips and took a healthy pull.

The whiskey had long since lost its burn, but it was still doing a good job keeping him in a dazed, emotionless state.

There was an ugly war waging.

A war he was determined to win.

That was why he'd drunk himself into a stupor then worked hard to keep himself there. Drunk meant he wouldn't leave his house. Drunk meant he wouldn't go to Hope, fall to his knees, and beg her to forgive him.

He knew better than to want more. He fucking knew not to pull her into his life, into the shit that constantly surrounded him.

Dumb fuck.

His head pounded and his eyes screwed shut as pain ricocheted around his brain.

"Open the fucking door!"

It took a moment for Jangles' liquor-drenched mind to understand it wasn't his head pounding—though it sure as hell felt like it—it was someone banging on the door.

"You got two seconds before I'm coming in."

Merlin?

What the fuck?

Jangles didn't bother trying to get up, Merlin could let himself in if he wanted in.

A minute later, Jangles craned his neck and watched his team prowl through his house.

Fuckin' perfect.

"You're shitting me," Duff growled.

Now, that was surprising. He didn't think Duff would be the one to open…whatever this was.

"Jesus, when was the last time you fed your cat?" Zip asked. "Only way I know you still have her is the ammonia smell from the litterbox."

My cat? He'd fed her that morning, fuck you very much. Yeah, he had Buster back. She got out during the kidnapping but came scratching at the door after he returned from taking Hope to her RV. *Probably should have let the cat go, too.*

"Talked to Hope," Merlin announced.

There it was.

Jangles remained silent.

"She's shattered."

His body tensed but he made no move.

"Locked out Gwen totally, took one call from Nori, now it's radio silence. She won't take any calls. Not going into work, BF said she won't leave her RV, and when he tried to get in, she refused him, too. I went out there, she opened the door, and Christ, Jangles, she's fuckin' demolished."

Direct hit—straight through his chest.

With his jaw clenched, his hand tightened around the neck of the bottle, he fought the urge to throw it across the room.

"What the fuck?" Merlin shouted. "Just like that, you don't care?"

Oh, he cared, he fucking cared so much his insides bled.

"Why'd you do it?" Zip asked.

Because I love her.

"You're joking, right? Please tell me you're not gonna sit there drinking yourself stupid while your woman is ten miles away, destroyed."

"She's not my woman," he lamely rasped.

"He speaks," Woof said, his words dripping with sarcasm. "And when he does, he spews bullshit."

"Why, asshole? Tell us why you dumped her ass," Zip pressed. "And less than twenty-four hours after she risked her life to protect ours. You've always been a cold motherfucker. On the job—emotionless. But this? This is a whole new level of extreme."

"Jangles—" Merlin started but wisely closed his mouth when Jangles' dead gaze slid to him.

"You know why."

"I do?" Merlin's shoulders jerked. "I don't have the first clue—"

"You do," Jangles argued. "You *saw* her."

"Yeah, brother, and I saw *you*. I saw you when we heard those shots. I was right behind you as you were running so fast I could barely keep up so you could get to your woman. I watched you pick her up and carry her three miles. I saw it all. Fuck, Jangles, I felt the relief rolling off you when you found out she was the one who unloaded that magazine. I'm also the one who walked in here on a Sunday morning and saw her in your tee and you looking like you'd won the lottery. So, no, with everything I saw, I do not get why you'd send her away."

Jangles surged to his feet, his stomach pitched, and he needed more than a moment for the wave of nausea to roll through him.

"Head to toe in *fucking* blood!" Jangles roared. "Stained with it. And I did that to her. Me. I can't have her...Fuck."

His head spun, whiskey and guilt churned in his gut and burned as it threatened to knock him on his ass.

"It wasn't hers," Merlin reminded him. The softness in his friend's tone infuriated him.

"So?"

"It wasn't hers," he repeated, and Jangles side-armed the bottle and sent it sailing across the room. With a bang, the drywall dented, the bottle shattered, and whiskey exploded everywhere.

"Head to toe in fucking blood. She begged me to get it off her. And you don't know. You don't know her. You have no idea what she's been through. I can't do it to her. I have to let her go."

"Do what?"

"Put her in danger."

If Jangles hadn't been nearing blackout, he might've felt the air in his living room change. He might've felt the hostility rolling off his teammates. But his mind was clogged with Jack and his heart was in pieces, so he missed it.

"What happened wasn't your fault," Woof rejoined.

"Keep telling yourself that."

"What the fuck?"

"None of them would've been in that fucking bunker if it wasn't for us. My woman wouldn't have been in a position to give herself up and she wouldn't have had to kill

Demir. I'm not doing that to Hope. I let her go. She'll get over me."

"You think I'd put Ivy in danger?" Duff growled, and Jangles' gaze slowly went to his. "You don't think all of us weren't scared? You don't think all of us aren't feeling this? The difference is, the rest of us have the balls to admit it. The rest of us know the risk is there but it's small. We also know what we found and none of us are going to live in fear and let it go. Wake up, Jangles, before it's too late and you lose her. Just because I never said anything doesn't mean I'm blind. We've all seen how you look at her, we've all watched the two of you for months. You're acting like a pussy. Wake. Up."

"You have no idea—"

"Jesus, grow a pair. And take a fucking shower, you stink worse than the litterbox." And with that, Duff turned and stalked to the door.

"He's right," Merlin told him. "We were all scared and I'm man enough to admit it. Just to add, if you think Hope's just gonna get over you and move on, you're fucking blind. That woman is in deep. She loves you and you're hurting her."

With a lift of his chin, Merlin stomped through his living room, Zip and Woof on his heels. The front door slammed and Jangles fell back on his couch.

"Fuck!"

Fucking hell.

His elbows went to his knees and his head bowed.

Christ. Such a coward.

Two days later, Jangles rolled off his couch. His head was throbbing with the worst hangover he'd ever had. He looked around his living room and was disgusted with what he saw and smelled.

The moment he stood, shards of pain engulfed his entire body. After what he'd done, he deserved nothing less. On shaky, weak legs he made his way through his house, down the hall, and into the bedroom he'd yet to have the courage to enter. Everything was exactly the way it had been the morning Hope was taken.

He glanced around the room and fear flooded him. His stomach roiled and he barely made it to the bathroom before he lost the contents of his stomach.

Don't ever do that again.

Hope's beautiful brown eyes and pretty smile flitted through his mind. The vision morphed and he saw her lying on the ground in the tunnel covered in blood. Her eyes were closed and she wasn't smiling. Red dotted her face, coated her arms, torso, bare legs.

His tee and her panties.

Fuck.

He retched again and willed all memories of Hope to vanish.

CHAPTER 23

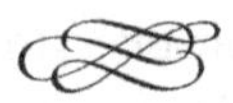

"You look miserable."

Hope turned to look at Jake, one of the other bartenders at the Ugly Mug, and flipped him off.

"*And* you're in a mood."

"Good of you to notice," Hope snapped. "You should go back to your end of the bar."

It had been almost two weeks since she'd been kidnapped. Ten days since the calls had stopped from Gwen, Ivy, Destiny, and Nori. She'd ignored every call but one. It was a bitchy thing to do and she knew it. But she couldn't be friends with Jangles' teammates' women. No way, no how. It would hurt too much.

This was exactly why she'd never been overly friendly with them, and other than the one outing with Gwen, she'd never seen them outside of the bar. They were good women, sweet, kind, funny, and Hope knew she'd become attached. And after spending time with them locked in a prison, she knew she'd been right to keep her distance. She liked them all, too much. And now she couldn't have them.

Jangles was gone.

And Hope was back to square one, picking up the pieces of her broken life. Only this time, she had BF and he wasn't allowing her to wallow in her misery any longer. She was actually surprised he'd given her as much time as he had. But yesterday, he'd gone to her RV, banged on the door, and didn't stop until she showed her face. Whereupon he promptly, mercilessly, and very dramatically told her to get her shit together. That was BF's way. He knew she was hurting, he didn't like it, but he was a man without a woman in his life, therefore he didn't have the first clue how to be gentle. But Hope knew he cared and was worried about her.

After he delivered his speech about pulling herself together, he told her she was going back to work. Hope argued until she lost, then she asked if she could work at the shooting range instead of the bar for the foreseeable future.

His reply was, "Girl, you think I'm letting you loose around guns, you are crazy."

Then he rolled away.

So there Hope was, behind the bar of the Ugly Mug. She was there under extreme protest, but after everything BF had done for her, she couldn't deny him. So, she had spent the rest of yesterday looking at apartments in El Paso. The six hundred and thirty miles felt necessary. She loved BF, loved Killeen, loved working at the bar and range, and even loved her little RV. She'd felt safe there, it was home. But now she needed to get away.

The mere thought of seeing Jangles and his team made her cry herself to sleep. Of course, Jangles would wait, he wouldn't come in for a good long while, he'd make sure the sting of their breakup had waned. Then he'd start coming back in to hang with his buds, and eventually he'd pick up a woman or he'd bring one in. That thought had driven Hope into hysterics.

The sting would never wane.

She'd never forget what he promised her, then took back.

No length of time would heal what Jangles had broken. Her only option was to leave. Everything she owned would fit in her car, and since BF had refused rent on the RV, she had a good amount of money saved. She'd barely feel the hit the move would cost.

"You're finally back."

Hope lifted her eyes from the glasses she was stacking and took in Nori's smile.

Yep, she needed to move.

Seeing the other woman hurt worse than she thought it would.

"And you're still in Killeen." Hope returned her smile but she knew it fell flat. "Bet Woof's happy about that."

"Yeah. I had to go back to D.C. for a couple of days but now I'm back. Lots of changes going on."

"All good, I hope."

"Definitely." Nori's smile widened.

"You look happy."

Hope immediately regretted her words when Nori's smile faded into a frown and her eyes went soft.

Yep, she was moving. Maybe even out of Texas—suddenly six-hundred-plus miles didn't seem far enough. She needed six hundred *million* miles between her and Jangles' team.

"We need to talk, Hope."

Shit.

No, we don't.

Hope grabbed a towel, dried her hands, and nodded to the far side of the bar. Nori caught her hint and met up with Hope as she moved from behind the bar to the empty back room. Hope looked at the pool tables, the dartboards, and her stomach clenched. She'd snuck many glances of Jangles bent over the pool table lining up a shot. She'd watched from her spot at the bar admiring his ass, at the way the material of his T-shirt stretched over his muscular back. She'd watched him laugh with his buds, throw darts, seen him smile.

"Hey," Nori called softly.

"Sorry. I was thinking about the liquor inventory."

"Liar." Hope jerked in surprise. "I know that look. I used to see it in the mirror."

"Nori—"

"Please, just give me five minutes."

Wordlessly, Hope pulled out a chair. Nori did the same and they sat.

"I did the same thing Beau's doing," she started. "I left Heath."

"You did what? Why would you leave him?"

"Not now," Nori corrected. "When we got back from Kazarus the first time. When I was in the hospital after I was shot. I suspect my reasons for doing it were different than Beau's but I did it all the same. I kicked Heath out of the hospital and out of my life. I thought I was doing the right thing, I thought I had to let him go. I was miserable. I was heartbroken. I hurt him. And I was very wrong."

"Jangles and I are not you and Woof. What you have is very different."

"Beau."

"What?"

"He's Beau to you."

Pain sliced through Hope, leaving her panting. *Sweet Jesus, that hurt*. He was Beau, now he wasn't. He wasn't anything to her. Nothing. She knew when he'd left that was it, he wouldn't call her or make any attempt to see her. She just didn't know how much his absence would tear her up.

"Please listen to me, he's not Beau. He's not even Jangles. Whatever we had is over. And really, what we had wasn't much." The lie rolled off her tongue and pierced Hope's heart. "We started off hooking up when we could, then we graduated to me cat sitting when he left for work. That's all we were. Now it's over. It was good, it was fun, but I've let that go."

"What happened to you?"

Hope's shoulders snapped back and a chill hit her skin. "What do you mean?"

"When we were in Kazarus, you said you know what it's like to live with guilt. What do you feel guilty about?"

"It doesn't matter."

"I got all day, Hope." Nori sat back in her chair but her eyes never left Hope's. "When we were in that bunker, I started going down a path—"

"I don't want to talk about Kazarus."

"Too bad, you need to. We all do. While we were there, we were all trying to make the best of a seriously shitty situation. But under all the lighthearted banter, each of us was scared. Not only for ourselves, but for the guys, too. I was so terrified Onur was going to kill me in front of Heath before he either killed himself or tried to kill Heath. You knew it, too. You knew when the lights came on and Onur was in the room with us he wanted me. That's why you gave yourself to him. You protected me. Now I'm returning the favor. And, Hope, you're gonna let me."

Tension coiled in Hope's shoulders. The tightness spread up her neck and she felt the beginning of a headache coming on. Not a good thing to have at the start of her shift on a Friday night, when in a few hours the bar would be packed, the music loud, and the crowd rowdy.

"Seriously, Nori—"

"Seriously, Hope," she snapped back and Hope's temper flared.

Fine.

If Nori wanted the story, she'd give it to her. Then she'd understand why a man like Jangles didn't belong with a woman like her in the first place. Nori would be relieved Jangles had cut and run.

Promise me, Beau. Swear it. You won't let me go.

Swear, Hope, I won't let you go, baby.

Push hard, Beau. Even when I fight you, push. Don't let me leave you.

Look at me.

I am.

You're looking, but you're not seeing me. I'm not gonna let you go.

The agony of Jangles' deception settled over Hope. Lies —all lies. The worst part was she'd known better. She knew he'd never give her more, knew she didn't deserve it, knew she'd never have it, yet she still fell for his lies.

No, it was better this way.

"Hope?" Nori's voice pulled her back to the present.

"Fine. You want it, here it is. When I was seventeen, my boyfriend killed my parents." Hope heard Nori's gasp but kept going. "Then he turned his knife on me."

Nori's eyes went to the long, puckered scar on Hope's forearm. The daily reminder of what a horrible person she was.

Hope lifted her arm to give the other woman a better view. "He did this, right before I got his knife from him and stabbed him in the throat."

"Hope—"

"Don't feel sorry for me. It's my fault they're dead. They told me he was bad news. Told me to stop seeing him. They threatened to pull me out of school and send me away to a boarding school. And it was my fault for telling Went that. He went ballistic. Totally insane. I thought him wanting to take me away was the most romantic thing in the world. That he loved me so much he wanted to run off with me and protect me from the bullies at school. He said he couldn't live without me. He said I was the best thing that ever happened to him. Then he killed my parents. Killed them so they couldn't send me away and he could have me.

"I don't deserve anyone's pity. I brought it all on myself and my parents died because I'm a selfish, horrible person. And don't think what I did in Kazarus was some brave, heroic act. It wasn't. You're a good person. Ivy, Gwen, Destiny, all of you good. I had nothing to lose. I have nothing."

"Honey, that's not true."

"All of it's true. I don't get Jangles because he deserves someone better. It's good he realized that and let me go. Now he's free to find someone that will make him happy. Someone good and clean and worthy. I'm happy for him."

Liar.

"It's not your fault—"

"Please, Nori, please stop. It *is* my fault. I chose Went. I kept seeing him after everyone told me to stop. And truthfully, I knew he wasn't a good guy. I knew it and I didn't break it off and I didn't for selfish reasons. Now, I have to get back to work. I'm sorry you wasted your time coming here but nothing has changed, nothing *will* change."

"I'm gonna kill Beau," Nori muttered.

"Please don't be mad at Jangles. He did the right thing, and in time, you'll see I'm right."

"You're not right. You are so very, very wrong. And, honey, it kills me that you think he deserves someone better. It hurts that you carry this guilt around when you shouldn't. But what really hurts is knowing you're not going to let it go when you absolutely should."

"I tried," Hope whispered. "I trusted him. He told me he wouldn't let me go. He told me he wanted more. He said he didn't want us to be a secret. He said he wanted the woman he loved on his arm and not have to hide. He broke every promise he made. But I understand and I'm begging you to understand, too. He's a good guy who knows what kind of woman he deserves."

"You're wrong." Nori shoved to her feet, the chair scratching on the wood floor as she stood. Then she leaned over the table, a deep scowl etched on her pretty features. "You're too fucking good for *him*. Think about that, Hope. You survived hell. And I don't care if you invited that Went person into your life, you didn't invite him in to murder your parents. You didn't ask him to end their lives. You were seventeen. You survived that and you didn't let it break you. Don't you think your parents would want you to move on, have a good life, be happy? Don't you think they loved you? No parent would want their child to throw away their life holding on to guilt that's not theirs. I know what kind of person you are, I know how good and courageous. You were willing to give up your life to save mine. That doesn't say horrible and selfish. That says good and brave. And I'm pissed as hell at Beau, and if you don't think I'm not gonna tell him exactly how disappointed I am, you're wrong about that, too."

Nori straightened, picked up her purse, and told Hope, "And by the way, I'm moving to Texas. One of many changes. Which is a good thing, since I figure it's gonna take me a fair amount of effort to sort your head."

Oh, no.

That didn't sound good. Hope had underestimated Nori. She'd thought the woman was competent, professional, and strong. Now she knew Nori was really a wild snarling dingo, and if Hope wasn't careful, she'd sink her feral teeth into Hope's life.

"I'm sure Woof and the others will be thrilled."

"But not you?"

"I would be if I was staying in Killeen."

Nori's eyes narrowed and her chin dipped before she asked, "Where are you going?"

"I found a place in West Texas."

"You're not gonna tell me where?"

Hope shook her head and smiled. "I'm happy for you and Heath. But mostly, I'm happy for you. Be well, Nori."

Before the other woman could say more, Hope stood and hightailed her ass out of the pool room and dashed into the back of the bar.

It was too soon to be back at work. Too soon to have to plaster on a fake smile and pretend her life wasn't in the toilet.

She'd planned on giving BF two weeks' notice. Now she was giving him twenty-four hours. And she knew he'd understand. He wouldn't be happy, but he was a man who'd lost everything, too. He'd also run from a life that was full of promise when he'd come back from war missing his legs. So he'd absolutely understand why Hope needed a fresh start.

CHAPTER 24

JANGLES LOOKED around his empty house and all he felt was relief.

"That's the last of it," Zip told him unnecessarily.

"'Preciate your help."

Zip looked around the living room before he gave Jangles a few bone-crushing pounds on the shoulder.

"Anytime. You know that, right?"

"I do."

"You gonna call Hope?"

"Not yet."

Zip sighed his disappointment. "It's been almost a month, brother. You heard what Nori said, she's packing up and moving."

Yeah, Jangles had heard the woman—loud and clear. That was because Nori had very loudly told him what a jackass he was, then very clearly told him that he was an idiot, and she'd done that for a very long time. When she'd finally stopped ranting, she gently coaxed him into talking. The conversation had started much the same way it had with his team but ended with him admitting he was scared.

And that's what he needed to talk to Trigger about. Not that his team didn't understand—they'd all been in the same position—all of their women had been taken. But his team was too close to the situation. It was hard to talk to them about blaming himself and not make them feel like he was blaming them, too, which he wasn't.

Intellectually, Jangles knew the sole responsibility rested on Demir. But he was still struggling to get past what Destiny had said to Hope—*don't ever do that again.* That one innocent statement had fucked with him since she'd said it. The thought of there being a next time plagued his dreams.

The chances were slim, yet it had happened. Jangles had brought his work stateside, literally to his door, and Hope had been taken, held captive, then she'd been forced to kill someone—again.

After Nori was done reaming his ass, leaving him to ponder all the ways he'd fucked up, he went to his bedroom, a place he hadn't been in since the day he woke up hungover, and immediately gathered the bedclothes and threw them out the front door. After that, he carried out the bed, the frame, and drove them to the dump. Three trips later, all of his bedroom furniture was gone. That had been the first time some of the weight started to lift.

Then he got on his laptop, found a house two blocks away that was move-in ready, and within a few hours, he'd signed a new lease, wrote a check to his old landlord getting him out of his current one, and started moving his stuff over.

He'd had to wait a week for the guys to be free to help him move the stuff he couldn't carry himself, and now that he'd let his disgruntled cat out of her carrier at the new place, he was done.

Gone would be the physical reminders of the house

that Hope was taken from, leaving the mental ones he'd yet to overcome. That was why he needed to speak to Trigger. He couldn't go to Hope until he knew he could move past his fear.

But he couldn't tell his friend that, so instead he asked, "She still planning on leaving tomorrow?"

"According to Nori, yes."

Good. I have time.

"I hope you know what you're doing."

"So do I."

"Jangles—"

"I need a few more hours to sort my head. She deserves that much, trust me. I cannot go to her and hope she forgives me if I'm not sure I can let go of the fear. Either way, I'll talk to her before she leaves."

"Either way?"

"I know you of all people will understand this. I love her enough to know that if I can't be the man she needs, I need to step aside. If I can't have her, at least I can let her go find her happiness."

"That's a lonely road," Zip quietly warned.

"You walked that road for twelve years, I suspect you know better than I do. But seeing as I feel like my heart's been ripped out of my chest, and the thought of her finding a man and spending her life with him makes me want to murder some imaginary dude, I think I have a good idea what the rest of my life would be like without her. She's it for me, I know it. Just like you knew Destiny was yours. But you stepped aside so your brother could be happy, so Destiny could be, too. So, I know you get it, Zip. I can't have her unless I know I'm man enough to push the fear aside."

Zip stared unblinking at the bare wall and nodded. "I get it. But just so you know, I wish I wouldn't have let her go. I can still remember lying in my bed listening to Sean and Destiny telling my parents they were getting married. It felt like I was dying inside, but I owed him. He was my brother—my twin. My best friend. He'd saved my life. So I owed him to stay upstairs in my bed and keep quiet even though I wanted to go downstairs and take Destiny away from him. So, while I understand, our situations are not the same. I regret losing those years with Destiny. I regret not having her by my side. I shouldn't have waited so long after Sean died to go to her. If you think Hope is the woman you want to spend the rest of your life with, then don't let anything stop you from going to her."

"I know she is."

"Then you better find a pair of knee pads, because I have a feeling you'll need them when you grovel." Zip clapped him on the shoulder and made his way to the door but stopped before he opened it. "And, Jangles?"

"Yeah?"

"You're man enough." Zip paused and smiled. "That is, when you're not acting like a pussy."

With that, Zip was gone.

Jangles didn't bother doing another walk-through of the house.

Thirty minutes later, Jangles pulled into Twinny's parking lot and found Trigger's car already there. He grabbed his cell and wallet, folded out of his truck, and made his way inside.

Thankfully, Trigger had the foresight to get a booth in the back corner of the restaurant, away from prying ears.

"I already ordered," Trigger started. "Didn't figure after we had this conversation you'd have a stomach for food."

The other man was correct, Jangles hadn't had much of an appetite for anything the last month, and he'd sworn off Jack Daniel's for the rest of his life.

Now that Jangles was sitting across from Trigger, he wasn't sure how to start the conversation. Actually, he knew what he wanted to ask, he just didn't know how to frame it without sounding like the pussy Zip had accused him of being.

"You ever hear the story about what happened when Gillian was shot?"

Jangles shook his head in the negative.

"I'll spare you all the details. The bottom line is, I heard the shot, took off to take down the shooter, Lefty covered Gillian. After the situation was under control, I went to Gillian and there was blood pooling on the concrete around her. My world stopped, all I could see was the blood. Without assessing her injuries, because at the time, all I could think about was if she died, I would never go on. Gillian was wheezing, her eyes dazed, and there I was on my knees begging my woman not to leave me—not to die. I can't remember everything I said, though if you ask Grover, he'll repeat it verbatim. The point is, I thought she was dying. She wasn't. She was hit, but it was a graze to her arm. Grover and the guys were giving me one hell of a ribbing. I didn't care what they were saying, how I looked begging my woman not to die from a graze. All that mattered to me was she was alive and she'd be in my bed that night.

"My point is, you're sitting across from me with a look on your face that tells me you need to talk, but what you're worried about is what I'll think of you. And I say this as a man who loves his woman and doesn't give the first fuck that others know or what they think. So, spit it out."

"I'd ask you how you could read me so easily, but I suspect I'm not hiding it."

"You're not," Trigger confirmed.

"How do you do it?"

"I love her," he returned immediately.

"I get that. So how do you do it?"

"I love her." Trigger held his stare and remained quiet.

It couldn't be that easy, could it?

"I'm scared," he finally admitted.

"Yeah?"

"I'm scared it will happen again. I'm afraid that something we do will follow me home and next time, she won't be so lucky."

"The odds—"

"I know the odds. I know they're nil. Yet, I can't stop being afraid. That's why I'm asking you how you do it."

"I do it because the fear of not having her outweighs the fear of a mission gone wrong. It's easy because the alternative means I don't have her. I don't go to sleep with her, I don't wake up with her, I don't see her smile, or tease her, or hear her laugh. I think the question you should be asking is, what are you more afraid of?"

"Not having her."

"Then why'd you let her go?"

"Told you why."

"That's not why. What's the real reason you cut her loose?"

Jangles felt the pressure starting to build in his skull, his ever-present headache making itself known.

"What if in a few months from now, or a few years, she decides I'm not enough, the life I can give her is not what she wants? The constant call-outs, the training, the inconsistency, the possibility I don't come home from a mission. Then what? I know she's it for me. I know what it feels like not to have her, I know the pain of the constant throbbing in my chest. I can't live like this."

"Then don't. You have the power to end your misery, yet you're not. Love's a gamble. But every morning when I open my eyes and see Gillian next to me, I feel like I've won. You're letting fear and what-ifs rule your life. If you love her like you say you do, I suggest you get in your truck and get your ass to her place and do it quick."

Jangles nodded. "I'm going there in the morning. I wanted to talk to you and—"

"If you love her, you'll go right now and pray you're not too late. She's leaving this afternoon."

"Come again?"

"She told me last night she was packed and ready and heading out a day early."

"You didn't think maybe you should've started with that?" Jangles snapped, and started to slide out of the booth.

"Nope. I figured the way you jacked her around, you needed to sweat a little. Good luck, friend."

Jangles didn't bother with a post-heart-to-heart good-bye. If he missed Hope he'd have to face BF, which he didn't mind doing, but it would take for-fucking-ever to get the old man to tell him where she went. Which he deserved, of course, but he didn't have the patience when he needed to get to his woman.

CHAPTER 25

HOPE LOOKED around the RV she'd called home for the last eight years and doubt started to creep into her heart. She'd refurbished every square inch of the motorcoach. From reupholstering the captain's chairs to the two-seater couch. She'd pulled up the ugly nineteen-sixties linoleum and replaced it with laminate wood flooring. A newish fifty-five inch flat-screen TV fit above the sink so she could relax on the couch and watch a movie. Not that she had time for that, but she could.

The kitchenette had been updated, along with the bathroom and the back bedroom area. All done by her, using the skills that BF had taught her. The old man was the first person who'd shown her any kindness after her parents died. He was an odd mixture of father-figure, grandfather, brother, confidant, and teacher. And she was going to miss him.

With a heavy sigh, she walked back to her bed to grab the last suitcase and wondered if she was doing the right thing. She was honest enough with herself to know she was running away from everything she loved, everything she'd built, because she couldn't face Jangles. Not that she'd seen him. He hadn't come into the bar even though Woof, Zip, Duff, and Merlin had.

The first time the guys had come in, they'd all said hello, but they gave her a wide berth. The next time, they sat at the bar and chatted with her. No one brought up the five-hundred-pound elephant in the room, but they made it clear they all liked her and didn't want things to be awkward. It was the third visit that had been the hardest. Nori, Gwen, Ivy, and Destiny joined them. The men played pool, the women sat at the bar. None of them dared to utter Jangles' name, but they made it clear Hope was one of them and tried their damnedest to pull her into their girl posse.

So, she was leaving for a variety of reasons. Her resolve to stay remote and not get sucked into the friendship the women were offering was one. The men glancing at her with sympathy was another. But mostly, she was leaving because she couldn't be in the same town close to Jangles. It was only a matter of time before he joined his buds at the bar. That would kill. But when he found himself a woman and brought her in, that would demolish Hope.

She'd done a lot of soul-searching over the last few weeks. After years of BF telling her she wasn't to blame for her parents' and brother's deaths—something the two of them had talked about in-depth over tequila many times—times where he'd have a shot or two, wait for her to drink enough to loosen her tongue, then impart his wisdom. Over and over, he'd told her the guilt she carried would destroy her. He'd begged her to burn the letter Peter had left. Nothing had penetrated. She held on to her past. But it was something that Nori had said that got her thinking. *You survived hell.*

Survived.

She had survived, the others hadn't.

Hope had spent so many years punishing herself for their deaths she'd forgotten something until Nori had reminded her. They loved her. Her parents might not have had a butt-load of money in the bank, they did what they could to get by. But they were rich in a way that had nothing to do with money. She and Peter were loved. She knew it, she felt it, and she still allowed her teenage self to get dragged down by what people at school said about her.

She'd allowed herself to become a victim. But not Peter. While their parents were alive, he knew he was loved and it didn't matter what others said.

It had taken a few days for Nori's words to settle, and when they finally did, Hope snatched her brother's suicide note from her nightstand where she kept it and burned it. Then she found the framed family photo her mom had proudly displayed in their old home and set it out. At first, seeing that picture sent Hope into a sobbing mess. But as the days slid into a week, it felt good having them back.

New life. New start. New home.

That was what Hope was after. And while she was finding that, she was going to let go of the guilt. Not that she'd ever forget, but she was determined to start living.

Hope heard the crunching of tires on the gravel outside and groaned. She'd already said goodbye to BF and she'd barely held the tears back the first time. Before she could grab her suitcase to go out and meet him, the door swung open with an almighty crash and Hope turned to see who'd entered.

Time stood still and her breath stopped when she caught sight of Jangles.

He looked horrible, disheveled, and he was staring at her like he had in the hotel room back in Kazarus. He also looked huge standing in the small space—imposing, angry—but his blue eyes held something else. A month ago, she would've tried to decipher the look, she would've wanted to ease what she saw. But now he was not hers. Whatever was bothering him wasn't her business.

Pain stabbed at her insides, and then and there, she knew she'd made the right decision leaving. She'd been wrong—just seeing him demolished her. Desecrated her heart.

She had to go.

Long moments stretched while neither said a word, but she couldn't look away. He held her captive. Everything she wanted stood before her. Only a few feet separated them but it might as well have been an ocean.

Yeah, she had to leave.

"Jangles—"

"Beau," he snarled.

Oh, no, not that again. He'd never be Beau again.

They went back to silence and it felt like an eternity before he spoke again. An infinite length of time where her heart pounded in her chest, breaking apart what was left of the organ.

"I fucked up."

Hope locked her knees and fought to stay upright. What she would have given to hear those words the day after he'd dropped her off. Hell, she'd secretly, stupidly, held on to hope for the first week after he left her, desperately wishing he'd come back.

Now it was too late.

New life.

New start.

"I don't know what to say to that," she admitted.

"Please, hear me out."

Now, she knew the answer to that one.

"No."

"Hope, baby, please—"

"Stop. Just stop. I don't want to hear anything you have to say. It's done. Whatever we had is over."

"I tried." Two words that sounded incredibly painful for Jangles to admit but even more painful for Hope to hear. "I tried to do the right thing. At least when I was doing it, I thought it was right. I failed to protect you. My job had leaked into your life and put you in danger."

"Jangles—"

"After we got word Destiny and Nori had been taken, something inside of me snapped. I didn't realize it at the time because all I could think about was getting home to make sure you were safe. Then I walked into my home, my fucking *home*, a place where you were supposed to be safe, and found you gone. Snatched from the bed we slept in, where I held you, where I made love to you, where hours before, I tucked you in before I left for work. And you were fucking taken from it, wearing my goddamn T-shirt and a pair of fucking panties. *Taken*!" he roared the last word, and Hope jerked in surprise.

"I know," she whispered.

"After that, I felt nothing but death and destruction and more fear than I've ever felt in my life. It consumed me. For thirty-six hours, I was scared to fucking death that something was going to happen to you because of my job. I love you, Hope. I love you so damn much that I thought I had to let you go to keep you safe. I tried to let you go to be free to live a life where you never had to worry about when your man was going or where to, or if he'd bring that kind of danger home. But I can't give you up. Those thirty-six hours have nothing on the pain I've felt the last month. I'm so sorry. Christ, baby, I'm so sorry."

"When I woke up tied and blindfolded, I was scared."

"I know you were."

"No, Jangles, I was *scared*. And when we were in that bunker I was *scared,* too. And when Onur took me into the tunnel, I was *scared*. But through all of that, I knew you'd come. Then I wasn't only scared for myself, Nori, Ivy, Gwen, and Destiny, I was scared for you and the guys. But never, not once, did I blame you. Never did I think about leaving you. When you found me, all I felt was relief that I was in your arms. Then you washed away the blood and I felt clean. I felt loved. I felt safe. I believed in you, in the promises you made me. You asked me to believe and I did. Then you took it all away. You broke every promise you made me. We're done, Jangles, in a way that cannot be fixed."

"I can fix it. I swear, Hope, I'll fix it."

"You promised me you'd never let me go. *Promised*. Yet, you did. So I hope you understand I don't believe anything you have to say."

Pain slashed across his face and it sucked, but Hope felt that pain, too. She didn't want it to affect her the way it did. She didn't want to care he looked like she'd fired a kill shot, but she did.

He was everything she'd wanted but would never have.

"Baby, I'm begging you, please give us a chance. Give me a chance to make this right. I was wrong. I know I was. I let fear cloud everything. I can't let you go."

"You're too late." She shook her head, needing to get away from him before she broke down. "Please leave."

"I'm not leaving."

"Fine. But I am."

Determined to get to her car and drive away from Killeen and Jangles, she started to move toward the door, which meant she was moving in his direction. The struggle not to allow him to touch her when he lifted his hand and reached for her was harder than she thought it would be. But she did it.

"Don't touch me."

They were close, so close she could smell the lingering scent of his laundry detergent, the faint pine of his soap. She loved the way he smelled, outdoorsy, rugged—all man.

"I'm begging," he repeated and dropped his hand. "Please, give me an hour."

"A month ago I would've given you anything you wanted. Now, you're too late."

"You love me."

Arrow straight through her heart.

Hope's eyes drifted closed and she fought to find her breath.

"I do." She didn't bother denying it. "I love you. I always will. But something you taught me is, I deserve better than to be thrown away." Hope opened her eyes and took one last look at Jangles. She lifted her hand and placed it on his chest. She felt the strong, fierce beat of his heart under her palm and wished he hadn't broken his promises. "Be well."

Hope stepped around him and made her way down the stairs, but stopped when he said, "I'm not letting you go. You can run but I'll find you."

Hope's step faltered but miraculously she kept her feet. He had no idea how badly she wanted to give in. Turn around and hear him out. But she couldn't. He lied, and it might've taken eight long years, but she finally believed she deserved better. She wasn't a secret, or a toy for someone to throw away until he decided he wanted it back.

"I won't hold my breath," she muttered quietly and opened her trunk to toss in the suitcase.

She reversed her car slowly and didn't look back. She couldn't. It was time to only look forward.

But if she had, she would've seen Jangles sitting in the doorway of her RV, feet propped on the top step, elbows on his knees, and his head hanging. What she wouldn't have been able to see were his tears falling silently as she drove away.

CHAPTER 26

JANGLES HEARD the man approach but didn't lift his head.

"You're a dumb fuck."

BF was not wrong, therefore he didn't bother defending himself.

"Yep."

"You gonna fix this?"

"Yep."

"You got twenty-four hours. Then I'm hunting you down and you'll find buckshot in your ass."

"Think it'll take more than twenty-four hours, BF."

"Then you're a bigger dumb fuck than the dumb fuck I already thought you were. You let this go on too long, you give her anymore time, she'll be lost to all of us."

His jaw clenched, not liking being called a dumb fuck multiple times, even if he was one. But more than not liking being called out, he knew the old man was right. He'd let his stupidity and fear ruin his relationship, and in the process, he'd hurt Hope.

"Only reason I haven't shot you yet is I figure you know you're a dumb fuck."

"Let that shit slide 'til now, BF, but that's enough," he barked.

"Yeah, is it, Jangles? Is it enough that you crushed that girl? Is it enough that after I worked my ass off for eight years tryin' to get her to a place where she could finally find some happy, and she finally found it with *you*, then it took you all of five fucking minutes to unravel it?"

"Enough!" Jangles roared. "I know what I fuckin' did."

"Look at me, boy."

Jangles appreciated being called boy even less than he appreciated being called a dumb fuck but still he lifted his eyes. He flinched at what he saw.

"Yeah, you see it. You see an old, broken man in a chair. You think I don't know what it's like to lose? And I'm talking about more than just my legs. You think I don't know what you're feeling? I know a dumb fuck when I see one because I'm the king of dumb fucks. I've been in this chair thirty-eight years, but thirty-seven of those I've been living in hell. Not because I don't got no legs. Fuck my legs. Fuck the chair. I'm in hell because I pushed away the finest woman I've ever known. A woman who loved me unconditionally. I made it so she had no choice but to walk away because I was busy feeling sorry for myself. Thinking I was doing her a favor by givin' her a reason to leave so she could find a man who had legs. A man who wasn't a fuckin' cripple. Stupid fuck. Dumb fuck. She never found that man because she was too busy lovin' me. Loved *me* until the day she died. Never found herself a man but I never went back. Just like Hope will die loving you, lost and lonely. And then you'll be me, King Dumb Fuck."

Jangles' chest burned as he listened to BF.

"I know, Jangles. I. *Know*. Because Hope looks at you like my Norma looked at me. I know because just like Norma, all Hope wanted was a man to help her beat back her demons, love her, and let her be her. Be the beauty she should've always been. She didn't care you'd be rolling out of bed in the middle of the night, because she knew you'd come home to her. And just like my Norma, she wouldn't care if you came home missin' an arm or both your legs because she loves *you*. I don't care why you did what you did. I don't care what was in your head when you were doing it. I suspect your reasons for leaving were the same as mine. All I care about is that you fix what you broke and bring my girl home."

"I'm not bringing her back here, BF."

"Didn't think you were stupid enough to do that, Jangles. Just bring her home and make her happy. It'd suck spending my last years on this earth in a five-by-five cell, but I'll gladly do it if you don't fix this."

"Not a big fan of being threatened."

"And I'm not a big fan of you fucking over my girl. Yet, here we are. And I think I'm being pretty fucking generous considering the state you left her in. It wasn't you that listened to her cry. And something you should know, not a single tear was shed about her being kidnapped and whatever the hell happened after that. They were all for you. Every last one rolled down her pretty cheeks because of what *you* did."

The burn turned into a raging fire of regret and misery. Jangles didn't bother to fight the emotions. They were nothing less than what he deserved.

"I'll fix it," he bit out.

"Good."

BF wheeled himself around and left, but Jangles remained where he was.

Then he pulled his phone out of his pocket, scrolled to the name he never thought he'd use again, and hit go.

"Jangles," Tex greeted.

"I need your help."

"Whatcha need?"

"I need you to track Hope Mitchell. She left Killeen about an hour ago. I believe she's headed to El Paso. I need to know every place she stops and if she's signed a lease."

"You fucked it up."

Tex wasn't asking a question so Jangles didn't bother confirming.

"I'll pay you or you can hold a marker. Your choice."

"Marker."

Tex disconnected and Jangles waited.

He had no doubt Tex would come through.

HOPE HAD ONLY MADE it two hours before it was no longer safe for her to drive. The hundred and fifty miles she'd driven with tear-filled eyes was as far as she could go. So when she saw the exit to Junction, she decided to call it a day. The city seemed fitting enough. After all, she *was* at an intersection of sorts. Right, left, forward, or reverse—all roads led to heartbreak, and more of it.

Damn Jangles.

Damn him for showing up right before I left.

For thirty-six hours, I was scared to fucking death.

God, why did he tell her that?

I'll never let you go.

Broken promises.

Lies.

Hope found a hotel and pulled in.

Forward

That was the direction she was going.

CHAPTER 27

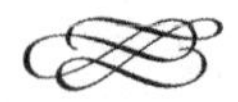

THE KNOCK at the door startled Hope. She sat up and looked at the clock then around the cheap hotel room. Bland and outdated. No personality. Nothing special. Bleak. It was the perfect room for her current mood.

She ignored the door and laid back down. No sooner did her head hit the pillow than the knock came again. She hadn't ordered food, no one knew she was there, and she wasn't expecting anyone so she ignored it again.

Another knock, only this time the pounding was accompanied by, "Hope. Open up."

What the hell?

"Baby, I know you're in there."

Hope's blood turned to ice and her body stilled.

This couldn't be happening.

How was this happening?

A few seconds later, she heard the door creak open and her temper flared.

"I'm coming in," Jangles announced even though he didn't need to.

As soon as the door opened she saw him. She lay there

stunned, wondering why she hadn't flipped that metal bar thingy, though she didn't think that would've stopped him from getting in.

"Go away," she groaned and shoved her face in the pillow.

"Baby—"

"Stop!" Hope shot upright in the bed and kicked off the threadbare comforter, then stood. "Get out, Jangles."

"Not until we talk." Jangles' gaze zeroed in on her face and his eyes narrowed. "Are you crying?"

Hope hadn't looked but she didn't have to. No doubt, hours of crying had turned her face into a puffy mess.

"Get. Out."

"Why are you crying?"

"Why am I crying?" she huffed. "Are you serious?"

Jangles took a step forward and Hope took a step back, skirting the edge of the bed. Space. She needed as much space between them as possible.

"Hope—"

Rampaging emotions slammed into her, every inch of her vibrated with unspeakable pain.

"I don't understand why you're doing this to me. You left. You promised me you wouldn't let me go and you did. You wanna know why I'm crying? Because you've destroyed me. I didn't think it could get any worse." Hope angrily swiped away the tears she didn't want him to see fall. "This last month has been awful. It hurt, Jangles. Hurt so bad I wasn't sure how I was going to make it. But I did and I picked up my life and now you're back. Why? Why are you doing this to me? Haven't you hurt me enough?"

"You don't think it's been hard on me?" Jangles pointed to himself and Hope felt her ire skyrocket. "I didn't want to let you go."

"Well, you did," she spat. "You lied to me."

"I've never lied to you."

"You promised never to let me go. You promised we'd see it through. But you—"

"I'm not letting you go."

"Too late. You already did."

"I'm not letting you go," he repeated.

Hope needed him to leave before she stupidly believed him.

"You did this to us. I was taken against my will..." She let that hang, not wanting to say the rest. She'd been kidnapped, scared, and she'd killed Onur Demir. "And the moment you could, you dumped me. I saw it, Jangles—you would've left me in Kazarus if you could've. I saw you shut down and start to distance yourself. You went through the motions of getting me home, then you walked out, not caring I was scared it could happen again. Not caring that I couldn't sleep. Not giving the first fuck I was reliving killing a man. You *dumped* me and walked out the door. So, no, I'm not going to listen to what you have to say. I want you to leave, and this time, don't come back. Stay away from me and let me move on."

With her palms sweaty and her heart pounding, she watched his body grow taut as she successfully landed blow after blow.

"Baby," he groaned.

"Too late," she shouted. "Get out."

"I love you, Hope. And fair warning, I'm not letting you go. I would, I'd step aside and set you free if I thought for one second you didn't love me. But I know you do. You're not the only one with a good memory, baby, so I remember. I haven't forgotten." He lowered his voice and gentled his tone when he said, "Push hard, Beau. Even when I fight you, push. Don't let me leave you. That's what you said to me. I'm gonna push until you break. I'm gonna stand and fight until I get you back. I'm not letting you go. And, Hope, that's not a promise—that's a guaran-*fucking*-tee."

Jangles turned, opened the door, and without looking back, he left.

Hope didn't make it to the bed before her legs gave out and her knees hit the hard floor.

JANGLES HEARD the sob from the other side of the door and forced himself not to break into her room again so he could hold her. Instead, he stood outside and listened—let the sound wrap around his heart until the tightness turned agonizing.

His penance.

He'd earned the soreness in his chest and the torment her tears brought. It was his fault they were both suffering and in pain. He knew he had a long, hard road in front of him, one that had been paved with love and happiness until he blew it up, leaving only rubble in his wake.

Total dumb fuck.

Minutes later when the sounds from Hope's room quieted, he moved next door and let himself into his room, tossed the keycard on the table, sat on the bed, and pulled out his phone.

The phone rang twice before a familiar voice picked up, "Hello?"

"Hey, Ghost, it's Jangles."

"Heard you're in a situation."

"Trigger call you?"

"Nope. Merlin. He's worried and wanted me to reach out but you beat me to it."

Jangles sighed and remembered Trigger's wisdom. "I'm in love with her. I fucked up, thought I was doing the right thing, and pushed her away. I never imagined my job would intrude into her life, and when it did, I couldn't handle it. I was…I am…scared. I want to protect her but I can't live without her. I totally fucked up, she's rightfully pissed and shutting me out. I need help."

"Sounds familiar," Ghost muttered. And it would—once upon a time, his mentor had shut out his wife, Rayne. At the time, she was his girlfriend and she thought he was sparing her worry after he'd been badly injured on a mission. Rayne didn't take kindly to Ghost being a dick and had no issues telling him so. But she'd forgiven him. "What do you need?"

"I need to speak to your wife."

"Come again?"

"I need to talk to Rayne," he repeated. "I need to ask her how to get Hope to take me back."

"Smart man. Hang on, let me get her."

There was rustling on Ghost's end of the line and Jangles took the wait as an opportunity to figure out how much he wanted to tell Rayne. She was the wife of a fellow operator, she understood operational security. She also was fully aware of the inherent danger of her husband's job.

"Beau?"

"Hey, Rayne. Did Ghost tell you why I'm calling?"

"He said you're having some trouble with your girl. What's going on?"

Rayne's sweet voice was full of understanding. But by the time he finished the story from start to finish leaving nothing out—not even how they met, Hope's parents, the kidnapping, how he felt, Hope killing Demir, all of the dumb mistakes he'd made, and finally ending with him begging Hope to forgive him and her kicking him out—

Rayne no longer sounded sweet when she muttered, "Men."

Jangles gave her a moment, but when she didn't speak he called, "Rayne?"

"Give me a minute. I'm trying to decide if I should give you advice or let you continue to wallow in the misery you created."

Fuck, but I deserve that.

"I need help, Rayne. I'm willing to do anything. What did Ghost do to get you to forgive him?"

"He loved me."

Jangles groaned. He knew he loved Hope and she loved him but that wasn't going to be enough. She was stubborn, and to top it off, she was right. He left her when she was vulnerable and scared after what'd happened with Demir.

The more he thought about it, maybe he didn't deserve her forgiveness. He wasn't just a dumb fuck, he was a supreme asshole.

"I forgave him because I understood," she gently told him. "The day he kicked me out of his hospital room, it hurt, but I knew why he did it. I felt the same way when he'd rescued me in Egypt. I was tied to a bed, scared, and nearly…never mind, the point is, I didn't want him to see me like that. I wanted off that bed and out of that room, but I didn't want the man who I loved to see me like that. The difference was, I couldn't kick him out. But *he* could kick me out of his room and he did. But deep down, I knew he was doing it because he was protecting me from seeing him injured. There was nothing to forgive, not really, we just had some stuff to work out."

Shit. None of that was going to help him. Jangles' situation wasn't about communication and settling into a relationship. He'd fucked over the woman he loved.

"What I can offer you is this—if you love her, don't give

up. From everything you just told me about her, what's happening right now isn't just about you and her. She has old wounds that by the sound of it have never healed. Maybe you need to heal those before you try to get her back."

"I can't heal them if she won't let me in."

"Sure you can."

"I don't know how, Rayne. If she keeps kicking me out, I can't help her."

"You're a Delta, Jangles. I have no doubt you'll figure it out."

None of his military training would help him win Hope over—or would it?

The light dawned and he realized the first thing he needed was a plan.

"Thanks, Rayne. You've been a big help."

"Not sure that's true, but you're welcome all the same."

"Tell Ghost I'll call him later, there's something I need to do."

"Will do. And good luck."

"Thanks."

Jangles disconnected and went to the window to peek out at the parking lot. He would've heard Hope leave, but he needed to double-check. Then he sat at the shitty, worn table for two and started to formulate a plan, and a backup plan, then just to be on the safe side, a contingency plan just in case the first two went to shit.

Come hell or high water he was getting Hope back. But more than that, once and for all, she was letting go of her past.

CHAPTER 28

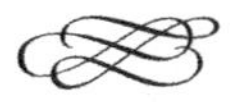

THE NEXT MORNING, Hope woke up with a splitting headache. *Lack of sleep, dehydration, and crying all night would do that to a girl.*

God, my life sucks.

Why had Jangles decided to come back? And why was she thinking about Jangles the moment her eyes opened?

The stale air in the hotel room got her moving, that and the thought of Jangles returning. She had no idea how he found her and she wouldn't put it past him to drive back to Junction, uncaring the drive was over two hours each way and she'd repeatedly told him to leave her alone. Jangles didn't seem to care about anything she had to say and less about what she wanted.

She tromped to the tiny bathroom and slapped on the shower spigot, turning it all the way over to hot and on full blast. The heat would do nothing for her red, blotchy face, but it would work out some of the kinks in her neck. She'd tossed and turned and lamented most of the night about Jangles and how much of an asshole he was. Then she'd dissolved into tears because she remembered he wasn't an asshole, not really. Hope wanted to forgive him, she really did, and when he explained how scared he'd been and the reasons why he left her, she wanted to jump into his arms and make *him* feel better.

The only thing that had held her back was her resolve to move on. A fresh start and a new life were what she needed. And to get that, she had to leave Jangles in the past.

Don't I?

She couldn't keep moving forward if she accepted his apology.

Right?

Nori had made her remember a lot about her parents that she'd pushed down and locked away. The most important thing was how much they loved her. It was easier to remember them arguing about Went and what a stupid teenaged bitch she'd been than remember the good times.

There had even been a time when her grandparents had loved her. They'd spoiled her and Peter. A night spent at Grandma and Grandpa's meant staying up late watching movies with big bowls of buttery popcorn and an extra scoop of ice cream.

At one time, they'd been a happy family. Then Hope had succumbed to the bullying and became a shell of herself. That was on her. She'd been weak, she stayed with a guy who was a jerk and she knew it. But never in her wildest dreams had she thought he'd murder her parents. That single act was bad enough, but it had set off a chain reaction that had ruined her family. Destroyed everyone. She hadn't wanted him to do it, she hadn't asked, and she hadn't made him do it. Hope loved her mom and dad even if they'd been fighting.

Now her family was gone. Mom, Dad, brother, grandfather, all dead. She knew her grandmother was still alive, or she had been the last time she drove to Austin to visit Peter's grave on his birthday. Hope had seen the older woman walking back to her car after placing flowers on the graves. The same ones Hope had been to see. Each year since Peter's death, she'd seen her grandmother, but she'd never approached her. Hope waited out of sight in her car, not wanting to upset her grandmother.

Why hadn't she ever confronted her, tried to make amends? It had been years, her grandmother was all alone. Maybe it was time to reach out, try to heal the break in their relationship.

Hope stepped into the shower, the scalding water burning her back and shoulders, but she remained under the spray, welcoming the heat. She tipped her head back, drenching her hair, and thought more about visiting her grandmother. And the more she rolled the idea around, the more she came to understand there was no going forward if she continued to allow her past to hold her back.

She needed to let it go. And there was only one person who could release her.

JANGLES WAITED in his truck in the far corner of the parking lot. He had no intention of letting Hope see him. He'd been out there for hours, and when she finally exited her room, he sucked in a breath. Even from a distance, he could see she looked wrecked and he mentally berated himself for not going to her last night when he heard her cries through the paper-thin walls. He'd lain in his bed and listened to her toss and turn with intermediate spells of crying.

Once again, he'd done the wrong thing. He planned to follow her to El Paso, make sure she made it there safely, then he'd explain that he wasn't giving up but understood he needed to prove his sincerity. After that, he'd start by asking her for her friendship. Not the kind they'd had before that had also included a good amount of time in his bed and multiple orgasms. This time, they'd start with good old-fashioned friendship. Then, he'd set about making himself an integral part of her life. He'd tie himself to her until she couldn't deny they were meant to be together.

And if that didn't work, he had a backup plan, if that went FUBAR, he'd make a hundred more until one worked.

Jangles watched as Hope backed out of her parking space and headed through the lot. He waited up until she made a right onto Main Street before he followed, keeping a safe distance so she didn't spot him. He went back to thinking about his Mission of Forgiveness until Hope changed lanes and made a sharp right onto the I-10 east on-ramp. To get to El Paso, she needed to go west. Betting she'd made a mistake and would take the next exit to turn around, he didn't merge lanes even though she had. It wasn't until she'd made her way to the far left lane that he moved over.

He could call her and warn her she was driving in the wrong direction but that would reveal his operation. Instead, he settled in for a long detour until she figured it out. Fifteen minutes later, she took an exit and Jangles had to swerve across three lanes of traffic to follow her. Being new to Texas, he still didn't have all the interstates down and had no idea what was in Fredericksburg, he just knew that's where the sign he passed said he was going. Five minutes after that, Hope blew past a turnabout that she could've used to make a U-turn. Then he decided with a long stretch of Texas highway in front of him not to wonder where he was going. It was pointless. He'd follow Hope anywhere she wanted to go.

~

IT WASN'T until nearly two hours later when Hope passed the sign for Cedar Valley that she started questioning the validity of her plan, and by the time she'd gotten off the highway, her stomach was in knots. And when she turned onto East Yager Lane she felt ill. Her grandmother still lived in Copperfield, a middle-income neighborhood. It was the same house she and her brother had visited growing up, the house he'd moved into after their parents had died.

She pulled to a stop across the street and took in the aging brick exterior. It needed to be pressure washed and two large tree limbs needed to be trimmed back before a storm hit and they broke off and landed on the roof. The yard needed to be cleaned and raked and the flowerbeds that had once been a riot of color were now barren.

Guilt started to eat at her, and for once it had nothing to do with her parents. She should've been looking out for her grandmother. She was getting up in age though not yet at a point where she couldn't get around, but one look at the state of her house told Hope she needed help.

Hope took a few cleansing breaths and gathered all the courage she could muster. She'd let the rift between them go on too long. She knew it, and she also knew it was she who needed to make the effort. They'd both lost huge. Hope, her mother, father, and brother. And Marybeth, her daughter, son-in-law, and grandson. Neither's burden was worse. But is was on Hope to reach out. She might've been slowly accepting that she wasn't to blame for her parents' murder, but she still held some culpability in the heartbreak.

The muggy afternoon air made it that much harder to breathe as Hope made her way across the street. And by the time she found herself on the front porch, she felt like she'd run a marathon. Her legs were jelly and her heart thumped frantically.

It took a few moments for Marybeth to answer the door. When she did, Hope was grateful the older woman hadn't called out a "who is it" because if she'd known beforehand it was Hope, she never would've opened. It didn't take a mind reader to know her grandmother wasn't happy to see her.

Marybeth's face said it all.

Disgust, clear as day.

"Leave."

"Grandma—"

"Don't you dare call me that," Marybeth sneered.

Tiny shards of pain sliced at Hope.

This is your only chance.

"Please talk to me."

"You have some nerve coming here. First, you kill my Patty and your father, and if that wasn't bad enough, you took my Peter from me. Go to hell, Hope."

Marybeth tried to close the door but Hope's hand shot forward and stopped her.

"I didn't kill them," she whispered. "Wentworth Collins did."

"You killed them. You, Hope. I don't care it wasn't your hand that held the knife. I ain't never gonna forgive you for takin' my girl."

"I lost her, too," Hope sighed, realizing her mistake. She never should've come. Some things were better left alone.

"You didn't lose her, you killed her. Always was a selfish child. Not worth spit, that's what your granddad always useta say. He was right. Now leave and don't come back. Not ever again, Hope."

"We're family—"

"You ain't my family, girl. My family's dead, all a 'em, and it's your fault."

Marybeth looked past Hope and jerked back in surprise. Her face pinched tighter, which was a feat considering the woman had worn a deep scowl since she'd opened the door.

"Oh, I see. You come around, bringin' another one of your criminals to my door. What? You bring him here so he can kill me, too?"

Hope had no idea what Marybeth was talking about. She craned her neck and almost had a heart attack. There he was, two feet behind her, arms crossed over his broad chest, blue eyes spitting fire, and he was frowning. Combine all of that with the angry vibes and he looked seriously freaking pissed.

Jangles.

Shit.

Did the man ever *listen?*

"Baby, I think you've taken enough abuse. It's time to go."

"She ain't got near enough of nothing. If you're here to kill me, get on with it. She already took everything from me. Got nothing else left. So if you're—"

"Woman! Shut your trap. Hope, baby. Come on," Jangles coaxed. "You tried. That's all you can do."

Hope blinked then blinked some more. After she'd

ascertained that Jangles wasn't a figment of her grief-stricken mind, she turned to face her grandmother.

"Beau would never hurt you," she defended. "And neither would I. I came here to say I was sorry, to ask you if we could move on—together, like a family. We're all we have left. I miss you."

"A family," Marybeth snapped the words like they tasted dirty. "You ain't my family. I don't accept your apology. You're a murderer."

"They loved me," Hope whimpered. "They loved me and you know they did. They told me all the time. Your daughter was a good mom and she loved me and Peter. You loved me, too. I'm sorry I brought Wentworth into our lives. I didn't know he was capable of *that*. I loved them. I miss them every day. I think about them and my heart bleeds."

"Good. It should bleed. I hope it bleeds you dry. I hope you die feeling the same pain your momma felt when he cut her throat. I hope you—"

"Enough!" Jangles roared. "Jesus Christ."

Then Hope was no longer standing on her grandmother's porch. She was cradled in Jangles' arms and he was stalking across the street.

Next thing Hope knew, Jangles was opening his truck door.

"What are you doing?"

"Baby."

He set her in the passenger seat and she asked again, "What are you doing?"

"Breathe, Hope."

"I am."

"No, baby, you're panting. You're gonna hyperventilate. Take a deep breath."

I am?

It was then Hope saw the worry written on his face. He was no longer angry, he was worried.

She glanced away, not wanting to see it, not wanting to feel it.

All she wanted was to be numb.

CHAPTER 29

Christ.

Jesus Christ.

Jangles saw it, the moment everything crashed down around Hope. Her eyes shifted from side to side not meeting his and wetness started to pool.

"I shouldn't've come."

"Why did you?"

"I wanted to apologize."

"To the woman who spit on you?" Hope's eyes snapped to his. "Yeah, baby, I remember what you told me. That woman's determined to hold onto hate, honey."

"She's my grandmother. She used to love me."

Fuck.

"I thought…" Hope stopped speaking, not because she didn't have anything else to say but because her torso jerked and a sob tore through her. Jangles slid closer and wrapped his arms around her while her body trembled and her tears soaked his shirt.

Jangles waited until he thought the worst had passed before he pulled back and started to buckle her in.

"Wha…What are you doing?" she hiccupped.

"Taking you home."

"I don't have a home."

"You sure as shit do."

"My car—"

"Don't worry about your car. Someone will come to pick it up."

"I'm not leaving my car here."

"Baby, even if I trusted you to follow me home, I still wouldn't let you drive. You're shaking like a goddamn leaf. Your eyes are swollen damn near shut. And that bitch just took a pound of flesh out of you. One that was not hers to fucking take. You're gonna stew on that, and it's gonna hit you again. When it does, you will not be behind the wheel of your car. I'm taking you *home*. You don't want me there with you after I get you settled, I'll leave. But you're staying there."

"BF's—"

"I'm not taking you back to that goddamn RV. You're going *home*."

Jangles knew Hope was gearing up to fight him, but this was one argument he would not lose.

"Why'd you come here?" Hope clamped her mouth closed and looked everywhere except at him.

"You're searching for family," Jangles told her. "But what you don't get is, you already have one."

"I wanted to move forward."

"By leaving everything you love behind?"

Hope shook her head. "I wanted a fresh start."

Fuck, that killed.

"I just wanted to move forward and I thought if I could make things right with her I could let go of the past and make that happen. But she's right—"

Hell to the motherfucking no.

"The fuck she is, baby. She spewed some seriously jacked shit. *You* were right, *you* didn't kill them. If she needs someone to blame and wants to live in misery, that's not your problem. And I'm not letting you go back to blaming yourself. I heard what you said, they loved you. Do you think your mom would be happy about the way that woman just treated you? I'm not a dad—one day, God willing, I will be—but I would be rolling over in my grave if my own blood spoke to my child the way that bitch just spoke to you."

"She's hurting, too."

The tears were back and it was time for Jangles to get on the road.

"I get that, baby, I really do. But that doesn't make it okay. Do you need anything from your car?"

"My purse," she answered absentmindedly.

"Keys in it?"

"Yeah."

Jangles was no fool and took advantage of the haze of sorrow that surrounded her.

He buckled her in, shut the door, and jogged to her car.

Jangles quickly located her purse and opened it to make sure her cell was there. He grabbed the keys from the cupholder, looked in her back seat, then glanced around the neighborhood. It wasn't the worst but it also wasn't the best. He wasn't leaving her suitcases exposed. Two trips later, he had the contents of her car loaded into the bed of his truck. When he got back into the cab, Hope's head was resting back and her eyes were closed.

"Everything's gonna be okay."

"Uh-huh."

"It will be," he promised.

"I don't believe you."

"I know you don't, but I'm gonna prove it to you."

~

TEN MINUTES INTO THE DRIVE, Hope could no longer hold her emotions in check. Her hands went to her face, the heels of her palms pressed against her cheeks, she bent forward, rested her forehead on her knees, and let go. The sounds of her sobs filled the interior of the truck and her body shook with the devastating heartache.

Marybeth's angry words replayed on a constant loop. Over and over she heard the conversation in her mind.

I hope it bleeds you dry. I hope you die feeling the same pain your momma felt when he cut her throat.

Hope had already been bled dry.

There was no denying she was alone. No family. Marybeth was as good as dead to her. She'd made it abundantly clear she wanted nothing to do with her granddaughter.

She felt Jangles' hand on her back but it did nothing to calm her, nothing to cut through the cold that had seeped into her bones.

Numb.

When the tears finally dried, Hope sat up and was surprised to find them back in Killeen. However, they weren't on Jangles' street, though still close by.

Jangles pulled into a driveway and cut the engine.

"Whose house is this?" she asked.

"Yours."

Hope's back snapped straight and she turned to look at Jangles.

"I don't—"

"For now, it's yours. One day it will be ours."

"Jangles—"

"Beau," he corrected. "Let's get inside and get settled."

"I'm not going in there."

"Babe, you are. You're going inside, I'm gonna fix you something to eat, and you're gonna get some rest."

"I don't need to rest."

"You tossed and turned all night. You've had an emotionally exhausting morning. You need some sleep and when you wake up, we'll talk."

"How do you know I tossed and turned?"

"Because I was in the room next to you. The walls were so thin I might as well have been in the bed with you. Every time you moved, I heard you. Every time you got up to pace the room, I heard. You were up more than you were sleeping."

Welp, that explains how he found me at Marybeth's.

"Why'd you follow me?"

"I wanted to make sure you got to El Paso okay."

"That's insane."

"Maybe." He shrugged his shoulders.

"How'd you find me?"

"I had a buddy track you. As soon as you used your credit card to book your room, I had your location."

Hope blinked away her shock. He was insane.

Why the hell would he track me?

"Isn't that illegal?"

"Probably."

"Why are you doing this?"

"I told you why, because I love you. I fucked up and I'm determined to prove to you not only am I sorry, but I will never make that mistake again."

"So, it doesn't matter what I want?"

"Baby, you're all that matters. But right now, I'm gonna give you what you need, not what you want. And we're starting with food and a bed. After that, we'll sort the rest."

"I think I know what I need," she snapped.

"No, Hope, you don't. You have no idea what you need. You're runnin' on emotion. I fucked you over—"

She'd had enough. More than enough, therefore those emotions Jangles had accused her of running on exploded out of her and she told him as much.

"I've had enough. I don't need to be reminded that you fucked me over, I feel it every damn day. I can't get away from it no matter how hard I try. It's in me, the pain, the anger, the heartache. You gave me everything then took it away. Stole it from me and left me empty. I don't want to be anywhere near you. Seeing you hurts. Being next to you hurts. Being at the bar hurts. Everything fucking *hurts*, Jangles. And you did this to me."

With escape on her mind, she unbuckled and threw the door open. Her feet were barely on the concrete of the driveway before Jangles was on her side of the truck grabbing her hand and leading her to the front door.

Hope didn't protest only because she had no options at that point. Her car was an hour away in front of her grandmother's house, she was bone-tired, and maybe after she slept for a hundred years, she'd be clear-minded enough to come up with a plan.

Jangles opened the door and gave her a gentle push. It wasn't until she'd cleared the foyer and stepped into the living room and saw Jangles' big black leather couch, his stylish coffee table, his TV mounted on the wall, and his bookshelves did she note, "You moved."

"Couldn't be in that house anymore. Couldn't even go into my bedroom. After I left you, I spent the first couple of days in a drunken stupor. When I sobered up and realized what I'd done, the first thing I did was haul the bedroom furniture to the dump. I couldn't bear to look at the bed you were taken from. I couldn't look at the sheets that I'd tucked around you before you were torn from them. I couldn't breathe in that house knowing what happened there. I didn't want you to ever step foot back in that place. If I couldn't stand being there, I'd never ask you to. So, I found this place and moved in."

Hope was stunned. Her heart beat wildly and her throat clogged. It was too much.

"Why..." she started but stopped.

Her gaze slid around the living room, then to the dining room where he'd also replaced his worn table with a large eight-seater. She couldn't see the kitchen but assumed it was through the large archway. She glanced to her right and there was a hall, the walls the same warm taupe as the rest of the house. Freshly painted white trim, the combination along with the wide plank wood floors gave the entire space a warm feel.

Jangles' old house had white walls, white trim. It was nice but a bachelor pad. This place felt like home.

"I explained why," he gently answered her question.

"No. Why couldn't you breathe in your old house?"

"Seriously?"

Hope nodded, not wanting to admit that his reason was important. Unwanted butterflies started swarming in her belly and that lump in her throat got bigger.

"Baby, you were taken from that house."

"I know I was."

"I know you know, but I don't think you're understanding. You were *taken* from our bed, in that house. Taken from *me*. When a man comes to realize all the ways he's vulnerable, when he comes to realize that he loves something so much that he now has a weakness, and that love can be exploited, taken, used against him, he does one of three things. Makes moves to protect it and in the process suffocates it because he's scared. Moves to protect it by walking away. Or, he mans up and does the right thing—

talks about his fear, protects his woman in a healthy way, and together they make moves to keep each other safe.

"I made all the wrong choices because I wasn't man enough to admit I was scared. I went back to that house and sat in the living room and all I could think about was how scared you must've been. I sat there with a bottle of Jack and I visualized how they got in, how they walked through my house, how they ambushed you while you were sleeping. From start to finish, over and over, I made myself think about it in an effort to punish myself for what I'd done. And I did a good job, Hope. I tortured the fuck out of myself. I deserved it. But when the fog cleared and it hit me that I'd made the worst mistake of my life, no amount of self-torture or alcohol could stop the pain.

"I knew I needed to fix what I'd broken, and the first step was to get the fuck out of that house. I needed to have a home to bring you back to. For you and for me. We both needed a fresh start. A place where we could begin again, this time with no boundaries, no hiding, no bad memories haunting us when we walked in the door or went to bed."

Hope liked that, all of it, but she was still wary.

"Are you still scared?" she asked.

"Shit, yeah."

Her heart stilled. So nothing had changed. He could turn at any time, and she'd never live through another breakup.

"I'll always be scared. There will never be a time when I'm not afraid for your safety. But I'm man enough to admit it. I'm fucking scared, Hope. I love you so much I don't know what I'd do if something happened to you. I'm also not so arrogant as to think I can protect you from everything. So, all I got is the knowledge that I cannot live without you. I love you, and I'm not letting you go. That leaves us one option—working together to make each other safe."

"You broke your promise," Hope said.

"I know I did." His honesty made it difficult for her to hold on to her grudge. "And I'm sorry."

"I won't survive if you leave me again."

"Bullshit. You're strong, Hope. You can survive anything and come out on the other side still standing. But I won't ever make you go through me leaving you again."

Survived.

Hope had to admit she had survived a lot. But surviving and thriving were two different things. She didn't feel like she'd accomplished much. All she'd done was get through each day.

"Hope?" Jangles pulled her from her introspection.

It was then the walls came crashing down. And with them, Hope.

CHAPTER 30

"WHOA, BABY. WHAT'S HAPPENING?" Jangles caught Hope around the waist as her body swayed and he lifted her into his arms as her legs started to give way.

"I…I…" Hope stuttered but said no more.

Jangles sat on the couch and settled Hope in his lap. To his surprise, she didn't fight him. Her head rested on his shoulder, one of her hands went to his chest, and she allowed him to hold her.

A step in the right direction.

"I thought it was my grandmother," Hope mumbled. "But I was wrong."

"Wrong about what?"

"It was me."

"I'm not tracking, honey. What are you talking about?"

"I needed to let go of the past so I could move forward. I thought I needed Marybeth to release me, forgive me, but I was wrong. The person I needed to release me was—*me*. The person I needed forgiveness from was *myself*."

"Yeah, Hope. It was you."

"I forgive myself," she whispered.

Thank fuck.

"I survived. I might've tiptoed but I did it. I picked myself up and I tiptoed until I could walk. Some days the steps are small, but I take them. That counts, right?"

"Absolutely."

"I cried and cried, but I wiped my own tears and I didn't give up."

"No, baby, you didn't give up."

"I remember how much they loved me. I forgot for a while but now I remember."

"Good."

Jangles had no idea what that meant for them but he was relieved as fuck she'd untwisted the guilt. He hated that her grandmother had gutted her, the woman was an absolute bitch, and while it seemed Hope gave the cow a pass, Jangles would not. He couldn't. Not after the venom she'd vomited. He got she'd lost a daughter, but that was not an excuse to decimate your granddaughter. But if the pain Marybeth had caused was the final incident that Hope needed to realize her strength, then he was glad for it.

"And I survived you leaving me."

The breath left his lungs, and his body grew tight.

"Hope—"

"It wasn't easy, but I wasn't gonna give up. I started tiptoeing again, picking up the pieces. I wasn't gonna let that stop me from moving on. I wasn't gonna let heartbreak, *break* me."

"Baby—"

"I wouldn't have been able to go back to that house," she declared, and his taut muscles turned to stone. "And not because I'm not strong. But because knowing that you sat in that living room and made up a story that was probably worse than what really happened so you could torture yourself kills me. I don't ever want to see that place again. And I'm glad you took that bed to the dump because you don't need to sleep on the mattress where I struggled. Though I don't remember it, I can't imagine I just willingly got out of bed."

No, she hadn't, she'd fought. And Jangles was happy she couldn't remember.

"You didn't give me a chance," she continued.

"Honey, please—"

"If you would've, I could've told you that I was scared, too. But I knew you were coming. I was locked in that bunker but I was wrapped in you. I can't say it was fun sitting there without pants or shoes, but I had you all around me. Your smell, your promises, your love, and I knew you'd come. So I wasn't as scared as I could've been. I'd take the fear over the possibility it could happen again over not having that fear because that would mean I didn't have you. God knows I didn't make it easy. I was holding on to the past with an iron grip. I thought I needed to. I thought that the best way to honor my parents was to hurt for the rest of my life. But I was so wrong. They loved me, and they'd want me to be happy."

"Yeah, they would."

And just as some of the stiffness started to leave his body, she continued. He'd started to relax, therefore he didn't brace. He should have. He should've prepared himself, because what came next rocked him to his core.

"I survived you once, and if you leave me again, I'll survive that, too. I will *survive,* Beau, but I will not come back. This is our one shot at getting it right. I deserve—"

Jangles didn't let her finish.

Instead, his mouth crashed onto hers and he showed her exactly what she deserved.

He kept their kiss slow and tender. Soft glides and

gentle licks. He kept at her until urgency crept in, then he ended the kiss with a soft peck.

"I love you, Hope."

"I know you do. But love's only gonna get you so far. I also need your honesty, you can't hold anything back." Jangles nodded and before he could ask for the same in return, she continued, "I'll give you all of me. I'm a little broken, honey, but I'm a whole lot determined. I figure you can work with that."

"Yeah, I can work with that."

"I think we need to figure out how to get my car up here."

"In a minute."

"Beau—"

"Say it again."

"Say what?"

"My name, say it again."

"Beau."

Jangles' eyes drifted closed and peace settled in his soul. *Christ, that felt good.*

"I'll call Merlin after I feed you and ask him and Gwen to go pick up your car."

"We can do it."

"Hell no. I don't want you ever going back there, and I barely controlled my temper the last time. Let's not tempt fate."

"I'm not scared to face her."

"Of course you're not. You're strong as fuck. But that doesn't mean this isn't one of those times where I can protect you. So, I'm not gonna let you go back there on the off-chance she's outside and tries to get another dig in."

~

HOPE TOOK in the fierce expression on Beau's face and relented. The truth was, they'd both had enough for one day. And while she believed she could face her grandmother and not break, Beau was giving her the option not to, and she appreciated that.

"Okay," she relented.

"Wanna see the rest of the house?"

The butterflies that had taken a nap awoke and started to flutter.

"We're doing this?"

"If by 'this' you mean we're together and you're home, then yes, we're doin' this."

Something big started to cover Hope. It coated her skin, and for once in her life, it felt good, it felt like a protective coating. Not one made of guilt and loss to shield her from the world, but one made out of love and concern that would give her the future she wanted.

Hope sat on Beau's lap in a home he made for her, and she let the galloping in her heart slow. Then she let the fear unknot and slide away. Her future was unknown, but she knew it would include Beau, and really that was all that mattered to her. She was telling the truth when she told him she could survive him leaving her. She'd do it with a broken heart and empty soul, but she knew she wouldn't break. The realization allowed her to be brave, to take a chance, to forgive, and finally to move on.

No more blood-soaked dreams.

"Yeah, show me the house."

Hope felt Beau's body tense. Every muscle coiled and bunched, his eyes turned the deepest blue, and she saw it—a sheen of wetness.

Then he gave her the words, even though they weren't necessary. He'd laid himself bare for her, he'd given her the greatest gift—himself, completely vulnerable and open. Beau hid nothing.

"I'm gonna fill that empty, baby," he whispered. "I'm gonna fill it until it floods out of you and spills over, then I'm gonna keep going. I swear, you'll never regret forgiving me."

"I know."

"You know?"

Hope adjusted herself on his lap and brought both hands up and cupped his handsome face.

"I know," she repeated.

"Fuck," he rasped. "Fucking hell, I love you so much."

"I know that, too."

And she did, she knew a hundred percent he loved her.

JANGLES STOOD in the doorway and stared at a sleeping Hope.

She was in their bed.

Where she belonged.

He'd shown her the house, fed her, and lay down with her until she'd fallen asleep. Then he'd slipped out of bed and moved across the room to look at her. Holding her felt better, but watching her in her slumber settled something inside of him that he needed settled. She was safe in their bed, in their home, and he'd stand sentry while she rested. One day, the need would pass, but until it did, he'd watch over her.

Jangles' cell vibrated in his pocket. He stepped into the hall and gently closed the door to take the call.

"Hello?"

"Heard she's home."

Tex.

"Yeah. Thanks for your help."

"Don't mention it."

They disconnected and Jangles smiled. Ghost had been correct, Tex was a man you could trust.

Before Jangles could decide whether to continue to stand watch, climb back into bed, or clean up the lunch dishes, there was a knock on the door. Not wanting to wake Hope, he quickly made his way through the house and checked out the front window to find Merlin's truck at the curb.

"Hey," Jangles greeted when he opened the door.

"Her car's in the driveway." Merlin held out her keys and dropped them into Jangles' palm.

"Appreciate you and Gwen driving down there to get it."

Merlin's lips twitched before they curved into a broad smile.

"Happy for you."

"I'm happy for myself."

"Happier for her," Merlin continued. "The women are planning something at the bar before Nori and Woof head to D.C. to finish packing."

"When?"

"Tonight."

"I'll talk to Hope."

"I'd be persuasive if I were you."

"Why's that?"

"Seems the women are over Hope pulling away. And, brother, I mean they are *over* it. She's not there tonight, I wouldn't be surprised if they plan a full assault. I'm talkin' full Winchester, Jangles. They'll make us look like baby operators the way they'll storm this house."

Jangles wanted to demand Merlin tell the women to stand down and let Hope go to them when she was ready, but he knew his friend wouldn't succeed. He also knew that Nori, Destiny, Gwen, and Ivy were good women and they'd take care of Hope.

"Baby operators?"

"While you've been living in your Castle of Catastrophe, the world has still been spinning around you. I see that you missed a few things so I'll enlighten you—the women have been studying up on military tactics. And Gwen passed around Sun Tzu's Art of War. Being as they're women, they're a fair bit smarter than us, so we're all fucked."

Castle of Catastrophe?

Where the hell did Merlin come up with this shit?

"Noted." Jangles smiled, and damn if it didn't feel good.

"See you tonight, brother."

Neither man moved. Both stood rooted, eyes locked, identical smiles.

"Feels good, doesn't it?" Merlin muttered.

"Damn good."

And with a lift of his chin, Merlin turned and made his way across Jangles' yard and got into his truck. Jangles didn't watch him leave.

He had something better waiting for him in the house.

CHAPTER 31

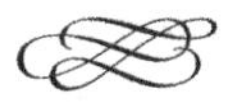

"THIS FEELS ODD," Hope shared.

"What does?" Jangles returned, and cut the engine.

"This. Us going out together, hanging with your friends at the Ugly Mug. A bar I used to work at."

"You gonna ask BF for your job back?"

Hope bit her lip and contemplated Jangles' question. She needed a job and couldn't imagine working anywhere else, but she was afraid to ask BF.

"Do you think he'd give it back to me?"

"Considering he told me I had twenty-four hours to bring you home or he'd shoot me, I'd say yes, he'll give you your job back."

"He did what?" Hope gasped.

"He loves you, baby. He considers you family. I hurt you and he was telling me in no uncertain terms he was displeased. He wanted you home where he knows you belong and he was letting me know that it was my job to bring you back. Luckily for me, I accomplished that before Zip was digging buckshot outta my ass. I'd like to think the man wouldn't aim to kill, but there's no doubt he would've shot me if I came home empty-handed."

"He wouldn't have shot you," Hope said, even though she knew it was a lie.

Baby Face totally would've shot Beau.

He loves me like that.

"Yeah, he would've."

"You're right, he would've." Hope smiled.

"You sure you wanna do this? We could go home, crawl into bed, and watch some TV."

Hope's smile grew. "Watch TV?"

Then she watched her man's lips tip up in a dazzling, bright, happy, sexy smile.

"What, you don't like TV?"

"No, I love watching TV. TV's great." She played along and shrugged her shoulders.

Jangles leaned over the center console, brushed an errant strand over her shoulder, and whispered, "When you're ready, all you gotta do is say the word."

"Word."

"You sure?"

"Why wouldn't I be?"

Jangles went silent and Hope pulled away so she could look at him. It was dark outside, the only illumination in the cab was from the lights in the parking lot. But Hope could still see the pensive look on his face.

"What's wrong?"

"Nothing. That's the thing, nothing is wrong. Everything's perfect."

"Then why would you ask if I was ready to have sex with you?"

"I'll do anything for you."

Hope felt her heartrate tick up, not knowing where

Beau was taking them but trusting that wherever it was, it would be good.

"I know."

"I'd wait a lifetime if that's what you needed."

God, I'm so happy I stopped running.

"I know, Beau. Where are you going with this?"

"I know down to the pit of my soul, you're it for me. I know you'd survive losing me. You're strong and resilient. But I wouldn't survive losing you. I wouldn't go on. There is no risk worth—"

"Beau, honey, *I know.* Stop fretting." Hope saw the smallest crack in his worried gaze. But it wasn't enough. She needed it gone. "Do you love me?"

"Yes."

Solid. No hesitation. Not that she needed to ask the question but there it was, more confirmation she'd made the right choice.

"Do you know I love you?"

"Yes."

"Then take me inside, buy me a drink, then take me home. We have a new mattress to break in." She watched Jangles' lips twitch. "Oh, and one more thing. Normally, and I promise this, I won't be the nagging girlfriend bitching about her man out with his buds tying one on. But tonight, you have a three-beer maximum. And you better suck those babies back quick."

"You in a hurry or something?"

"Hell yeah. For the first time in thirteen years, I've gotta home. A real home. My man's hot, and as I said, we gotta new bed to break in."

There it was. All the worry slid from Beau's features, replaced with sheer magnificence—pure beauty, badass style. He shook his head, dipped his chin, and belted out the most beautiful laugh.

Hell to the yes. She'd made the smartest decision of her life.

They'd just stepped into the bar when something dawned on Hope and she yanked Beau to a stop.

"Where's Buster?"

"What?"

"You better not've gotten rid of her, Beau," Hope said and narrowed her eyes. She hadn't seen the cat anywhere. As a matter of fact, she'd been so wrapped up in her whirlwind of a day, she'd actually forgotten Beau had a cat.

Oh, no, did she run away during the kidnapping? Poor Buster.

And for the second time in the space of a few minutes, Beau busted out laughing.

"Woof has her. I didn't know how long I'd be gone, so I forced him to take Buster."

"Well, I'd like her back."

"You like my cat, baby?"

"Yes."

"You like her so much, you can have her."

"Why do I feel like this is a trap?"

"No trap. I'm just being nice. You like Buster so much, she's all yours."

Hope tilted her head and studied Beau. "You know it doesn't matter whose cat Buster is. We live together, she's our cat."

"I insist, she's all yours."

"There you are." Gwen interrupted the ridiculous cat conversation.

"Hey," Hope greeted her friend.

"The guys are playing pool," Gwen told Beau. "I'm taking Hope."

But before Gwen could pull her away, Beau caught her around the back of the neck and turned her to face him.

His lips lowered to hers, and front and center in the crowded bar, Jangles claimed his woman. He made it long, wet, and thorough.

"Three drinks, baby," he said.

"Three drinks," Hope agreed, then in a daze, she followed her friend to the table.

"Woman down. Sheesh," Destiny exclaimed. "That was hot."

"Glad you're not working tonight so you can sit with us the whole time." Ivy's comment momentarily took Hope off-guard.

"'Bout time. It sucks when we only have you for a few minutes at a time," Gwen agreed.

"So, did you like the new house? So much better than his bachelor pad," Destiny rejoined.

Hope glanced around the table and she felt her nose start to tingle.

Accepted.

Not a single one of them acted like she didn't belong. Like she wasn't one of them. Just easy acceptance.

Her gaze caught on Nori's and warmth spread like wildfire.

"Welcome home," Nori mouthed.

"I owe you," Hope returned.

Nori waved her off and winked.

"What are you two talking about?" Destiny asked.

"Nothing. How are the wedding plans?" Nori redirected.

Hope soon found out Nori was more of a genius than she'd thought. And Hope already thought Nori was pretty freaking smart. This was because Destiny was seriously excited about marrying Zip. So excited, she could—and did—speak about it for hours.

It was awesome.

Normal.

Easy.

"Are you ready to start your new job?" Ivy asked Nori.

That was when normal and easy slid straight to deep and binding. Hope settled in and listened to Nori tell them about her new job, about how excited she was to be moving close and there would be no more traveling.

"I still can't believe you're going to be a professor." Gwen smiled.

"Me neither."

"Heath's gonna be hot for teacher, hope you stocked up on rulers," Destiny quipped.

The table erupted into laughter. When the hilarity died down, Nori caught Hope's attention.

"Hey, before I forget, are you going to be around tomorrow morning? Heath and I need to drop off Buster before we leave."

"Yeah, I don't know Beau's plans but I'll be home all day."

"Did Beau tell you about her?"

"About Buster?"

"Yeah, that she's pregnant."

"Son of a bitch," Hope muttered. "Excuse me for a second."

~

Jangles was lining up his shot when he heard Woof mutter, "Incoming. Nine o'clock."

He lost sight of the cue ball when he tipped his head to the left and saw Hope approaching. Her eyes were narrowed into slits, her sexy lips pressed together, and there was an enticing, pissed-off sway of her hips.

Christ. Beautiful.

"Hey, baby," he greeted and smiled.

"Buster?"

Jangles fought back his grin. "Buster? You mean, your cat? What about her?"

"She's *your* cat."

"Oh, no, you said you liked her. She's all yours."

"She's *pregnant*," she spat like an accusation, and Jangles lost the battle.

A wide smile tugged at his lips. "What a hussy."

"Don't be funny, Beau. How in the world did an indoor cat get knocked up?"

"Don't look at me, I didn't knock her up."

"Ha. Ha."

Jangles heard the guys' laughter behind him but tried to refrain from joining them.

"She's gonna have kittens," Hope informed him.

"Yep. It'll be good practice."

"Good practice? You planning on quitting the Army and becoming a cat breeder? Kittens are hard work."

"I wouldn't know. But I imagine you're right."

"What are you practicing for?" She went back to her ignored question.

"For babies."

"Babies?"

"Yep."

Hope's already narrowed gaze pinned him in place. "Are you talking about human babies or feline babies?"

"Human ones."

"Women don't have a litter, you know."

Jangles shrugged.

"And as long as we're on the topic of babies, I want twelve so I hope you're ready."

"So, you do want a litter."

"Not all at once, dummy."

And for the third time in one night, Jangles laughed. Something a month ago he never thought he'd do again. He didn't bother trying to stop it. He let the splendor of it slide through him.

Then he kissed his woman.

CHAPTER 32

"BABY?" Jangles brushed Hope's hair off her shoulder and took a moment to revel in its softness.

Top to toe beautiful.

"Hmm," she mumbled and rolled to her back, taking the sheet with her, exposing two perfect mounds of flesh.

Without thought, his hand moved to cup one, his thumb brushing over her nipple until it pebbled. *Good Lord, she's sexy.*

The soft glow from the hall gave Jangles just enough light to watch her full lips spread into a smile.

"What's gotten into you?" Her question made him chuckle.

Their sex life had always been good, both in frequency and deed, but since she'd forgiven him and come home, they couldn't keep their hands off each other. Sometimes it was in a frantic rush—a race for pleasure. Other times, it was less about release and more about them craving the connection. Minds, bodies, and souls fusing together.

She was spectacular.

Every part of her.

"Open your pretty eyes, baby."

Slowly, she gave him what he asked for, and just like all the times before when the intensity of their beauty hit him, it took his breath.

All his.

"You're dressed," she whispered. "Call out?"

"Yeah. I shouldn't be gone long. Week, tops."

"Go save the world."

It wasn't the first time he'd heard her say that. It wasn't even the fifth. Every time he'd left her in bed in the middle of the night, she'd said those same words. But this time, he savored them.

"You're still going to the bookstore today, yeah?"

"Yeah. Gwen got in a new shipment. I'm gonna help her sort through the boxes before my shift at the bar."

"Good."

Jangles was pleased as fuck all the women got along. Their friendships had grown over the months, and now that Nori lived close and Hope was home, they wasted no time arranging weekly get-togethers. The five of them were thick as thieves.

He loved that all five had that. But mostly, he loved that Hope had them, especially while he was gone.

"Be safe, Beau."

"Always, baby."

His palm slid up to her throat, then her jaw, and finally to her cheek. He leaned down and Hope craned her neck to meet him. Jangles brushed his lips against hers and listened to the sweet mew his touch had provoked.

"Love you," he whispered against her lips.

"Love you."

~

"THAT'S EVERYTHING," Gwen said and looked around the room.

Hope's gaze followed her friend's and she pulled off the white cotton gloves.

"I still can't believe you let me open the book," Hope returned, and took in the new shelves they'd spent the last few hours arranging.

"Eh, it's just a book."

Just a book?

"You say that like the three volumes aren't worth my yearly salary."

Gwen flashed one of her signature smiles that made her eyes dance with excitement.

"They're *so* cool, aren't they?"

"God, you're a nerd."

"A nerd? Those are first edition Tolstoy. Less than five thousand copies were printed. And it took him seven years to write that book." Gwen pointed to the three leather-bound books. "*And* it's in the original Russian. Now, if I can just get my hands on a copy of Anna Karenina, my life would be complete."

"Yep. Nerd. And you better not let Merlin hear you say that. It might bruise his ego."

Gwen waved her hand and smiled. "Please, Luke's ego is just fine."

Hope suspected it was. She'd seen the change in him since he'd met Gwen. The two of them were two book-loving nerds in a pod. Though Hope wouldn't call Merlin a book nerd to his face. The man was positively menacing—just like his teammates.

"Speaking of the guys, since they'll be gone at least a week, we can get together for dinner a couple of nights."

"Sounds good to me, but I work three nights this week.

I'll text you my schedule. And speaking of that, I gotta roll. I have a liquor order to check-in."

"Thanks for all your help."

"Anytime. I love helping you."

And Hope meant that with all her heart. She loved spending time with Gwen, helping her in her bookstore. But more, she just liked hanging out with her friend.

She had those now. Honest-to-goodness friends.

It was awesome.

Ten days later

"Problems?" Hope asked as Trigger slid onto a barstool.

"Brain cheats," he grumbled, and Hope bit back a smile.

"I take it you lost."

"No. Brain cheated."

"Right." Hope chuckled.

"Stop laughing at me and get me a beer, woman."

Hope would've taken offense if anyone else had demanded a beer while calling her woman, but instead, the broad smile on Trigger's sore-loser face made her bust out laughing.

She grabbed a glass from under the bar and held it under the tap. "Didn't anyone teach you to lose?"

"Hell no. And don't tell me that there's such a thing as a good loser. That's bullshit. If you're losing and happy about it, then you're a shmuck."

Shmuck?

Damn, Trigger's funny.

"Whatever you say, big guy." Hope set his beer in front of him and caught Trigger staring at her. "What? Do I have something on my face?"

"Yeah. Happiness. And it looks good on you."

With that, Trigger took his beer and started back to the billiards room.

Hope stood rooted to the spot and let Trigger's statement roll around in her belly.

She *was* happy. Extremely so.

And not just because she was with Beau. Though it was because of him and Nori she'd allowed herself to let go of her past so she could enjoy her future.

A future that included Beau, a home, good friends, and hopefully children. Nearly two weeks ago, she'd tried to scare Beau when she'd told him she wanted twelve babies. She was joking, but he hadn't batted an eye. He'd give that to her, she knew he would. The crazy man would give her a dozen babies and whatever else she wanted.

Yeah, she'd made the right decision. If she'd continued to hold onto the guilt, she would've missed out on the magnificence of life. *Her* life. The one she and Beau would create together.

Hope walked to the other end of the bar where her girls were sitting.

My girls.

Man, that feels great.

"Another tequila shot?" Hope asked Destiny.

"God, no. My head is already spinning. I'm done."

"I'll have one," Ivy happily chirped.

"No way, Ivy's cut off," Gwen cut in, and Hope looked at her. "She's over here waxing poetic about Magnus. I do not need to know his skill level, if you catch my drift."

Destiny giggled and Nori joined her.

"Well, maybe *I'd* like to hear about Magnus's talents," Hope teased.

"No, you wouldn't." Hope's eyes lifted to the door and her heart soared.

Beau.

"You're home!" Hope shouted. She dashed to the bar hatch and opened it with a crash.

Beau met her at the side of the bar and she jumped into his arms. He caught her with a grunt. Hope's legs wrapped around his waist and his hands went to her bottom. The tips of his fingers dug in and she sighed.

"You're home," she repeated.

Beau didn't respond, not with words anyway. His mouth took hers in one of his deep, wet, claiming kisses and Hope responded in turn.

Her man was home.

CHAPTER 33

Two years later...

Heath rolled over, taking Nori with him. He loved the way she slept in his arms, not letting go of him in the night or pushing him away if she got hot. Two years, and he still didn't think he'd ever get enough of her.

He ran his hand up her warm thigh and around the curve of her sexy ass. Nope. Wouldn't ever get tired of waking up with her in his arms.

His eyes went to his overnight bag in the corner where a ring burned a hole in the side pocket. His buddies had taunted the hell out of him for waiting so long to ask her, especially since they'd been living together now for over a year.

Still, he'd wanted to be sure Nori had a chance to make decisions for her life without the pressure of feeling like she had to follow him around or change her career for him. Shortly after they started dating, she moved from D.C. to Georgetown, taking a job as a professor at a university. She told him she hadn't been happy with her job, but part of him worried she would regret the move and grow to resent him.

But he couldn't deny how much happier she seemed in her new role. When he saw her on campus talking to her students or giving a lecture, she seemed so energized. She would get excited when one of her students really seemed to connect with a topic. She'd come home and talk about their achievements; who got what internship or where one of her students was interviewing.

If she missed her work at the State Department, she didn't show it.

And when he'd told her he was being recruited by HALO Security in Austin, she'd told him she would support him no matter what he decided. He wasn't sure he was ready to leave the military at the end of his current tour, but the idea of a little steadier lifestyle and being able to settle into a life where he wasn't called out halfway across the world routinely, appealed.

Not that a job at HALO would be a walk in the park. Sure, some of what they did was routine protection detail, but Nan and Ris had told him the company did quite a bit of kidnap rescue work nowadays, too.

He didn't know if he was ready for civilian life, but knowing Nori would have his back no matter what he decided, meant everything to him. His dad had never supported him the way this woman who stole his heart did.

Bruno hopped onto the bed and nuzzled Heath's neck with the top of his head before circling twice and lying down.

"Hey, buddy," Heath said, scratching under the dog's chin. They'd been talking about getting a brother or sister for the little dog.

He grinned. Whether that was a four-legged sibling or a two-legged one remained to be seen.

Nori stirred and let out a contented sound, making his heart trip in his chest. Fuck, it was probably a caveman mentality, but he loved knowing he made her happy. Wanted to make her happy for the rest of her life.

"Morning," she croaked as she rolled in his arms. She always sounded like she'd swallowed a sand milkshake overnight, and not in a good way. It wasn't that sexy bedtime voice men fantasized about. He could seriously mistake her for a fifty-year-old trucker who smoked a pack a day, but he loved it. He loved that she was uniquely Nori. That he got to see and hear her like this with her hair mussed instead of everything buttoned up and in place the way she was with the rest of the world.

He grinned and ran his hand down her leg again. "Morning, babe."

Tonight, they would get dressed up and he'd take her to the Italian restaurant the owner of the bed and breakfast had recommended when he'd contacted her the week before. The restaurant was holding a table for them in a private corner of the outside patio. He would ask the woman he loved to marry him under the stars of the Lake Tahoe night sky.

For now, he was happy to look into her sleepy eyes and let her see how much he loved her.

"What are we doing today?" she asked.

He ran his mouth over her temple and breathed in the sweet scent of her hair. "I thought we'd grab a picnic and a bottle of wine from that little deli down the street and spend the day hiking."

"Yeah?" she ran her hand up his chest as she wriggled against him, and that was all he needed.

He'd been half-hard already just from holding her in his

arms. Her touch did what it always did to him. Set him on fire and had him ready for her in an instant.

He rolled, apologizing to Bruno when the little dog slipped to his side. Bruno threw an affronted look their way.

Nori laughed, but her breath caught when he lowered his mouth to her nipple. He loved the way she arched her back when he ran his tongue around the stiff tip and how she sighed when he took her breast into his mouth and sucked gently.

"Heath," she whimpered, pressing her hips toward him.

His laugh was rough and low. She had very little patience for his teasing. Unfortunately for her, he planned to make this last. He wanted her begging for release before he entered her. Wanted to feel that moment when she toppled over the edge as he entered her. Hear her as she panted out his name while she grabbed his hair and pulled hard because she lost all control.

He settled between her legs and worked his way down her body with his mouth. He loved the softness of her stomach, the way her legs came up around him, trapping him in place when his mouth made it to the apex of her legs.

She bucked beneath him when he closed his mouth around her, the taste of her making his cock pulse with need. Only after he had her writhing and moaning, he rose above her and pressed himself to her center.

No way could he stop his groan as he entered her. She was warm and wet and so damned right for him. *Everything* about this woman was so damned right for him.

She met him thrust for thrust, her nails digging into his ass as she pulled him into her.

"I...Heath...more," she panted.

"Anything you need, baby," he said, meaning it. He

would give this woman anything she needed, for the rest of their lives if she'd have him.

He stilled inside of her as he watched her face.

She opened her eyes and smacked at his chest, never hesitating to tell him when she wasn't happy in the bedroom. He loved that.

"Marry me," he said, but it came out almost a whisper. "Marry me," he said again.

She stopped squirming under him and stared.

Heath couldn't help but grin at her, even though he knew she might kill him for it.

"This is all wrong," he said, still not moving inside her. "I have a ring and we have reservations for dinner tonight. I was going to ask you there. I had it all planned out. But I don't want to wait. I love you, Nori Bonham. I have for a long time, maybe since we were kids. It's not ever going to go away. I want a life with you. Kids, more dogs. Everything."

She thrust her hips at him. "You could get going on that kid part right now."

He laughed, putting a hand to her hip to hold her in place. "Not until I get my answer, woman."

The laughter left her face then and she held his gaze. "In a heartbeat, Heath Davis. I'll marry you in a heartbeat."

His heart kicked into overdrive, swelling so damned much he didn't know how it wasn't busting through his chest.

"I don't know how I got so lucky, Nori. I don't know what I did to deserve this second chance with you, but I'm the luckiest man in the world."

She put a hand to his cheek and smiled. "Your luck's going to run out if you don't start moving, mister."

He laughed at that and did as he was told. He moved slow and deep, losing himself in the feel of their bodies joined together. The feel of them coming together—mind, body, and soul. The feel of the promise they'd just made to each other and what it meant for their future.

"I love you, Heath," she said, never looking away from him.

"I love you, Nori. Always."

And after he'd loved her thoroughly and completely, he retrieved the ring from his bag, got down on one knee, and proposed to her the right way.

Thankfully, her answer was the same. She'd be his wife and make his life complete.

Five years later...

Destiny could smell the herbal tea and smiled inwardly even though she grumbled as she smashed her face deeper into the pillow.

Trent chuckled as he set the cup on the bedside table and laid a hand on her hip. "You're stalling."

"Mmm-hmm."

He rolled her onto her back, brushed her hair from her face, and set both hands on her enormous belly before leaning in to kiss the tight skin. "Have I told you lately how gorgeous you are?"

She let her lids flutter open and met his gaze. "Every day, you liar."

He shook his head. "Not a lie. You're radiant."

"I'm a whale, and the last thing I want to do is get all dressed up and go to a party. Can't I just stay here in bed for the last two months?" she joked.

He smoothed his hand over her belly again. He was always touching her like that, as if he were still in awe and shock over what they'd created. "My mother has been planning this baby shower for months. She'd be terribly disappointed if the guest of honor didn't show up. And your grandmother would be, too."

Destiny rolled her eyes. "You lie again. Your mom has been planning this shower for thirty years."

Trent laughed. "True. Look at it this way, you know the shower will be amazing. She never fails when it comes to celebrations. She managed our entire wedding without a single glitch."

Destiny finally smiled. He was right about that. She was extremely lucky to have Nancy Dawkins as a mother-in-law. The woman had loved her as if she were her own mother for thirty years. She was the best. "Who's on the guest list?"

Destiny hadn't given more than a passing thought to this shower. For the past few months, she'd been dedicated to quitting her job, breaking her lease in Dallas, and moving her belongings to Killeen. She and Trent had lived in two separate cities for five years and they'd made it work, but with a baby on the way, it was no longer feasible.

She would miss not working for Open Skies. She loved being a flight attendant. But she loved Trent more, and this baby, of course. She was ready to become a full-time mom and wife. The best part was waking up every day in Trent's bed. He wasn't always there. Sometimes he was on a mission, but at least she no longer had to worry all the time about her schedule matching up with his. Often, they only saw each other a few nights a month.

"In addition to everyone my mother has ever met and all our friends, everyone on my team will be there and their significant others. Merlin and Gwen, Woof and Nori, Duff and Ivy, and Jangles and Hope."

Destiny pulled Trent down for a real kiss. On the lips. It seemed he spent more time kissing her belly lately than her mouth. He was already in love with their baby and they didn't even know the gender. She knew he was going to be an amazing father. She also knew this was a special day. It was rare for everyone on his team and their wives to be able to gather in one place.

"So, are you going to get out of bed?" he asked, his face inches from hers, a twinkle in his eyes.

"Thinking about it." She glanced at the herbal tea. "Maybe after I down some of that ridiculous decaf tea, I'll find the strength."

He sat up, pulled all the pillows from his side of the bed to stuff behind her, and handed her the tea.

"You spoil me," she pointed out as she took a sip.

"That's because I wake up every day remembering how damn lucky I am to have you, and this baby on the way." His hand smoothed up and down her belly again, pausing when the baby suddenly kicked.

She winced. The little guy or gal was strong already.

Trent grinned. "I'll never get used to that. It reminds me that there is actually a human in there. Inside you. It's mind-boggling. I can't wait to meet him or her."

"I can't wait for you to either, because it will mean he or she is no longer kicking me from the inside out."

Trent kissed her belly and then her lips one more time. "I'll turn the water on. We can shower together." He wiggled his brows.

She couldn't imagine why he still seemed to find her so attractive, but he apparently did. She sure wasn't going to complain about sharing the shower. She loved it when he bathed her. It meant all she had to do was stand there while he ran his hands all over her body. It usually ended with them back in bed though. "You sure we have time for a shared shower?" she asked, glancing at the clock.

"They can't start the party until we get there," he teased. "And I'm not going to complain if we're late because I was busy making you scream my name." He stood and hurried toward the bathroom.

Destiny stared after him. She wasn't going to complain either. Even seven months pregnant, she hadn't lost a single bit of lust for him. It seemed like it had increased since moving in and having the promise of sex readily available far more often.

She heard the shower turn on and then she smiled as Trent started humming. It was time to face the day. The idea that it would start out with Trent's hands on her making her writhe made the thought of attending the baby shower far less daunting.

She finally set the teacup on the bedside table and heaved herself to standing. As she shuffled toward the bathroom, she pulled her nightgown over her head. The look on Trent's face when he turned around and found her leaning on the doorframe naked was everything.

God, she loved him. And there was no doubt he loved her back just as fiercely.

Ten years later...

Gwen stood at the sink, rinsing off vegetables for the salad to go with dinner when Enid's loud screech made her look out the window into the backyard. The nine-year-old fraternal twins were playing tag, and her brother, Bran, had caught her. They were growing up so fast and getting more independent and inquisitive by the day. It was rare that they played together these days, but since it was so close to dinner, they had to stay in the yard.

Their lives were so different. Gwen wouldn't change a day of it. She had an amazing husband and two children who meant the world to her. But she had never believed it could happen before Luke walked into the bookstore that day. Her life was everything she'd dreamed of and more.

After the twins were born, Gwen had cut back on her hours at the bookstore and worked mostly from home, managing the online store. Remembering how she'd complained about being tired at the end of the workday back then made her giggle. After chasing the kids and playing Uber driver for soccer practice, karate, and dance classes, she'd learned the real meaning of exhaustion. She'd even learned how to cook, much to the relief of her family.

The timer beeped, and Gwen pulled the lasagna out of the oven and put it on the island to cool. If she'd timed it right, it would have just enough time to rest before Luke got home. She didn't miss the days when he was on the Delta Team and had to leave at a moment's notice. Not knowing when he'd return home had been the hardest part. It hadn't been easy when he was off saving the world, but she'd understood the drive that burned inside him. When he missed the twin's birth, he'd been so upset, but he'd more than made up for it.

Luke's days as a Delta ended three years ago. Gwen would never forget how the world had stood still when Roe called. Just hearing his voice meant something awful had happened to Luke, but hearing the words—wounded in action—made the world stand still. Thank God Roe had also called Destiny. She'd come over with Nori, Ivy, and Hope before the words had sunk in. Their help kept her sane until she could see for herself that Luke would be okay. After he'd healed, he'd taken the promotion they had offered him—a desk job. At first, Gwen worried he'd hate it. But that never happened, and he seemed to enjoy all the research and planning he did now.

Gwen checked the time and leaned out the window to

find the kids. "Hey, guys. Daddy will be home soon. C'mon in, and get ready for dinner."

"Too late, he's already here." Luke's deep voice raised goosebumps on her arms. Not only was she still head over heels in love with him, but their passion hadn't cooled at all.

"I can't believe you snuck up on me," Gwen said as she turned away from the window and looked up into her husband's handsome face. "Did you have a good day?"

Luke wrapped an arm around her waist and pulled her close. He slanted his head, and when his warm lips touched hers, she moaned with desire.

"Eww, gross. We don't want to see you kissing," Bran said as the twins skidded to a stop in the kitchen doorway.

Luke smiled against Gwen's lips as he pulled back to greet the children. Bran had been growing like a weed and looked more like Luke every day. Enid took after Gwen down to the red hair and freckles across her little nose.

"Daddy, what are the flowers for?" Enid asked as she ran up to her father and hugged him around the waist.

"What flowers?" Luke asked.

Gwen tried to peer around him to see what Enid meant, but Luke blocked her.

"The ones in your hand. Daddy, you're silly."

"Shhh, they're a surprise for Mommy."

"You messed that up, E," Bran teased his sister.

Gwen winced. They had about ten seconds until the explosion. Whoever said twins were inseparable didn't mean hers. "Why don't you go wash your hands for dinner? No fighting," Gwen admonished.

"Okay," the twins answered, then turned around to go to the bathroom.

Luke chuckled as the two of them argued all the way up the stairs.

"How long until they grow out of that?" Gwen leaned into Luke and inhaled his scent of pine trees and mint.

"I don't know? Maybe by the time they go to college." Luke laughed and then handed her a huge bouquet of wildflowers. The orange, yellow, and pink assortment filled her with joy.

"What are these for? Not that I'm complaining." Gwen opened a cabinet door and reached for a vase.

"I put in my retirement papers today," Luke said.

Vase in hand, Gwen twirled to face him, staring into his caramel eyes. "What? Really? Are you okay? Did something happen?"

"I'm fine. Nothing happened, but it's time. I thought we could take over the bookstore from your parents. The last time they were here, your dad hinted about wanting to retire and do some traveling with your mom. They haven't been happy since we grounded them."

Gwen giggled. They'd more than deserved it after almost getting them all killed in Egypt. Her grandparents had died within weeks of each other the previous year, and that had left an enormous hole in her heart.

"You want to run the bookstore? Your sisters will kill you. They've begged you to work with them."

"I know, but I don't want to run a chain of department stores. And you know how I feel about books." Luke's eyes warmed to molten amber, and she shivered with desire as she recalled their first meeting so long ago.

"Yes. Yes, I do," Gwen whispered as she pulled his head toward her. She needed another kiss.

"God, woman, you're killing me. I want to lay you out on the table and make love to you. But we'd scar the kids for life."

"Yes, we would," Gwen said with a giggle. "Besides, dinner is ready, and I made your favorite."

"Lasagna? I guess I'll have to ravish you later." Luke's stomach growled, and they both grinned. "But I do have one more surprise for you."

"You do? What is it?"

Luke brought her flowers all the time, but the retirement announcement was huge. She didn't know how he'd be able to top that one.

"I'm taking you to Camelot." Luke's grin was huge as he held up a pamphlet.

"What?" Gwen's head spun with shock. He'd already given her Camelot—at least the one she'd dreamed of as a child. Luke had made all of her dreams come true.

As if he could read her mind, he shook his head. "Not all of your dreams, princess. I did some research, and we're going to tour Wales and visit all the likely locations where King Arthur could have lived and ruled."

Gwen jumped into his arms and slid her hands through his silky hair. "I don't even know what to say. I love you with everything that I am. But you still make me fall even harder."

"I told you, princess. You are my one love, my life, my everything. If I could give you the moon, I would, but Camelot will have to do." Luke lifted up and she wrapped her legs around his hips.

Gwen smiled at the man who'd made all of her dreams come true.

"I love you, princess," Luke murmured and slanted his lips over hers. His tongue slid into her mouth, tasting like mint. Even after all these years, his kisses still curled her toes.

"That is so gross," Bran groused from the hallway.

"One day, you'll kiss a girl like that," Enid told him.

"Never."

. . .

FIFTEEN YEARS LATER...

Ivy held the cellphone to her ear. "Maggie's not answering."

Duff laid a hand on Ivy's arm. "She's probably reading a bedtime story to the twins." He smiled. "They'll be all right. Trust our daughter. She learned from you."

"But this is Maggie's first time babysitting all five of them."

"She'll do fine. They love her as much as they love you. I'm sure they'll behave."

Ivy rolled her eyes. "They love me, but there are times they run all over me, leaving skid marks."

"Relax. It's been a long time since we all had a chance to get together at the Ugly Mug." He pulled into the parking lot. "Looks like the old place got a new paint job since the last time we were here."

"Lord, when was that?" Ivy asked.

"Two or three kids ago," Duff said. "It's been a couple years since we were all in the same town."

"I can't wait to see everyone," Ivy said, her smile spreading across her face as she looped her purse strap over her shoulder.

"And the best part is we get to see everyone without kids." Duff sighed. "Real adult time."

Ivy glanced back at her phone. "I'd feel better if I could get Maggie to answer."

Duff switched off the engine and walked around the mini-van to open the door for Ivy. "They'll be fine. Maggie knows how to call 911."

"Sweet Jesus, don't jinx us," Ivy said as she let him help her to the ground.

He pulled her into his arms and held her there. "We could run away, you know."

"Don't tempt me," she said, and rose up on her toes to press her lips to his in a brief kiss.

He shook his head. "Uh-uh. I need a lot more than that." His arms tightened around her and he bent to claim her mouth the way he did when they weren't surrounded by children.

Oh, he loved his children, but alone-time with this woman was hard to come by.

He kissed her long and hard, wishing it would never end. When he came up for air, he stared down at her. "You're as beautiful today as the day you kissed me in Gwen's bookstore."

She laughed. "I was a lot younger then, and a bit more adventurous."

"I'd say you're still just as adventurous, and I love you even more now." He smiled down at her. "You don't look like a woman who has six children."

"They keep me running. I don't have time to think about getting old." She cupped his cheek. "And you don't look any different than the day we met. You're still my handsome guy."

"You two gonna stand out here sucking face? Or are you coming inside to do some serious adult drinking?" Merlin grinned as he led Gwen up to the door of the Ugly Mug and waited for Ivy and Duff to join them.

Duff shook Merlin's hand while Ivy and Gwen hugged.

"Can you believe we got out of the house without children?" Gwen said. "I feel like we're playing hooky."

"Me, too." Ivy grimaced. "I feel bad dumping all of mine on Maggie."

Gwen shook her head. "Maggie's amazing. Whenever I have her babysit my hellions, I know they'll be in bed on time, fed, bathed and stories read."

"She'll make an amazing commander someday," Merlin said.

Duff's chest puffed out. "Damn right she will."

"*If* she goes into the military," Ivy said.

Gwen grinned. "She wants to be like her daddy."

"She can be," Ivy said. "In the security business. Or she'd make a great private investigator."

"Or an attorney, like her mother," Merlin said.

Ivy grinned. "She can be anything she wants to be. She's that smart."

"How's the child advocacy law going?" Merlin asked.

Ivy's smile slipped. "Sometimes I wonder how I'll make it through the next day. Other times, I know I have to. Those kids need someone who gives a damn to defend them."

Duff slipped an arm around Ivy, his heart swelling. He was a very lucky man to have her in his life. "She's an amazing attorney and mom."

She smiled up at him. "Couldn't do it without you, babe."

"Merlin, Duff, ladies," Zip called out, as he and Destiny climbed out of their vehicle and joined them in front of the bar.

Hugs were exchanged all around.

"I've been looking forward to this for months," Destiny said. "Seems like we don't get together often enough."

"Jangles and Woof are inside with Nori and Hope," Merlin said. "We should move this party indoors."

Inside, they all greeted each other and sat around a large table at the back of the bar. Hope helped the bartender with the drinks, laughing as she carried the heavy tray across the floor. "It's been a while since I made drinks. They might be a little stiff."

Once everyone had their drinks in hand, Merlin stood and lifted his beer mug. "To friends."

"No," Duff said. "To family."

Zip chuckled. "Says the guy with the biggest one. What are you up to now?"

"Six, and holding," Duff said, raising his mug to take that gulp.

Ivy leaned close and murmured low enough so only Duff could hear, "Uh, we need to bump up that number."

Duff spewed beer. "What?" He spun to face his wife. "Are you—?"

She nodded. "Pregnant." Ivy bit her bottom lip. "I didn't want to say anything until I was at least three months along. You know. I didn't want to worry you if they weren't viable."

Duff shook his head, feeling suddenly dizzy. "Wait… what…they?" He gripped her arms. "*They*?" he said a little louder.

She nodded. "Another set of twins." She gave him a weak smile. "I know, I'm getting a little old for this, but we didn't think we could have anymore…and, well…we haven't been practicing birth control…" She looked up at him, her brow furrowing. "Are you mad?"

"Mad, no. Stunned?" He drew in a deep, shaky breath and turned to his friends, raising his mug. "I'm going to be a daddy!"

Everyone laughed.

With a grin on his face, Merlin said, "Hate to break it to you, but you've been one for the past fourteen years. I'd say six kids qualifies."

Duff shook his head again. "No…I'm going to have two more." He downed the rest of the beer and dropped hard into his seat. "Eight children." A grin spread across his face. "I'm having more babies."

Woof clapped a hand on his shoulder. "You're going to have to up your client list and hire more security agents."

Gwen left her seat to rush over to Ivy. "I told you he'd take it all right."

Ivy grimaced. "I'm not so sure. He looks a little pale. Sweetheart, do you need to put your feet up?"

"Yeah, old man. You already had enough children for a basketball team," Jangles said. "Are you going for a football team?"

A glance at Ivy's worried face made Duff pull himself together. He stood, pulled her into his arms, and kissed her in front of everybody. "I love you, Ivy. It's a good thing we put an offer in on that ranch with the big house. We're going to need it."

She smiled. "Yes, we are."

He stepped back and laid a hand across her belly. "I can't wait to meet the newest members of our clan. They'll be as beautiful as their mother."

"Or as handsome as their father," she said. "Promise me one thing." She stood before him.

"Anything." He gathered her close again.

"You'll love me and all eight of our children for as long as you live."

"That's easy," he said.

"And promise me," she continued. "That you'll get snipped before the twins are born."

He laughed and swung her up in his arms. "Are you sure you don't want to go for an even dozen?"

"With you…" she smiled down at him, her eyes glassy with unshed tears. "I'd do it. But I think we'll have our hands full with eight."

He kissed her and set her back on her feet. "We'll love them all, and I'll make that appointment first thing

Monday morning." He turned to his group of friends. "I guess my mission days are over."

"No," Merlin said. "The mission has only changed. Congratulations, old man. You're a very lucky man."

With Ivy in the crook of his arm and firmly rooted in his heart, he nodded. "I am…a very lucky man."

Twenty-five years later…

Beau sat on the edge of his bed and stared down at his wife. It had been a long time since he'd received a middle of the night call-out.

Though they'd been expecting this call.

"Hope, wake up."

His wife stirred, then sat up so quickly he had to move out of the way or court getting head-butted.

"Did she call?"

Yeah, they'd been expecting the call, and his wife was excited.

"She did."

"How'd I miss the phone ringing? Don't answer that. It doesn't matter. Move, Beau, we have to hurry."

Hope was practically vibrating with nervous energy. He reached over and clicked on the lamp, bathing the room in a soft glow. What he didn't do was move so Hope could jump up and get dressed.

"We have plenty of time."

"No, we—"

"Hope, baby, we do."

Beau watched as she came up on her knees. The T-shirt she'd worn to bed fell over her hips, the edge of the material skimmed her thighs, and after all these years, he knew better than to fight the urge to take in his beautiful wife. So he didn't. He allowed his eyes to take her in fully.

So. Damn. Stunning.

Time had done nothing to diminish his desire. His hair had long ago started to gray, but there wasn't a single silver streak in Hope's shiny brown. Over the years, she'd changed the style but never the color. Now, her once-long locks were cut into what Hope had called a bouncy bob with lots of texture—whatever the hell that meant. All he knew was it gave him access to her neck without having to brush her hair aside. So, he simply called it sexy.

"Okay, fine. We have time, but I want to be there for Chelsea."

Twenty-three years ago, Hope had given him the second-best gift he'd ever received. She'd given him three really great ones and since there was no way to decide which one was best, he categorized them in the order Hope had given them. The first was the day she'd married him. The second, the day his daughter was placed in his arms. The third, the day his son had been born.

Three miraculous events. Life-changing moments that he'd never forget.

This would be the fourth-best moment of his life, and he wanted a moment to enjoy it before all hell broke loose. And Beau knew it would. His daughter, Chelsea, was a lot like her mother. She'd take today in stride, but Chelsea's husband, Hank, was a lot like Beau. Therefore, he would not.

Hank could fly an Apache into enemy territory and not break a sweat, but since the day Chelsea had announced she was pregnant, Hank had gone from the cool, reserved pilot Beau had allowed to marry his daughter to a man possessed, proving to Beau he'd made the right decision giving the Army officer his blessing.

Chelsea had found a man who subscribed to Beau's brand of love, loyalty, and protection.

"I know you want to be there for our daughter," he told Hope. "But before we leave for the hospital, I need to tell you something."

"What? Is Jake okay?"

Damn, that reminded him he needed to call his son to tell him his sister was on her way to the hospital. And he needed to do that soon. Jake had not found a woman to settle down with—not that Beau would expect a young man in his early twenties to tie himself down—but that didn't mean Jake was ever lonely.

"I'm sure Jake's fine."

Hope scowled before she said, "I wish that boy—"

"Baby, he's twenty-one. He's smart, he's happy, he's safe, he's got a good job, he pays his bills. He's living his life, and part of that is him playing the field. You can wish all you want, but when Jake finds what he's looking for, he'll know. And when he does, like his old man, he will not let her go."

"You're right."

"I know I am."

"You know what's amazing?" Hope groused.

"I know a lot of things that are amazing."

Hope's eyes squinted and she shook her head.

"Annoying," she huffed, and Beau smiled.

"What's amazing, Hope?"

"That twenty-five years later, I'm still finding things for you to add to the list of stuff you do that irritates me."

Beau's deep chuckle filled the room.

"Baby, I threw that list away a long time ago and started a new one."

"Can we please stop talking about this and get to the hospital?"

"Not until I tell you how grateful I am." Hope's face softened like it always did when her husband was being sweet. "You've given me a good number of gifts over the years, baby. Three that are at the top of my list, but there are nine-thousand one-hundred and twenty-five that are equally important. Every day with you is a gift. But those three at the top are special. Those are the times when you tipped the scales. When you gave us something I could never balance. And today will be the fourth. The birth of our first grandchild."

"I think Chelsea's giving us that," Hope whispered.

"There is no Chelsea without you. There's no family without you. There's no happy times, birthdays, graduations, weddings, Christmases, without you. Chelsea, Jake, and I have all that we have because of you. Thank you, baby. Thank you for giving us *you*."

"Beau?"

"Looking right at you, Hope."

"I know you think that, because you've told me and you've somehow convinced our kids that's the truth. But you're wrong. It's not me. It's not even you. It's us. *We* did it. We created it. We worked to keep it good. We raised good kids."

Beau took in a breath and allowed Hope's argument to settle in. It was not the first time she'd said those exact words or a variation of them. And right then, just like all the other times, he loved that Hope thought that. But she was wrong. Sure, they'd created a beautiful family together, but it was only possible because Hope had found it in her to forgive him.

It was Hope who'd single-handedly given him everything he'd ever wanted.

And there were no words to express that kind of felicity.

"You ready to be a grandpa?" Hope smiled.

Hell, yes, I am.

"Sure am. You ready to be a granny?"

"Um, no. We've agreed on Mimi, remember?"

"Right. Mimi." Beau shook his head in amusement.

"Thank you, Beau. You still never let go."

Fuck.

That still burned. And nine-thousand one-hundred and twenty-five days had done nothing to lessen the scorch.

"Let's go meet our grandbaby," Beau suggested.

Hope pushed off the bed and flew into his arms. She tipped her head and peppered his face with happy kisses.

"I'm so excited."

"I can see that."

"We're gonna be grandparents. Our baby's having a baby."

"Yeah, she is."

Beau was shocked to find he didn't feel any sadness about his baby growing up and having a family of her own.

He felt nothing but elation.

A feeling he knew well.

On behalf of all of the authors of the Delta Team 3 series, Lori, Becca, Lynne, Elle, and Riley…thank you for reading our books. Working together on this series was a lot of fun, and we loved being a part of Susan Stoker's world, at least for a little bit.

If you haven't picked up *Shielding Kinley, by Susan, do so! You'll get to meet Duff, Jangles, Woof, Zip, and Merlin for the first time and see how they interact with Delta Team 2!*

If for some reason you haven't read the other books in the

Delta Team three series, I've listed all the links here so you can go and get the others! :)

Nori's Delta by Lori Ryan
Destiny's Delta by Becca Jameson
Gwen's Delta by Lynne St. James
Ivy's Delta by Elle James
Hope's Delta by Riley Edwards

ABOUT THE AUTHOR

Riley Edwards is a bestselling multi-genre author, wife, and military mom. Riley was born and raised in Los Angeles but now resides on the east coast with her fantastic husband and children.

Riley writes heart-stopping romance with sexy alpha heroes and even stronger heroines. Riley's favorite genres to write are romantic suspense and military romance.

Don't forget to sign up for Riley's newsletter and never miss another release, sale, or exclusive bonus material.

https://www.subscribepage.com/RRsignup

Facebook Fan Group

www.rileyedwardsromance.com

facebook.com/Novelist.Riley.Edwards
twitter.com/rileyedwardsrom
instagram.com/rileyedwardsromance
bookbub.com/authors/riley-edwards

There are many more books in this fan fiction world than listed here, for an up-to-date list go to www.AcesPress.com

You can also visit our Amazon page at:
http://www.amazon.com/author/operationalpha

Special Forces: Operation Alpha World

Christie Adams: Charity's Heart
Denise Agnew: Dangerous to Hold
Shauna Allen: Awakening Aubrey
Brynne Asher: Blackburn
Linzi Baxter: Unlocking Dreams
Jennifer Becker: Hiding Catherine
Alice Bello: Shadowing Milly
Heather Blair: Rescue Me
Anna Blakely: Rescuing Gracelynn
Julia Bright: Saving Lorelei
Cara Carnes: Protecting Mari
Kendra Mei Chailyn: Beast
Melissa Kay Clarke: Rescuing Annabeth
Samantha A. Cole: Handling Haven
Sue Coletta: Hacked
Melissa Combs: Gallant
Anne Conley: Redemption for Misty
KaLyn Cooper: Rescuing Melina
Janie Crouch: Storm
Liz Crowe: Marking Mariah
Sarah Curtis: Securing the Odds
Jordan Dane: Redemption for Avery
Tarina Deaton: Found in the Lost
Aspen Drake, Intense
KL Donn: Unraveling Love
Riley Edwards: Protecting Olivia

PJ Fiala: Defending Sophie
Nicole Flockton: Protecting Maria
Alexa Gregory: Backdraft
Michele Gwynn: Rescuing Emma
Casey Hagen: Shielding Nebraska
Desiree Holt: Protecting Maddie
Kathy Ivan: Saving Sarah
Kris Jacen, Be With Me
Jesse Jacobson: Protecting Honor
Silver James: Rescue Moon
Becca Jameson: Saving Sofia
Kate Kinsley: Protecting Ava
Heather Long: Securing Arizona
Gennita Low: No Protection
Kirsten Lynn: Joining Forces for Jesse
Margaret Madigan: Bang for the Buck
Trish McCallan: Hero Under Fire
Kimberly McGath: The Predecessor
Rachel McNeely: The SEAL's Surprise Baby
KD Michaels: Saving Laura
Lynn Michaels: Rescuing Kyle
Wren Michaels: The Fox & The Hound
Kat Mizera: Protecting Bobbi
Keira Montclair, Wolf and the Wild Scots
Mary B Moore: Force Protection
LeTeisha Newton: Protecting Butterfly
Angela Nicole: Protecting the Donna
MJ Nightingale: Protecting Beauty
Sarah O'Rourke: Saving Liberty
Victoria Paige: Reclaiming Izabel
Anne L. Parks: Mason
Debra Parmley: Protecting Pippa
Lainey Reese: Protecting New York
KeKe Renée: Protecting Bria

TL Reeve and Michele Ryan: Extracting Mateo
Elena M. Reyes: Keeping Ava
Angela Rush: Charlotte
Rose Smith: Saving Satin
Jenika Snow: Protecting Lily
Lynne St. James: SEAL's Spitfire
Dee Stewart: Conner
Harley Stone: Rescuing Mercy
Jen Talty: Burning Desire
Reina Torres, Rescuing Hi'ilani
Savvi V: Loving Lex
Megan Vernon: Protecting Us
Rachel Young: Because of Marissa

Delta Team Three Series

Lori Ryan: Nori's Delta
Becca Jameson: Destiny's Delta
Lynne St James, Gwen's Delta
Elle James: Ivy's Delta
Riley Edwards: Hope's Delta

Police and Fire: Operation Alpha World

Freya Barker: Burning for Autumn
B.P. Beth: Scott
Jane Blythe: Salvaging Marigold
Julia Bright, Justice for Amber
Anna Brooks, Guarding Georgia
KaLyn Cooper: Justice for Gwen
Aspen Drake: Sheltering Emma
Alexa Gregory: Backdraft
Deanndra Hall: Shelter for Sharla
Barb Han: Kace
EM Hayes: Gambling for Ashleigh
CM Steele: Guarding Hope

Reina Torres: Justice for Sloane
Aubree Valentine, Justice for Danielle
Maddie Wade: Finding English
Stacey Wilk: Stage Fright
Laine Vess: Justice for Lauren

Tarpley VFD Series

Silver James, Fighting for Elena
Deanndra Hall, Fighting for Carly
Haven Rose, Fighting for Calliope
MJ Nightingale, Fighting for Jemma
TL Reeve, Fighting for Brittney
Nicole Flockton, Fighting for Nadia

As you know, this book included at least one character from Susan Stoker's books. To check out more, see below.

SEAL of Protection: Legacy Series

Securing Caite
Securing Brenae (novella)
Securing Sidney
Securing Piper
Securing Zoey
Securing Avery
Securing Kalee
Securing Jane (Feb 2021)

SEAL Team Hawaii Series

Finding Elodie (Apr 2021)
Finding Lexie (Aug 2021)
Finding Kenna (Oct 2021)
Finding Monica (TBA)
Finding Carly (TBA)
Finding Ashlyn (TBA)

Delta Team Two Series

Shielding Gillian
Shielding Kinley
Shielding Aspen
Shielding Jayme (Jan 2021)
Shielding Riley (Jan 2021)
Shielding Devyn (May 2021)
Shielding Ember (Sept 2021)
Shielding Sierra (TBA)

Delta Force Heroes Series

Rescuing Rayne (FREE!)

Rescuing Aimee (novella)
Rescuing Emily
Rescuing Harley
Marrying Emily (novella)
Rescuing Kassie
Rescuing Bryn
Rescuing Casey
Rescuing Sadie (novella)
Rescuing Wendy
Rescuing Mary
Rescuing Macie (Novella)

Badge of Honor: Texas Heroes Series

Justice for Mackenzie (FREE!)
Justice for Mickie
Justice for Corrie
Justice for Laine (novella)
Shelter for Elizabeth
Justice for Boone
Shelter for Adeline
Shelter for Sophie
Justice for Erin
Justice for Milena
Shelter for Blythe
Justice for Hope
Shelter for Quinn
Shelter for Koren
Shelter for Penelope

SEAL of Protection Series

Protecting Caroline (FREE!)
Protecting Alabama
Protecting Fiona
Marrying Caroline (novella)

BOOKS BY SUSAN STOKER

Protecting Summer
Protecting Cheyenne
Protecting Jessyka
Protecting Julie (novella)
Protecting Melody
Protecting the Future
Protecting Kiera (novella)
Protecting Alabama's Kids (novella)
Protecting Dakota

New York Times, USA Today and *Wall Street Journal* Bestselling Author Susan Stoker has a heart as big as the state of Tennessee where she lives, but this all American girl has also spent the last fourteen years living in Missouri, California, Colorado, Indiana, and Texas. She's married to a retired Army man who now gets to follow *her* around the country.

www.stokeraces.com
www.AcesPress.com
susan@stokeraces.com

Made in the USA
Monee, IL
27 December 2024